MISFIT MONSTERS

PACK OF OUTCASTS - BOOK 1

EVA CHASE

I

Periwinkle

Today will be a good day! Today, I won't kill anyone.

I chant my mantra to myself as I slink through the shadows, invisible to the mortal beings on the city street around me. With every iteration, I squeeze my conviction a little tighter.

It has to be true. I'm going to make it true, and there's no arguing with that.

All I have to do is take it easy-peasy. No situations that could turn traumatic or overwhelm me. I've totally got this.

Hunger prickles through my filmy body like the jabs of a hundred really annoying needles. But that's okay too. The ache gave me an excuse to come here.

There's nowhere I'd rather be than the mortal realm… even if somehow things always go wrong.

Nope, not thinking about that. Stuff those memories in a trash bag and throw them away. This is a brand-new start!

And it's a beautiful day for my most recent brand-new start. Beyond the patches of shadow I flit through, the sun beams down over the strolling humans. Its warmth stirs enough contentment in them for the emotion to touch me too.

Childish laughter carries from the next street over. I taste the edge of their joy, bright and shimmery like fizzy lemonade.

Mmm, delicious.

The needles of hunger jab deeper, and I pause. Yep, totally in control. I won't rush or leap before I look this time.

I reach the edge of a small park. A patch of trees stands on one side, a playground on the other.

A couple of kids are flinging themselves as high as possible on the swings, as if they're preparing to take off into the sky. I've never seen humans actually fly, but those two seem to believe it's possible. Their exhilaration trickles into me, tart and sweet as chilled apple cider.

Nearby, a toddler giggles nervously as he careens down the slide to his waiting mother. Two girls sway upside down on the monkey bars.

Playgrounds are perfect for my needs: a good, simple meal.

But I feed much better when I'm in physical form.

In the shelter of a cluster of trees, I solidify wearing a daisy print sundress and my favorite track jacket: rainbow stripes across the chest to represent all the light and color I want to bring with me.

I heard on a TV show once that you are what you wear.

The jacket's hood materializes already pulled up over my long, vibrantly turquoise hair, which I can't change and tends to draw attention I'd rather not have. Especially if it starts glowing.

That's something no human would do.

The fresh spring air floods my newly formed lungs, filled with the perfume of the flowers blooming on a tree by the playground. Magnolia blossoms. Wonderful!

But what I really want to savor is the delight of the romping children. The ravenous prickles inside me are already starting to soften.

I amble closer to the playground and stop near the magnolia tree.

With each whoosh of the swings and clamber up the climbing equipment, I absorb more emotion in little spurts. This boy's daring eagerness tastes like a sip of spiced hot cocoa. That girl's dizzy hilarity could be a mouthful of pulled taffy.

The little wisps don't soothe the deeper burn of hunger very quickly. Once I know I've got my balance, I can come more often. I won't wait until I'm on the verge of starving.

It'll be fantastic.

A little girl wanders over and gazes up at the magnolia's luminous flowers. She stretches her hand, but the nearest one is far above her head.

A glimmer of hope flutters in my chest. I can *make* her happy.

One more bit of joy to make amends for the thousands I've hurt.

I dare to step closer and smile. "I can get one for you."

It's been weeks since I last used my voice, but the words slide off my tongue with my usual bubbly cheer. The girl grins. "Yes, please!"

The human-ish body I can shift into has many appealing features, from its unique hair to its multitude of soft curves, but it's hardly tall. I have to stand on tiptoe to reach a flower.

The girl watches avidly. Lucky her, she'll grow with the passing years. The only thing I can change about my human-like form is what it's wearing.

As my fingers close around the base of the blossom, a different sort of ache jabs through my ankles and feet—not a hundred needles but one that's way bigger than any needle has a right to be.

Shadowkind can recover from plenty of injuries that mortal bodies can't. But some wounds aren't so considerate.

Suppressing a wince, I hold out the flower. "Here you go."

The girl plucks the blossom from my fingers with a gasp of delight that melts in my mouth like a gumdrop. She darts away to show off her prize.

Warmth tingles over my scalp. I tug my hood lower over my hair to cover the glow of satisfaction.

On the far side of the park, a procession of vivid colors catches my eyes. People are walking up to a large stone building, the women in swishy dresses, the men in suits.

They give off a cocktail of excitement and anticipation that tingles into me from even this far away.

I study the building. Arched windows, tall towers, intersecting lines carved into stone—

Oh! I've seen this before. It's a church. They must be coming to a wedding.

My heart skips a beat.

Weddings bring big emotions. Delicious, giddying, fill-me-up-in-one-gulp emotions.

It's so much easier to overindulge.

I hesitate and then gird myself. I'll only walk over to the fence between the playground and the church. Absorb the edges of the celebration from a distance. That's safe enough.

Pleased with the compromise, I stroll over. The wafting festive energy draws me in.

I rest my hands on top of the picket fence. Only traces of the largest emotions reach me, like standing outside a bakery and imagining pastries filling your belly from the scents seeping past the door, but it's a feast all the same.

The burn of my hunger eases. After another five minutes here, it'll be nothing but a smolder. Five more, and I'll be completely sated.

The stream of wedding-goers trickles to a halt. It must be almost time for the ceremony to begin.

A small wooden door on the side of the church opens, and a woman in a poofy white dress steps out onto the narrow lawn.

Her pale hair swirls around her head in a fancy arrangement of overlapping loops. Gold jewelry gleams around her neck and in her earlobes.

I stare at her. What's the bride doing out here?

How are all the people inside the church going to revel in the marriage if she isn't in there doing the getting married part?

A current of more concentrated emotion washes over me from her, so close by. Without trying, I can pick up on a sour tang of doubt and a bitter knot of guilt alongside the delicate tendrils of excitement.

Oh no. What does it matter if the people inside are happy for her if she isn't happy herself?

Is there some way I can help her?

My resolve to keep my distance wavers. I never want to come here and only take.

People who do that… People like that are the reason my feet hurt.

I walk along the fence until I'm directly across from the bride. "Are you all right?"

At the sound of my voice, she startles. She spins to face me with a rustle of her massive skirts and knits her brow. "Are you one of Ted's cousins?"

I shake my head. "I'm not a guest. You just look like maybe you need someone to talk to."

The bride droops. "I—I don't know."

She presses her hand to her forehead. "I thought I wanted this, but… we haven't been together for very long. Only a year. Everything's felt so *right*, and I didn't want to wait. But what if I'm being crazy? Who jumps into marriage like that?"

My understanding of human relationships comes mostly from fictional ones on screens, but that gives me context. "You're afraid you're rushing in too fast. You might not know him well enough."

"People don't normally do this. There's obviously a reason why."

Through her uneasiness and shame, the quivers of excitement still reach me. There's the edge of a richer, more substantial sweetness like a honey-glazed roast.

"He didn't *do* anything to make you feel that way, did he?" I say. "He's good to you."

A smile lights up her face.

"He is," she says, and it's in her voice, in her sparkling eyes meeting mine: the whole roast and a heap of buttery mashed potatoes and caramelized squash besides. "When I'm with him, I feel like I can do anything. And he'll be right there, cheering me on."

She lets out a choked sort of laugh. "Even if I went in right now and said I want to wait, he'd just hug me and reassure me that we'll sort everything out."

My breath catches in my throat. I haven't gotten to bask in this especially potent sensation very often. It's filling in every bit of empty space inside me.

I can repay her for that.

I reach across the fence to pat her arm. "You love him.

And you know he loves you. That's bigger than anything you're afraid of."

Humans are strange beings. They're the ones feeling the feelings, but so often they need to be told what's inside them before they can recognize it.

A brilliant smile crosses the bride's lips as a flood of relief courses off her. "You're right. The worries seem so silly when I think clearly. Thank you."

She turns and hurries back into the church, nothing but elation radiating off her now.

I sent her on that path. A surge of my own joy swells inside me.

Too quickly, too vast.

Panic jolts through me amid the rushing whirlwind. I only have an instant to push myself away from the fence before the hurricane of happiness bursts out of not just my hair but all of me in an explosion of light.

I crumple in on myself, hugging my knees, willing the blinding glow back under my skin. But it's blazing too wildly for me to catch hold.

Frantic voices yell. Tires screech. Sparks of other people's panic nip at me.

A metallic crunch reverberates through the air. The impact of the people hurt by my power stabs right down the center of my body: an acidic spurt of agony, a searing flare of anguish.

A crackling of pain before a life snuffs out.

A sob hitches out of me. I dig my fingers into the grass.

The light starts to contract back into me, and I dive into the first sliver of shadow I can reach.

I shouldn't have come over to the church at all. I should have known it'd be too risky.

Why didn't I walk away when I saw the bride?

But she looked so lost…

Now I have more injuries to make up for. More hurt to balance out.

I'll find a way. There has to be a way. For now—

A sudden force blasts straight through the shadows to slam into me.

I reel through the patches of darkness. Before I can get my bearings, another blast of the unexpected energy smacks me.

This time it digs in, like fingers clutching around my mind. The force wriggles through my thoughts.

I have the sense of a presence at the other end of that grasp, as if I'm a fish hooked on a lure.

The lure yanks at me. It's so snagged in my head I can't do anything except follow.

I stumble through the shadows, a silent wail building inside me. No, no, no.

It's been years since I felt this sensation, but I know it too well. It's one of them, one of the mortals with magic.

A sorcerer is reeling me in.

Not just me. As I'm dragged forward with increasing speed, my essence brushes against other beings in the shadows alongside me. We've all been caught up in this vast net of sorcerous compulsion.

An impression of words hum through my essence. *Come. Come to me.*

I squirm and flail, but my ephemeral body won't respond. It just flows on toward the call.

I'm trying so hard to fight that I barely notice my surroundings until my forward momentum slows.

Alongside the other shadowkind creatures hauled by the sorcerer's power, I dip under a rusty fence that surrounds a large, mostly empty lot. Weeds sprout up from the cracks in the pavement.

Five figures wait for us by a parked van. Three of them are human; two are higher shadowkind like me. The two shadowkind and two of the humans stand poised around a waist-high metal box.

An icy shiver passes through my being.

I know a cage when I see one.

The third human keeps reeling me in with his magic. When I'm about ten feet away, he loosens his hold just slightly, his dark gaze sweeping over the lot as if he can see us even in the shadows.

He's definitely not the other sorcerer I've known. This man is a lot younger—maybe mid-twenties, as well as I can judge mortal ages. Since all shadowkind pop into being fully grown and unchanging, I don't have a ton of observations to go by.

Even though he's younger, he's awfully strong. His power shows not only in the invisible force clamped around me but in his chiseled jaw and the muscles filling out his broad shoulders as well.

With a twitch of his hand, he flicks a strand of wavy black hair away from his eyes. Then he chants another command in a low murmur I can't make out.

His magic wrenches me right out of the shadows into my true physical form, not the human-like one I can use as a disguise in the mortal realm.

My translucent body shimmers with a passing gust of wind. It's nothing but light from the vague shapes of feet to my glowing blob of a head.

All around me, other shadowkind pop out of the darkness too: mostly lesser creatures with their animalistic bodies but a few scattered higher beings as well: an imp with purple skin and spiky ears, a centaur in the midst of rearing his horsey front legs, and a nearly transparent wind spirit whose blustery hair is having a really bad day.

The sorcerer looks only at me.

His voice comes out steady and hard. "That's the one. Take her in."

2

Periwinkle

When the door to my cage finally opens, I've been crammed in here for what must have been multiple days, lifted and jostled more times than I can count.

And I'm a very good counter.

I know better than to try to leap straight toward possible freedom. If someone's mean enough to put you in a cage, they'll probably be just as mean when you're out of it.

So I stay contracted in my shadowy form amid the searing lights that burn away every hint of darkness within the metal box. Beyond the door, there's a sliver of shadow along the base of the cage. It calls to me.

Off past the blazing lights, someone intones several syllables in a language that pummels right into my essence.

Come out and show your human-like form. Then stay until you're dismissed.

I can't resist the sorcerous commands. I flit out and solidify into the human-like figure that comes naturally to me, complete with my daisy-print dress and rainbow-striped hoodie.

Hmm. I'm not sure the room outside is any better than the cage.

Dour gray walls surround me. The only furniture is a big kidney-shaped table made of stainless steel with seven matching chairs set around the outer curve. I don't think the seats even have padding.

Could anyone be happy in this place?

Someone should introduce these people to the concept of interior decorating. How about cushions for comfort? Maybe a rug? Art on the walls could liven things up.

The beings studying me from the six occupied chairs don't look like they're in the mood for lifestyle advice. Proving my point about the atmosphere, the strongest vibes they give off are curdled-milk apprehension and stale-bread boredom.

Not a meal I could even subsist on.

The first face my gaze lands on makes me flinch. It's the sorcerer who dragged me into the cage—obviously he's the one who ordered me out.

His eyes, a deeper hue than his cedar-brown skin, hold mine from beneath his wavy black hair. His broad shoulders are rigid. But despite his stern appearance, a pang of his guilt hits me like a shot of lemon juice.

Huh. The other sorcerer I knew never felt guilty about anything. At least, not when he was around me.

Next to the young sorcerer sits a shadowkind similarly shaped to myself—female, youthful, short and curvy—with a head of blond curls and dimples in her cheeks where she's smiling widely.

I can't tell whether she's hiding happier feelings under her apprehension or her smile is a lie. Not knowing makes my skin itch.

Her other neighbor is a tall, wiry woman with a few silver streaks running through her sleek black bob. Like the sorcerer, she's human.

No smile from her—her lips press in a flat line.

The other three members of my audience are shadowkind.

One pushes her long, dark blue hair back over her slim shoulders with a melodic sigh. A big, muscular man gives me a feral impression, his thick fingers curving against the tabletop like claws—I think he must be an animal shifter.

Most of the boredom emanates from the last figure: a man in an old-fashioned suit whose skin is so pale it might be translucent. I suspect that if I stared hard enough, I'd see his bones through it.

Why would shadowkind lock up another being like them? Why are they working with a sorcerer?

Is there any way I can lighten this situation?

I push my mouth into a smile of my own. "I think this must have been a misunderstanding. What are we all doing here?"

The wiry human's lips press even flatter at my question. The shadowkind with the blond curls lets out a tinkle of a laugh.

The woman with the long blue hair leans forward. Her voice sounds as melodic as her sigh did. "Unknown shadowkind, you've been brought in for assessment because you've been causing inappropriate disruptions in the mortal realm." She motions toward the sorcerer. "What exactly did this one do again?"

The sorcerer sits up straighter. "We believe she's responsible for multiple incidents in Greenville in the past year. Mostly bright waves of light that temporarily blinded human citizens and caused car accidents, falls, and other damage. At least once, there was a flood of darkness with similar results."

Yikes. How long have these people been paying attention to me?

"I didn't do any of it on purpose," I blurt out. "I never wanted to hurt anyone, I promise."

The pale man's eyebrows arch. "An immediate admission of guilt. Convenient."

The blond woman beams at me. "Let's start with the basics. What's your name? What kind of being are you?"

A genuine warmth seeps through her words as if they've been spread with melted butter.

I like her. I don't think she wants to shove me back in the cage.

My answering smile comes easier. "My name's Periwinkle—but usually I tell people Peri, because it sounds less strange to humans. I don't know if what I am has a name."

The muscular man drums his fingers on the table. "What do you *do*? Other than blind mortals."

His hint of a snarl has me wincing. "I absorb emotions. I kind of… eat them. But eating them doesn't hurt people. They don't even notice."

The wiry woman gives me a skeptical look. "And yet you've managed to harm quite a few people just in one year."

My cheeks heat. "Those… those were accidents. I haven't had a lot of practice at this."

At keeping control over my reactions rather than having someone else drive them.

I shove away those chilling memories. "If I get full of too

much emotion all at once, it bursts out of me. I don't know how to stop it from happening. But I think I'm getting closer to finding the right balance—so I'm not hungry but I don't get overwhelmed."

Her gaze rakes up and down me. "And that's all you want? Just to eat some emotions?"

"And make people happy. Spread the good emotions around."

Bring joy into mortal lives until I can count more of those than the lives I've wounded.

I don't think these beings will be very happy if I mention my more distant crimes, so I keep those to myself.

The muscular man lets out a snort. The blonde shoots a quick glare at him before returning her attention to me. "If we could teach you how to control your power better before you go back around humans, would you like that?"

They kidnapped me to offer me lessons?

I hesitate. "Teach me how?"

The blue-haired woman takes over. "We run a school for shadowkind who are having trouble integrating into the mortal realm. We'd rather humans stay unaware of our existence—and that you don't give those who are aware any additional excuse to call us 'monsters.' Sometimes beings who could use our guidance are unaware of our… services."

"Which is totally not their fault!" the blonde pipes up.

The wiry woman narrows her eyes at her companion, but with a waft of ginger-snap affection that I absorb in one gulp. She isn't all dourness.

The blue-haired woman continues. "Either you commit to working through our program here at the Quinn Moody Academy for the Shadowkind until we judge that it's safe for you to mingle with humans again, or we banish you to the shadow realm."

Images swim up of the vast, blank darkness where I emerged into being and lurked between my visits to the mortal world. So much dreariness, so little to do other than marinate in your thoughts, listen to other beings drone about theirs, and make pointless power plays to own a tiny corner of the murk. Or avoid the ones making power plays, which is more my vibe.

Sunshine or gloom—why would anyone take the second option? We "monsters" might all come from the shadow realm, but the mortal plane is so much more delicious.

Before I can speak, the pale man makes a disgruntled sound. "Are we sure we should be giving her a choice, Shanty? It sounds as if she's caused a lot of harm already with her unpredictable powers."

A lump fills my throat. One death, seven major injuries, and twenty-three minor wounds just in the most recent incident.

I told you I'm a good counter.

The muscular guy hums in a rumble. "We've never taught a being like her. I've never seen her specific power before. She might disrupt the students too."

I fumble for my words. "I won't. I'll do whatever you ask me to do. I want to be better! I want to make everything better. Please. I'll starve if I can't leave the shadows— emotions are too hazy there. I can only feed properly in the mortal world."

Eyebrows rise around the table. My scalp tingles.

I didn't pull my hood up—my turquoise hair is emanating a desperate pea-green glow.

"Well, that's certainly something," the blue-haired woman—Shanty?—says in a dry tone.

Mr. Muscles pushes to his feet. "Are you trying to blast *us* with light? How dare—"

"No!" I clasp my hands in front of me. "My hair lights

up when I'm feeling something a little strongly. No one's ever gotten hurt from just that. But I can't help it. Unless… maybe you could teach me how to turn it off too?"

It'd be handy not to have to worry about my hair blinking on like a nightlight with every shift of my own emotions.

The blonde sweeps her hand in my direction. "Listen to her! She'll obviously work hard to avoid getting banished. We don't see that kind of dedication often. Or are you afraid you can't handle a little unruliness, Gnash?"

The muscular man glowers at her, but Shanty nods slowly. "Rollick founded the academy on the principle that every shadowkind deserves the opportunity to enjoy the mortal realm. He would say to give her a trial period. Especially if she's a type of shadowkind that needs something from the mortal realm for nourishment."

"He's not here to say it, though, is he?" the pale man says tartly.

The wiry woman glances around the table. "He hasn't made his convictions a secret, Al. Shanty's right."

"I agree," the sorcerer says.

My gaze flicks to him. It's the first time he's spoken since the questioning began.

He doesn't look at me, only his colleagues. A thin draught of emotion reaches me: a cluttered mix of sour, bitter, and a softly sweet tang that I can't untangle.

The blonde lifts her head with a triumphant air. "There you go. It's four to two even without Rollick's vote."

Gnash growls but gives a flippant gesture of acceptance. The pale man—Al?—inclines his head. "So be it. Jonah?"

The sorcerer fixes his deep brown eyes on me.

"I'm sorry," he says quietly. Then a few more syllables of sorcerous compulsion roll off his tongue and wind around my being.

As the command to remain within the school's grounds sinks into my mind, I stare back at him.

What was he apologizing for? And why does the emotion coursing off him now carry a stodgy porridge flavor of sadness?

3

Periwinkle

"I think you'll like it here," Pearl says with a swish of her blond curls as she leads me through the pale blue halls. "There are so many interesting students with different stories. Lots of emotions flowing. You won't go hungry!"

The most upbeat of my interrogators volunteered to show me to my dorm after her colleagues finished my initial orientation. At least this area is a little more vibrant than the dreary room where I met Pearl.

I peer around me at the various doors with their frosted glass windows. "And there'll be classes that will teach me how to control my power?"

"Yep! And all sorts of other support to help you exist among mortals." Pearl pats my arm. "Lots of shadowkind prefer hanging out in this world rather than the shadow realm. You're in good company. Just follow the rules, and you'll be fine."

The rules. I look down at the badge attached to my dress —the metal crest Shanty pinned there right before I left the interrogation room.

You start at level one, the more solemn woman told me, tapping the number imprinted at the top of the crest. Then she touched a triangle underneath it. *You're in the reform division, for beings who've been actively struggling with their behavior. The weekly schedule for each level and division is posted in the dorm areas. We expect you to attend all your assigned classes. Show commitment and perform well, and you'll graduate to the next level.*

There's something I forgot to ask. I glance over at Pearl. "How many levels are there?"

How much graduating do I need to do before I can be sure it's safe for me to leave?

"Five!" Pearl replies. "And level five is really just some final finessing. Once you make it even to three, you're well on your way."

A couple of other symbols mark the sides of the badge. One is a swirling line, the other a starburst with six points.

I tap them. "What do these mean?"

"Oh." Pearl giggles, but the cheerful vibe beaming off her like buttered popcorn dwindles. "That's to help the staff and other students know what precautions to take. The left side indicates how cooperative or defiant you are. The swirl means we're not sure yet. The right side tells people how dangerous you might be. The star means you've harmed mortals. They can have up to ten points."

I stare down at the imprint for a few more seconds. If the school's overseers knew how much more damage I've caused beyond the recent incidents they talked about, would they have marked me with all ten?

Pearl chatters merrily onward. "It's not a big deal here since almost everyone is shadowkind anyway. You want to watch your step around anyone who's got a ring around their star. That means they've hurt shadowkind too."

At least I can say I don't think I've ever done that.

When I look up again, we're passing several beings standing in small clusters in the halls. Their gazes slide over me with traces of curiosity, but no one speaks.

I smile at them. Most avert their eyes to go back to talking to their companions.

Well, they don't know me yet. I'll show them how cooperative and helpful I can be.

I'll learn everything I need to undo the damage I caused before.

We head up a flight of stairs. After a few steps, a jolt of pain quivers up from my ankles through my calves.

I suppress my wince, but Pearl catches my discomfort anyway. "Are you all right?"

I nod quickly. "It's not a big deal. My legs are just a little… weak. Sometimes I get wobbly when I'm in human-like form for a while."

Her mouth slants with a frown. "It's policy that students stay human-esque as much as possible, for practice. But if you need to take little breaks in the shadows here and there to look after yourself, that's totally okay."

I give her my brightest smile. "I'm sure it'll be all right. It doesn't bother me that much."

Not anywhere near as much as the memories of how my legs got that way, which I'll keep shut away in the back of my mind.

Pearl doesn't look totally convinced, but she accepts my answer. "If you need guidance any time, you can look for me or the other board members… Well, maybe Al wouldn't be the best bet—I don't know if it's a vampire thing, but he acts like emotions are cooties he might catch."

She rolls her eyes.

So the pale man at the table is a vampire? The comment reminds me of another name I never got to attach to a being. "What about Rollick? You were talking about him— who's he?"

Pearl's expression turns wistful. "He's the shadowkind who came up with the idea for this school and got it off the ground. He's been around for millennia, built up lots of resources to create awesome places like this. So he's the big boss—all the final calls go through him. But he's had some other important stuff to deal with, always very busy, so he hasn't been around much in the past few months."

I don't know how long I've been in existence—there's not much sense of time in the shadow realm—but I think my first trek into the mortal world was only a couple of decades ago. What would a thousands-years-old being make of me?

Maybe it's better I didn't have to find that out.

As we reach the top of the stairs, she taps her own badge: a simpler one than mine, bronze instead of tin, with a single symbol like a church spire. "You can turn to any of the staff —look for badges like this. It's better for all of us if you have everything you need to thrive."

On the second floor, late-afternoon sunlight beams through a series of skylights set in the angled ceiling. The illumination buoys my hopes.

Getting dragged into this school might be the best thing that could have happened to me. If I'd known it existed, I'd have come looking for them instead of the other way around.

They could have just asked nicely instead of throwing me in a cage.

What does that say about the other "reform" students if they did need to be hauled here?

We take a right, and Pearl motions to an arched doorway up ahead. "You're in the Lugosi dorm."

"Lugosi?"

"Rollick thinks he's funny." She winks at me as if there's a joke I've missed and peeks at her phone. "It looks like you've been assigned to room 5. The class schedule will be posted in the common area. Since the day's almost over, you can get started with your education tomorrow. Take some time to meet your dormmates and settle in."

She sashays back the way we came.

All right. It's the new kid's first day! Let's make it a good one.

With my lips stretched into a sunny smile, I reach to open the door.

In the wider hall on the other side, several doors line both walls. A line of sofas and armchairs stretches down the middle of the space with an occasional side table in between.

All sorts of beings lounge on and around the furnishings. Many of them look over to see who the new arrival is.

A flurry of understated emotions tickles me from across the distance—intrigue and irritation and anticipation swirled together in a jumbled stew.

My attention stalls on a group of students off to one side of the hall. Several beings have gathered around a tall, slim man who's propped against the wall in a cavalier pose.

I'd imagine many people's eyes would be drawn to him. He's handsome in a particularly striking way, with blond hair so light it's almost silver, sharp features that could have been carved out of ivory, and startlingly dark blue eyes gleaming amid all that paleness. Even leaning nonchalantly, he gives off an impression of cool authority.

Not only that, he has some interesting magic going on. Despite his dispassionate expression, a figurine that looks like a towering pine is forming over his hand with an icy gleam.

He's conjuring it out of the air while the beings around him exclaim with much more enthusiasm than he's showing.

That's what catches my attention more than his looks or his chilly power: the undercurrent of emotion drifting off him. For all his apparent nonchalance, frustration bubbles beneath his surface like a bitter curry.

One of his companions cuts off my view, stepping toward me with a graceful but haughty air. She's nearly as tall and equally gorgeous, her snow-white skin contrasting with her waterfall of black hair.

"We have a new rogue," she says in a smooth, crystalline voice that fits her looks perfectly. Her gaze flicks to my badge. "And a threat to humankind as well. What did you do to get tossed in here?"

I resist the urge to dive under the nearest sofa. It's time to spread some friendliness around, since it seems to be in somewhat short supply. "It was just an accident. I'm looking forward to learning with all of you!"

I catch a few muffled giggles and snorts, cotton candy fluffs of amusement. But everyone who's here made the choice to stay, didn't they? They must have thought it was a good idea.

Another shadowkind woman, shorter but similarly svelte, sidles up beside the haughty one. She sneers at me. "Sure you are."

The first woman taps her friend with her elbow. "We can be welcoming."

She holds out her hand to me. "My name is Gloss. I sometimes drop in on the reform division for the… invigorating company."

She tosses a grin over her shoulder toward the icily handsome man, and I notice her badge, pinned to the bodice of her sleek burgundy dress. It has a circle etched on it beneath the number 4, not a triangle like mine.

Does that mean she's a student who came voluntarily?

I give her hand a tentative shake and smile wider to make up for my hesitation. "I'm Periwinkle. But you can call me Peri. It's nice to meet you."

Another woman steps around Gloss to peer at me. "She doesn't seem like she could warrant a six-pointed star, huh?"

"Not at all. So sweet. We'll have to find out what she's made of." The look Gloss gives me seems a bit pointed, but she gives off so little emotion it's hard for me to tell. "What room did they give you?"

"Five!" I announce, relieved to find that piece of information stuck in my head.

"Hmm." Gloss taps a finger to her lips. "I think there might have been some informal shuffling. Tansy, why don't you check whether room five is actually free and which one has an opening if not?"

The shorter, sneering woman darts off down the hall to make her inquiries. The other shadowkind following our conversation watch Gloss avidly but with a prickle of anxiety.

I think they want to make sure they don't disappoint her.

She obviously has some authority, considering she's the one who greeted me and this isn't even her dorm.

"Where's your room?" I ask out of honest curiosity.

Gloss flicks her fingers vaguely toward the wall. "Oh, the voluntary students stay in the Citrine building. Reforms aren't allowed into other dorms until they're at least level four. Some of my friends are *very* bad at playing nice."

She tsks her tongue playfully and glances at the other women and the icy man. But for all her effortless confidence, a trickle of doubt seeps off her—a tart splash of insecurity only I can taste.

She's been welcoming enough to me that I want to reassure her. I should do something kind for her too.

"You don't need to worry," I say. "They really do care what you think."

Her attention snaps back to me. "What?"

I fumble under the sudden intensity of her stare. "I just mean, you've already impressed them. They want to listen to you. So you don't need to worry."

For a split-second, Gloss's eyes narrow. A jolt of fury hits me right in the throat, searing like charred peppers.

Then it's gone. She takes a step back with a crisp laugh, and my sense of her inner state dwindles to nothing.

"It sounds like the only one who's worried is you." She turns to Tansy, who's just hurried back to join her.

The other woman dips her head. "Mica moved into room five. But there's a bed in—"

"In room twelve." Gloss's eyes glint at me as if nothing went wrong, but several of the beings around her stiffen.

"Twelve," her other friend hisses. "Are you sure—"

Gloss clasps her slender hands together. "I think room twelve would be perfect for Periwinkle. Exactly the atmosphere she needs. Unless someone else wanted to claim that spot?"

The hall has gone silent, broken by a brief chuckle from the icy man. The pine tree he was conjuring flits apart into a puff of snowflakes. "Brilliant as always, Gloss."

Gloss's face lights up. She gestures for me to move on. "You won't have any trouble finding it. They're all in order."

I summon a smile that feels tighter than before. "Thank you."

As I weave between my watching dormmates down the hall, no one speaks other than a few murmurs. A hum of edgy anticipation has come into the air.

What are they waiting for? What do they think is going to happen?

The room labeled twelve is right at the end of the hall on the right side. When I turn the handle, it opens easily.

There isn't much point in locks when we can all slip through the shadows beneath the doors if we want.

I step inside.

The room appears empty—at least, of other beings. Two twin-sized beds with simple wooden bedframes stand at opposite ends, with even smaller desks just beyond their footboards. The walls are the same light blue as in the halls. A square rug in a darker shade covers most of the floor between the beds.

I'm not alone, though. My senses quiver with the awareness of another shadowkind nearby, merged with the patch of darkness around the lefthand bed.

A shadowkind that's radiating outrage.

Before I can even turn toward the impression, he materializes out of the darkness. The huge man looms nearly as high as the ceiling, ropey muscles bulging across his limbs and chest, his tan face that might have been stunning otherwise set in a fierce expression. Thick brown hair gleams like buffed bronze as it bristles from the top of his head.

His badge shows a number one like mine… and a ten-pointed star with a ring around it. Pearl said that means he's hurt shadowkind as well as mortals.

"What are you doing in here?" he growls.

My heart stutters. I hold up my hands appeasingly and step back toward the other bed. "I—they told me this is the room I should be in. With a free bed."

I can hear my voice going squeaky. A smattering of light touches the walls as my hair flickers with a sickly yellow flare of fear.

The immense man bares his teeth. "This is *my* room. I don't share. Get out!"

My pulse outright lurches. I back up, on the verge of fleeing, when a giggle reaches my ears from beyond the door.

My dormmates—and specifically Gloss—sent me into this situation on purpose. They knew the room's current inhabitant would be furious.

They're waiting for me to scurry out so they can laugh at me for failing.

My legs balk at the thought of playing the horrible game they made up. If I do what they want… what will they try to make me do next?

In my hesitation, the man lets out a snarl. "Can't you hear? Get the fuck away!"

With the words, another waft of emotion washes over me. Not rage this time, but fear that's not mine, as suffocatingly sour as a flood of cheap whiskey.

This being… is afraid of *me*?

That can't be right, but I know what I'm tasting.

I don't like the idea of abandoning a being in some kind of distress any more than I want to submit myself to my other dormmates' judgment.

I should show them I won't fail. I can be kind to *everyone* here. I can find ways to be happy no matter where I am.

I back up another step, but this time toward the bed. Sitting down on the mattress, I keep my hands raised and my voice softly bright. "I promise I'll keep my distance. I'm not going to bother you at all. I just need a place where I can sleep."

The man could lunge at me, and I'm not totally sure what I'd do then. But he stays where he is, confusion trickling through the unpalatable mix of anger and fear.

"You'd *better* stay away from me," he warns, and vanishes back into the shadows.

I lower my hands to rest on the bedspread. My pulse

keeps hammering away, but a knot of resolve solidifies in my gut.

These are the circumstances I've been given. I'm lucky to be here at all, so I'll just have to make the best of it.

I made Gloss upset—she thought I deserved this.

She doesn't know how much I can endure. I won't let her or any of the others shake me.

After all, I've lived through way worse before.

4

Raze

My new, incredibly unwelcome roommate appears to have fallen asleep.

How the fuck is that even possible? Doesn't she feel doom breathing down her neck?

All I have to do is walk through the school halls in physical form, and the other students scatter in my wake. Even the instructors tense up when they meet my eyes, despite the contacts I conjure to stifle my gaze's killing power.

But I outright demanded that this little ball of vivid fabric and hair get out, with all the brutality I could put into my stance and voice, and she just… sat down on the other bed and proceeded to ignore me.

It doesn't make sense.

I thought it had to be an act. She'd break down eventually in shivers or tears and take off the way I expected.

Instead, she's lain down on the mattress, pulled the blanket up, and taken a nap.

She really is asleep. My predator instincts pick up the shallow rhythm of her breaths, the slowed thump of her heart.

Somehow, even with me lurking in the shadows, she relaxed enough to drift off.

Maybe she was *really* tired? There's no way of knowing what she was doing before the administrators caught her.

Not that she seems particularly dangerous.

I didn't get close enough to tell for sure, but she looks so short her head would barely reach halfway up my chest. Even under the blanket, the slopes of her shoulders, breasts, belly, and hips give the impression of total softness.

I have the bizarre urge to go over and lean my head into the dip of her waist to see if she'd make as comforting a pillow as I can't help imagining.

Why is she in the reform division at all? What harm could this bit of fluff with glowing hair possibly do?

It couldn't be enough to protect her from me.

I hold steady in the shadows around my bed for several more minutes, as if the answers might present themselves out of thin air. All I get is my new roommate's scent, bubblegum-sweet, filling my lungs.

Making me wonder how good she'd smell if I did tuck my head right against her.

She shouldn't be so… so whatever she is.

Finally, my confusion overcomes my distaste for mingling with my dormmates. I slink along the edge of the room to the strip of shadow beneath the door.

There's no need to go into the hall and announce myself. Whatever frivolous or awkward conversations they're having I can hear just fine from here.

If they knew I was listening, they'd probably shut up anyway.

As usual, the other beings are giving the entire area around my room a wide berth. Maybe wider than usual, as if they're still expecting the newcomer to come bolting out at any moment.

It seems like they're as confused as I am.

The largest group is gathered around Hail, as usual, even though as far as I can tell the callous winter fae is about as warm and friendly as a blizzard. He even looks like an icicle, frost-pale from head to toe except those dark blue eyes.

Something about his chill draws other beings in, though, especially the female ones. A cluster of seven is hanging around now, chattering with each other and shooting him coy glances through their eyelashes.

At the moment, they're yattering on about some class for a level above my own. I shift restlessly in my shadow.

Then a couple of the women glance toward my room. One of them elbows Gloss, the fancy interloper who's always coming around to our dorms even though she doesn't belong here.

"What do you think happened to the newbie?" the first woman asks.

Another titters. "I'm surprised the door even closed without her scampering back out here."

Gloss shrugs as if the subject doesn't matter to her. Her tone is equally careless. "Maybe Raze has already eviscerated her. If he hasn't yet, I'm sure she'll be lizard kibble soon."

Even in the shadows, I have the sense of my hackles going up and my lips drawing back from my basilisk fangs. But my anger at her mocking words prickles with a deeper discomfort.

Of course that's what they think of me. I do "eviscerate" people, don't I?

I'm fucking poison, and everyone knows it.

Now they think they can use me as a tool in their mindless jostling for dominance, as if anyone should give a shit who rules this ridiculous school. The whole point of it is to prepare us to *leave* this place.

Not that it's likely I ever will.

A fourth woman makes a scoffing sound. "Did she really think she was going to get away with it, coming in here acting all sweet and then taking a jab at *you* of all people?"

Gloss offers a sharp smile. "If she hasn't learned her lesson quickly, she's an even bigger imbecile than she seemed. We'll just have to teach her what her place is as often as she needs it."

Hail dips his pale head to her. "It's always fun to watch you work."

She slips her hand around his elbow. "The dorm has gotten tiresome for today, don't you think? Why don't we see what the reform division is getting for dinner, and maybe I'll join you for that too."

As the clot of them saunters out of the dorm, I pull back into my room. My essence simmers with uneasy heat.

My attention slides to the small, curvy form tucked into the other bed.

I can't tell whether the fact that the newcomer stayed was a show of strength or idiocy. Either way, it's hard to imagine her insulting Gloss on purpose. She was nothing but respectful in her approach to me.

A gentle sort of respect that feels strangely different from the panicked variety I'm used to.

I've seen how Gloss operates. The snow wraith might not have fangs of her own, but she makes sure her targets are eaten alive one way or another. This bit of fluff doesn't stand a chance.

I don't want her in my room. But if she's going to insist

on staying for now, I can at least do my best to stop anyone from going out of their way to hurt her.

Staying in the shadows, I stretch out along the edge of the rug, making a barrier between the door and her. Still keeping a careful distance from her myself.

She might not have figured it out yet, but no matter how vicious Gloss gets… the being here who's most likely to hurt her is me.

5

Periwinkle

Two streams of impressions waft out of the reform division cafeteria to meet me: a jumble of mild but cluttered emotions in various flavors and a flood of savory, spicy, and sweet scents drifting off actual food.

So many beings combined with so much cuisine makes a chaotic smorgasbord. My head is spinning before I've even stepped into the vast room.

I study the cafeteria's layout carefully. The schedule said today's breakfast theme was "casual hangout." The tables spread throughout the room can seat anywhere from four to ten beings—no tablecloths, just paper plates and plastic cutlery set out for people to grab.

The students are swiping morsels off platters of sausages, boiled eggs, pancakes, toast, and cut fruit laid on each table. Some of the sweet scent carries from bottles of maple syrup, enticing enough that I lick my lips.

There's nothing specifying where any of us should sit. The students already eating are chattering away with their companions as if they chose to sit with friends.

Who do I hang out with when I haven't managed to make friends yet? My first attempt ended with my dormmates setting me up for violent murder.

I can do better with practice, right? Learning how to cheer on my fellow shadowkind should help prepare me for dealing with more fragile humans.

As I debate which group I should join, a slim woman with deep brown skin slips past me. She tugs at the black spirals of her hair in a nervous gesture, revealing violet scales gleaming on her forearms. We all have one bit of our monstrous selves that we can't conceal in human form, mine being my oddly colored hair.

Her obvious uncertainty draws my attention with a twinge of sympathy. She meanders over to one of the larger tables, pauses, and then reaches for a plate.

A beefy guy bumps his elbow into her arm. He wrinkles his nose at the sight of her. "Oh, it's the drip."

The woman cringes and slinks away, her head low. I march over to join her.

"Hey," I say. "I'm new here, so I don't really know what I'm doing. Maybe we can find a table together?"

Both the woman's face and the emotions trickling off her brighten. She turns toward me, and my gaze catches on her badge—level one, reform division, no harm done to mortals or shadowkind.

Why would anyone be mean to her? *They're* not getting very good practice.

Maybe I've got this school thing in the bag after all.

The woman glances around and points to a small table near the wall that no one has grabbed yet. "We can take an empty one if there are at least two of us. Since it's supposed to be a 'hang-out,' the staff want to see us socializing. Every meal has a different theme like the different ways mortals eat. You'll get used to it."

I beam at her. "I'm glad I have someone to explain the rules. I'm Peri. Have you been at the academy long?"

She rubs her face with a flicker of embarrassment. "Several months. I sometimes have… unfortunate reactions that I'm still having trouble controlling. Anyway, I'm Fen. Let's get some pancakes!"

I feel like I've already passed a test. I get to stack fluffy pancakes on my plate and drizzle them with syrup, I've made a friend after all, and nobody has died. Wins all around!

Physical food might not sustain me the way it does humans, but that doesn't mean it isn't tasty. I dig into my heap of cakey, syrupy goodness while peering around the cafeteria. I recognize a few faces from my dorm, but my growly roommate, who hasn't spoken to me since our first standoff, isn't among them.

Across the room, another guy jumps on top of one of the tables. Vibrantly red hair flares above his golden-brown face. His wide grin reveals canines narrowed into sharp little fangs.

As the dishes rattle around him, he lets out a whoop and springs into a handstand. "I bet I can eat more eggs upside down than any of you right-side up!"

The students around him either laugh or shake their heads. The fanged guy bounds around on his hands with impressive nimbleness, his legs wheeling in the air.

Fen giggles. "That's Mirage. He's always goofing around. He might startle you sometimes, but he isn't mean about it."

She says that like lots of other students would be. I guess I've already encountered a little of that cruelty.

A woman with a bronze staff badge materializes out of

the shadows. She gives the fanged guy—who's still upside down on the table—a stern look. "Mirage, you know mealtime is for *eating*, not acrobatics."

He cocks his head at her, his vivid hair standing on end with his pose. "Don't humans have fun with their friends? I'm following the theme."

She folds her arms over her chest. "They don't like that, not in the middle of breakfast. Get down, now."

Mirage pushes himself onto one hand and whirls around. For the space of a breath, four more identical figures spin on the table around him.

I blink, my jaw dropping, and the extra Mirages vanish. The real one leaps onto the floor and gives the staff woman a jaunty salute.

He's too far away for me to taste any emotions seeping out of him. But even though he's still grinning, I can't help thinking there's something tense in his expression.

"He can multiply himself?" I ask Fen.

"He can make you see pretty much whatever he wants. He's a fox shifter—they're usually good with illusions." Fen's smile stretches wider. "You should have seen, the other day in the gym he—"

The blare of a horn cuts off her story. All around the room, the other students snap to attention.

Fen fiddles with the cuffs of her sleeves. She glances at me and knits her brow. "I guess you don't really have to worry. Your hair is your holdover feature, right? A human could dye it that shade, so you don't have to hide it."

"I usually keep it covered anyway. When I'm around humans." I tug up the hood of my jacket. "Why, are they bringing humans in here?"

"Oh, no, definitely not. That was an adapt check. It goes off a few times a day, totally random to keep us on our toes. When you hear the horn, you make sure you'd fit in as a human as quickly as possible. It stops us from getting lazy if there are parts we need to remember to keep hidden."

Fen glances down at her arms, where her sleeves conceal all of her scales.

"It's too bad," I tell her. "Your scales are pretty."

Her skin is too dark for a blush to show, but her pleased awkwardness tastes like cinnamon toast. "Thank you. I wish they weren't so low down on my arms so they'd be easier to cover."

"Maybe someday scales will become a new human fashion trend, and then you won't have to."

Fen giggles. "I don't know about that, but it does seem like with mortals, anything is possible."

A gurgle of liquid draws my attention. A guy a couple of tables over is pouring himself a glass of orange juice from a pitcher.

Our table is tragically devoid of pitchers.

I spring up, grabbing my plastic cup. "They forgot to put drinks on this table. We can borrow from another one, right? Sharing is a friendly thing to do."

Fen pushes to her feet too, her dark green eyes glinting. "I'd think so. I am kind of thirsty."

I set off, but I've only made it a few steps when an elegant figure sweeps in front of me with a swish of sleek black hair. "*Excuse* me."

I lurch to get out of her way and set down my foot at an angle that sends a jab of pain lancing up through my ankle. With a stumble, I bump into the nearest chair.

As I grasp the chair to catch my balance, Gloss glowers down her nose at me. "It looks like the newbie is as clumsy on her feet as she is when she's talking."

The cluster of students following her titters with laughter. Half the cafeteria seems to be craning their necks to see what's going on.

My face flushes—and a tingle creeps into my hair.

Gloss covers her mouth with a guffaw she somehow manages to make sound dainty. "Oh, look, she's glowing with embarrassment. That peachy shine really isn't a good color on you."

I yank my hood farther over my luminescent hair, which is definitely not something any human has. "I'm sorry I almost bumped into you."

"You should watch where you're going," Gloss says with a benevolent air, as if she's doing me a favor by not dropkicking me for my transgression.

The glow of my embarrassment is already fading away, but her gaze flicks to my companion. Her crimson lips curl condescendingly. "You poor things—it's the hopeless leading the hopeless. Impressive that you've found each other so quickly."

I glance at Fen, who appears to have shrunk in on her already slight frame. Her voice shrinks too. "We were just getting some juice."

"Oh? I thought you had more than enough liquid in you already, Drip."

One of Gloss's friends snorts. "The way she piddles, she should be in puppy school, not here."

Gloss tsks her tongue. "Look, there she goes again."

The patter of falling water reaches my ears. It's coming from the hand that's dropped to Fen's side as she hugs her other arm across her waist.

Droplets of murky water dribble off her fingers and plop onto the white-tiled floor. The nearest students wince and move away.

Their reaction only makes the dripping thicken into a steady trickle. Fen squeezes her hand into a fist, but she can't contain the water leaking off her.

It must be something to do with her powers. This is what she was saying she can't control.

Gloss provoked her on purpose.

The shame radiating off Fen now chokes me with its vinegar sourness. She was perfectly happy a moment ago.

She shouldn't have to feel like this.

With a smile that feels fierce, I stare into Gloss's gleaming amber eyes. "It's just a little water. Water's good for everyone. I'm proud to be her friend."

Gloss rolls her eyes. "We'll see how far that pride gets you, I suppose."

She motions to her cluster of followers, and they all sashay off.

"Here." I take Fen's cup and hustle to the table where I fill it and mine with juice. When I return, she's left behind the puddle of marshy water and retreated to her seat.

I sit next to her. "I don't understand why people say things like that. You didn't do anything wrong. No one would be here if we didn't have more to learn."

Apparently a lot of the other students have amnesia about that fact. Let's hope it's temporary.

Fen takes a sip of her juice and lifts her shoulders in a weak shrug. "It's okay. Humans aren't always going to be nice either. The staff encourage us to hassle each other as long as there's no real harm done. It tests our tolerance, gives us practice at holding in our powers even when we're annoyed or upset." She grimaces. "Like you saw, I usually fail that test."

I let out a dismissive huff. "We'll figure it out. I'm here because I have trouble keeping my powers in too. We can work on our control together."

Finally, a glimmer of pleased relief seeps through Fen's gloom, sweet as a dab of strawberry jam. "You think so?"

"Absolutely. Everyone knows it's easier to tackle problems when you're not alone."

A streak of red at the corner of my vision catches my attention. Mirage is just loping to the cafeteria door, pausing to swipe a sausage off another student's plate and provoking an indignant yelp.

A burst of resolve raises my spirits. I can find out what's going on inside him too.

6

Periwinkle

As she leads me to the room for our Geography and Culture class, Fen perks up. "I wonder what place we'll be hearing about today. I think if I can ever really integrate, I'd want to visit a whole bunch of them."

I think of the many different landscapes and styles of humans I've glimpsed images of. "I want to see all of them!"

I have a brief daydream of gliding around the mortal world, sampling all its flavors… Brief because when we walk into the classroom with its rows of tables, I find myself staring at the sorcerer who compelled me into my latest cage.

My muscles tense so swiftly I nearly trip over my feet.

Jonah glances over from where he's standing by a whiteboard at the front of the room. He's smiling, white teeth bright against his cedar-brown skin.

When his deep brown eyes meet mine, his friendly expression falters.

I get a whiff of sour-stale discomfort that makes me wish I could chug more of the maple syrup we left back in the cafeteria.

Fen tugs my wrist. "We should sit in the front. Then we get the best view of the pictures."

It shouldn't be a surprise that the sorcerer has other roles at the academy. I wouldn't want there to be so many shadowkind upending mortal lives that he'd need to make a full-time career out of dragging them here.

When I risk another glance at Jonah, his smile has come back, though it's a little cautious. "It looks like you're already making friends, Peri. That's good to see. I know Fen will help you find your footing."

His tone stays steady and professional, but my new friend beams at the compliment anyway.

"I definitely will," she promises, and drags me over to the table that's front and center.

It's only after I've followed her lead that I realize sitting up here means I'm as close as possible to the sorcerer in our midst. Minor miscalculation.

I breathe slow and deep. The last thing I need is my hair shining with anxiety for all to see.

There's nothing to be afraid of anyway, is there? I'm *glad* I've ended up at the school.

I should be grateful Jonah stepped in, really.

It's just hard not to remember the strands of sorcery digging into my essence every time I look at him. And that memory stirs up echoes of so many other times…

So I do my best not to look at him at all. As our classmates file in, I check out them instead.

The icy man with the unnervingly dark blue eyes enters and drapes his lanky frame into a chair halfway back at the edge of the room. When he catches me looking at him, he gives me a smile so cold it feels more like a knife-stab.

Thankfully Gloss won't be joining us, since she isn't even in the reform division. I do spot a few of her other friends—they all sit by the chilly guy, like they're forming a barricade around him.

To my delight, Mirage bounds through the doorway, grinning with a flash of his fangs. He vaults over one of the tables to land on the chair feet-first. Spinning around, he drops into the seat. Conjured applause kicks in like the laugh track in a TV sitcom.

Jonah gives him a stern look. "Let's keep the illusions to a minimum today, Mirage."

"Just giving myself the recognition I'm sure I deserve," the fox shifter replies cheerfully.

A few dozen more beings drift in and take their seats until almost all the chairs are taken. None of them is the big sinewy shadowkind who yelled at me to get out of our dorm room yesterday.

That's strange. Shouldn't he have this class too? He was level one like me.

As I consider asking Fen, Jonah clears his throat. A shadowkind woman wearing a staff badge has arrived, now standing next to him.

Well, that solves one problem. I'll just look at her instead of him and still be perfectly attentive.

Jonah taps the whiteboard, which must have a computer display built in. Its surface flickers and forms what looks like a digital photo album.

"Today, we're going to be talking about Berlin. That's the capital city of the country of Germany, in the continent of Europe. The location is convenient for shadowkind, with a few rifts around the city if you need to quickly return to the shadow realm."

He brings up a map of the entire mortal realm to show

the city's exact location. It takes my breath away seeing how big the human world is.

I guess the shadow realm might be equally large, but it's so vague and dark that it's not as though any one part is particularly different from another. No cities or countries, just endless gloom.

I restrain a shudder.

Jonah goes on. "If you like an urban atmosphere, Berlin is one of the best cities to blend in among humans. Many alternative subcultures have a strong presence there, with a wide variety of unique fashion and personal styling. In some cases, your shadowkind features won't raise any eyebrows—people will assume they're body modifications."

The photos he flips through show young people with ink coloring their skin and hair all the colors of the rainbow. Metal glints from every place I knew you could insert piercings and a few more besides.

I wind a lock of my hair around my finger. No one would see the turquoise shade as strange in that kind of crowd.

At least, unless it starts glowing.

At the drumming of fingers on a tabletop, I peek over my shoulder. The icy man's lips have curved with amusement.

"I've heard they have clubs where you can be free with your desires, for those who might want to indulge," he says languidly. His cool voice gives away no suggestion that he has a personal interest, but he aims a suggestive look at one of the female students sitting near him. She flushes with a flirty giggle.

Oh. Memories flit through my head of club scenes I've seen on screens—limbs twining, mouths melding together. And more intimate embraces that always cut off so quickly…

A faint flush ripples over my skin. I dabbled in that kind of bodily play with a couple of other shadowkind years ago, but it was never as thrilling as humans make it seem. Maybe these people in Berlin are better at it?

It might be worth a quick trip just to find out…

My imaginings are cut off by the wasabi-bitter irritation that wafts off Jonah, though his expression stays mild. "That's a topic better addressed in your Personal Relationships class, Hail."

The icy man—Hail?—leans farther back in his seat with a blasé attitude, but I taste a lick of satisfaction like a dab of whipped cream. "It seems like a key feature of the place to me."

His remark provokes another giggle from his neighbor.

A slight edge creeps into Jonah's tone. "When you're teaching the subject, you can make that call."

He cuts off the conversation by turning toward the woman who joined him. "Our guest instructor, Crinkle, has spent the past few decades living among the mortals in Berlin. She'll be able to fill in details I can't and give you a shadowkind perspective on life in the city."

Jonah and Crinkle go back and forth discussing the benefits, the potential problems most likely to arise, and which types of supernatural inclinations Berlin can best accommodate. Throughout the presentation, the sorcerer encourages us to think about whether we could see ourselves fitting into this place.

"It might seem far off," he says, "but brief real-world practicums start at level two, and by level three we want you seriously considering and trying out locations where you might settle down for your first year of integration."

A lot of the aspects he mentions sound lovely, but I have another voice in my head from years ago: Gracie's awed tone as she told me about the city on the lake where she wanted to go as soon as she was old enough to leave home—the music festivals, restaurants with every kind of food you could imagine, so many parks and trees…

She drew pictures in my head with her words. I haven't seen *her* since that last night—since the night when I escaped—

I already know where I'm going when I'm ready to leave this school. As soon as I'm sure I won't accidentally blaze her away, I'll go find her.

If there's anyone I owe a heap of joy to, it's her.

The talk shifts to questions from the students. After the first few, the brawny woman behind me raises her hand. "Isn't there a higher chance of having a bad interaction with a mortal if you're living in a city? I mean, with so many of them around?"

"Being surrounded by a lot of people can actually make you safer," Jonah says. "If someone hassles you, you can slip away, and the chances of running into them again are a lot less than in a small town."

The woman lets out a jovial chuckle. "Right, of course. And it's not like any of them would stand a chance against us if push came to shove anyway."

Her posture is all bravado, but a current of lemony terror touches my tongue.

I turn in my seat to give her a reassuring smile. "You don't need to be scared of humans. Most of them aren't bad at all. They want to be happy just like we do."

The woman stares at me and then pulls her lips back in a snarl. "I wouldn't be scared of any puny mortal."

Her tablemate extends claws from her fingertips and flexes them at me with a menacing scowl. "A runt like you should think before you speak."

Even if she's trying to look and sound ominous, all I can taste from the second woman is more fear. I have to show them I mean well.

She doesn't have any starburst points on her badge—she's never hurt anyone before. Her implied threat is all defensive.

I try to make my smile even kinder in apology. "I only wanted to make her feel better. Neither of you need to be afraid of *me*, I promise."

The second woman growls and shoves to her feet. "What are you trying to say?"

I open and close my mouth, my thoughts turning into babble that won't help anyone.

I thought I'd said exactly what I meant. Why is she acting angry?

Jonah lifts his voice, calm but firm. "Sit down, Vim. I'm sure Peri wasn't trying to insult you."

A faint scoff carries from Hail's seat. "The newbie's going to have to fight her own battles sometime. From the looks of her, they'll at least be short."

Jonah shakes his head. "If we could get back on topic, please—"

The chime of the bell interrupts. Everyone pushes back their chairs.

As soon as I can tell we're meant to leave, I hurry to the door.

Fen touches my arm. "Don't worry about any of them. We've got an hour before the next class. Do you want me to show you the courtyard? It's really nice."

I don't want to upset her too, but my faith in my cheering abilities is shaken. I manage a smile. "I think I just want to rest in my room for a bit, but I'd love to see it later."

Despite my best efforts, Fen deflates a little. "Oh. All right."

I rush through the halls to the dorm area, my stomach twisting into knots.

Why do things go wrong when I'm trying to do something good? Why can't I fit in properly even here where I'm surrounded by beings who are supposed to be like me?

It's okay. Not *everyone* hates me. I'm still figuring things out.

It'll get better. It has to. I insist.

When I reach the dorm, I walk straight to my room. I'll take the next hour to sort myself out, and then I'll be ready to face whatever's next.

Except I'm not alone. The instant I walk into the small space, I pick up on my roommate's stormy energy from the shadows.

I turn toward the spot where I can tell he's lurking. The question tumbles out before I can think better of it. "Why weren't you at class?"

If he spoke from the shadows, I'd still hear him, if in a distant, blurry kind of way. Instead, he ripples out into his full, immense form, glaring down at me with his ropey muscles tensed. "Some of us have to go to different classes. Because there are more important things to worry about."

He points at his badge—the ten-pointed star, the circle around it.

"Oh," I mumble. "I just wondered."

He grunts and vanishes again. I sink onto my bed and draw my knees to my chest to hug them.

I seem to be pissing people off left and right, and one of them is a shadowkind so fearsome he needs special classes to make sure he doesn't hurt the rest of us.

All I can do is keep going, doing my best.

Because it's either that or starve in the shadow-realm gloom.

7

Hail

I close my eyes to the sun, letting the rays wash over my skin. The glare filters through my eyelids with a ruddy glow. My cheeks feel as if they're baking.

The mortal realm is a bizarre place. So many aspects of it waver on the line between pleasure and pain.

My essence responds best to the cold rather than heat. If I stand here a few minutes longer, like I sometimes do on the desert plain outside the academy, every inch of my skin will start to prickle with the impression of burning.

But then, why shouldn't I burn?

My instructor clears her throat to get my attention. I open my eyes to the sprawling green of the city park, scattered with looming trees and dotted with mortal figures lounging on picnic blankets.

A trace of acid creeps up my throat. I resist the urge to curl my lip in disgust.

If I'm ever going to establish myself in this realm the way I want to, I have to be able to tolerate humanity. As little as they deserve it.

"Shall we keep walking?" Shanty says pointedly. This excursion isn't much of a test if I don't have to come near anyone.

We both know the main reason I've failed my trial outings again and again.

I shrug as if unconcerned and start forward along the paved pathway. When I lift a potato chip from the bag of BBQ flavor I bought, I keep a close eye on the sleeve of my thin linen shirt to ensure the tight cuff doesn't ride down.

Who knows what the humans would make of the blue veins that wind across my milky forearms all the way to my elbows? They stand out as starkly as if they were painted on.

I pop the chip into my mouth and allow myself a small smile at the crackling flavor that spreads across my tongue. I'll give humans credit for one thing—they know how to make good use of spicing.

Nothing in the shadow realm ever offered this delicious shock to my system.

I suppose we do need to keep them around, if only for that reason.

I catch a couple of glances from the human women strolling past me, one with a slight flush in her cheeks. It seems my smile has drawn a familiar sort of attention.

It's become obvious even in my very short sojourns away from school that mortals find my human-esque form just as appealing as many of my fellow shadowkind do. Not an opening I'm inclined to pursue with *these* sort of beings, but worthy of a wider smirk.

Shanty drifts back behind me, giving me plenty of room as if I'm out for a walk on my own. I know she's tracking my every move.

I tune out her presence, drawing fresh air into my lungs, snacking on another chip.

If you ignore the humans draping themselves all over it, the park is appealing enough. The warm breeze carries sweet scents of spring growth. Plenty of more genial mortal creatures abound, from the squirrel scampering across the path to the birds chirping on the tree branches.

This place is much closer to where I'm meant to be—where my shadowkind essence craves to be—than the nearly barren New Mexico desert that holds the academy, that's for sure.

A child leaps after the squirrel with a high-pitched giggle. Watching the poor animal dart away in a panic, I grit my teeth but keep walking.

I simply have to make it from one end of this large park to the other. It shouldn't take more than twenty minutes.

A dog races past me with a tennis ball clutched in its jaws. It drops it at the foot of an elderly woman and bows down in a pose of appeasement it really should be ashamed of. She doesn't even look at it, too busy blathering on the phone pressed to her ear.

A little farther on, a group gets up from their meal in the midst of raucous chatter. They saunter away, leaving plastic wrappers and soda cans nestled in the grass around the picnic table.

Do they not even see?

No, the problem is that they don't care.

But that's not *my* problem. My only problem is finishing this test and getting out of here. None of them need to matter.

I follow a bend in the path past a parking lot half full of noxious human vehicles. A row of shops comes into view beyond the last of the trees up ahead.

I'm almost at the end. My goal is no more than a minute away.

Even as I think that, a sharp *bang* reverberates through the air. I jerk to a halt as I register what it was: a car door slamming.

Raised voices burst out. "What the fuck do you think you're doing?"

"You cut *me* off, you prick!"

My nerves scatter, and my pulse hitches to a frantic pace. Images flit through my head: red splashed on white, humans bellowing, a lance of pain—

I stiffen my body to stop it from trembling. Terror and humiliation over my panicked reaction jolt through me. My jaw clenches.

Before I can catch it, a spurt of my chilling power shoots out of me.

I glance over in time to see the two men in the parking lot skidding on the slick ice that formed out of nowhere beneath their feet. One topples and smacks his knee hard enough that I hear the crack of bone from where I'm standing. He groans in pain.

A car that was just pulling out of its spot skids on the spreading slick patch. Its tires screech in the instant before it slams into the trunk of a minivan.

Oops.

"Hail," Shanty growls at my shoulder. She yanks me off the path, away from the lot.

My pulse is already slowing, but the tang of adrenaline lingers, turning my thoughts and my tongue sour. "It was only a little ice. No one had any reason to think I caused it."

The siren glares at me. "No one had any reason to expect sudden ice in the middle of May. And you hurt that man. He wasn't even near you."

There were other men who did more than hurt. There were others where I didn't do *enough*.

All I was doing was putting the vermin in their place.

Saying that will only frustrate her more. My hand tightens around the near-empty chip bag.

I aim one of my charming grins at Shanty—the type that sets off giggles among half the female shadowkind in my dorm and a couple of the men too. "I was almost at the end of the path. Can't you find the goodness in your heart to give me a few points?"

She sighs. "You know it's not a point system. It's pass/fail. And that was a definite failure."

I flex my muscles subtly beneath my button-up tee. "You really are something to look at when you're annoyed. I could make it up to you."

She sputters a laugh. "Are you trying to seduce me now? *You're* really something, Hail, and I don't mean that in a good way. If you aren't even going to try, you might as well go on back to the shadow realm. The Academy's spots are for shadowkind who actually want to change."

A different sort of chill sweeps through me with a rush of denial.

No. This is where I'm meant to be, with the trees and the grass and the open sky. To go back to the suffocating darkness, alone...

"I am trying," I say with forced evenness. "My powers lashed out in an instinctive reaction. I didn't *decide* to throw ice at them."

"Do you really think that's better? Come on, let's get you back to school. I'll need to talk to the rest of the administration about this."

❧

When I walk through the arched front entrance of the reform building, Gloss is standing just inside, eyeing the bonus assignments posted on the bulletin board as if she'd ever consider taking them on. They aren't even for voluntary students like her.

She's waiting for me, of course. She's very good at not letting it on, flicking her smooth black hair over her shoulder and lifting her eyebrows slightly as if she didn't expect to see me coming in, but her interest in me has been obvious enough.

And she deeply wants me to move up in the levels so she can finally show me off over on her side of the school. I won't be allowed to cross between buildings until I'm at least level four.

My gaze travels over her svelte body. I think she'd let me take her to bed if I offered the invitation. But she's intense enough when we haven't exchanged more than a few flirty touches. It's easier to play around with the beings who don't want anything more from me than that.

I'm not sure I have any interest in playing a significant role in her life. I've seen the excitement shimmer in her eyes when she's just come back from a stint in the human world, hobnobbing with some elite group.

She wants to blend in. She's gotten stuck on the idea that I could be a major force in paving her way, but I want to build something in this realm that humans can't touch. There's not much overlap between our dreams.

Still, shame pricks at the back of my neck when she takes in the 1 marked on my new badge.

To give the snow wraith credit, she hides her flicker of disappointment with a cool to match my own and tsks her tongue. "You just don't know how to play nice, do you, Hail?"

I could say something about how she likes me better

when I'm being bad, but today's expedition hasn't left me with much interest in flirtation. I stride past her. "I never learn my lessons well enough, apparently."

I keep my tone flippant, and Gloss laughs as if it was a fantastic joke, although it isn't really one at all. As I head deeper into the school, she slinks after me. "You could burn off some frustration on the morphball court. Make sure you keep your top spot."

I wave her off. "I've had enough games for today. Feel free to find someone else to play with."

After the brush-off, Gloss doesn't follow me. She's got too much dignity for that.

I stalk the rest of the way to my dorm, letting a wintry chill course out of my body. Reminding everyone who passes me that I'm by far the most powerful fae at the academy, and they'd better respect that.

Fucking school and its ridiculous tests. I could have done ten times worse to those humans and their hunks of steel, and they'd have deserved it.

I'm sure as shit not going to let the administration chase me back to the shadow realm.

I push into the dorm, and my gaze lands on the only other being currently in the common room: the short-and-pudgy, teal-haired new arrival who thinks she can wield her perkiness like a weapon.

Periwinkle. A ridiculous name.

She's standing at the far end of the hall by the kitchen area, clinking a spoon in a glass. At the sight of me, one of those absurdly sunny smiles darts across her face. "Oh, hi! It's Hail, right? I was making iced tea. Do you want some?"

Is that supposed to be a jab about my powers? Or does she think if she sucks up to me, I'll get Gloss off her back?

I pitch my voice to be both languid and cold enough to

burn. "If you want to drink stuff that tastes like sugared piss, it's all yours."

Most shadowkind would wince. The wimpiest of them would scuttle away.

Periwinkle the whatever-the-fuck-she-is keeps smiling at me like I complimented her taste in beverages. "Let me know if you change your mind!"

Her aquamarine eyes sparkle like gems. Who the fuck has eyes like that?

I scoff and stride into my room, yanking the door shut behind me. Does the dimwit not have two braincells to rub together?

There's definitely something wrong with her. Even if the shine of her eyes lingers on in the back of my head like stars I can't quite reach.

8

Periwinkle

When I walk into the workout room where the self-defense classes are held, my heart sinks twice.

I see the burly, ruddy-haired shadowkind from the admin team standing at the front of the room, looking just as gruff as when he suggested I be banished to the shadow realm, and the thumping organ in my chest seems to drop to my knees.

My gaze slides over to Gloss standing by the far wall, and it plummets right to my feet.

What's she doing in this class? It's supposed to be for reform students.

"Wonderful," Fen mumbles next to me.

I summon all the good spirits I can for my friend's benefit. I should be cheering her up, not dragging her down.

"Maybe we'll learn something to defend against *her*," I murmur, and consider it a win when I earn a giggle.

As more students arrive, it gets harder to keep up my optimistic attitude. Mirage bounds into the room with a flip followed by a somersault, but the next beings who pass through the doorway are the brawny woman and her clawed friend, Vim, who got angry with me in the Geography and Culture class.

The moment they notice me, their eyes narrow, as if they're deciding how to best stomp me into kibble.

A few of Gloss's reform student friends sashay in next, giving her a wave and our teacher coy looks through their lowered eyelashes. Lust laces the air like overripe plums.

One of them takes on a sultry tone. "How are you today, Gnash?"

If she's trying to flirt, he doesn't appear to be interested. "Looking forward to finally getting this class started, Tansy," he says with a scowl.

More students trickle in, including a few who go to stand by Gloss. There are seven beings now who I haven't seen in my past reform classes, their badges with circles rather than reform triangles.

It's a smaller class than usual, only some of the level ones. Why would they bring in extra beings on top of that?

Fen must pick up on my confusion. She tips her head closer to mine. "For the self-defense classes, the teachers ask trusted higher-level students to help with the hands-on exercises. Unfortunately, we don't get any choice in who those students are."

Gloss glances our way at that exact moment. Fen clamps her mouth shut even though I can't see how the other woman could have heard her.

Gnash claps his hands together, and all twenty or so pairs of eyes in the room snap to our teacher.

He prowls from one side of the room to the other. Fen mentioned to me that he's a tiger shifter, and even in human form, the powerful feline influence shows in his movements.

"There are three types of humans who know of shadowkind and will approach us with malicious intent," he says. "Collectors, who focus on lesser shadowkind creatures as curiosities to cage. Sorcerers, who use us as tools for their own ends. And hunters, who we're talking about today. They buy into the myths humans have made up about the various shadowkind they've encountered over the ages—*most* of which are total lies—and see us as nothing but monsters. Many of them want to not just capture us but to outright destroy us."

A shiver races over my skin. The one upside to the shadow realm is that while I could starve there to the point of being the thinnest shade of myself, I'd never actually die. When we're completely immersed in the shadows that made us, they can sustain us.

In the mortal realm, even the darkest night can't quite match the atmosphere of our home. Here, we're all mortal too.

Mirage springs forward with a burst of his fox ears from his head and a sharp-toothed grin. "To end us they have a great thirst, but there's nothing to fear if we smash them first."

My lips twitch at the singsong rhyme and the illusionary applause that follows it, but Gnash simply glowers at the shifter. "Less smashing, more avoiding attention. Put your ears away."

Mirage complies with a nimble backflip. It'd be hard for any hunters to catch him in the first place.

Gnash's peeved expression doesn't change. He stalks over to the seven higher-level students and hands out batons with streamers of yellow fabric. I think gymnasts—those humans who tumble around a lot like Mirage does—use those.

Do hunters also perform gymnastics?

The tiger shifter gives us an ominous look. "One of the hunters' primary weapons are whips with streams of concentrated light. If the light hits you, it'll damage your essence—temporarily disabling you. So if you encounter a human wielding one, you dodge until you can make a run for it."

He motions the higher-level students forward. "Two students to each helper. Take turns avoiding the whip. The fewer times our helpers manage to make contact, the higher your grade will be."

Fen and I hurry over to join a skinny, pointy-chinned male shadowkind who's moved to the farthest corner of the room from Gloss.

"I'll go first!" I volunteer. It's just a ribbon—no big deal.

The skinny guy lashes it toward me. A sheen on the fabric gleams beneath the overhead lights as if it really is made of light.

I jump to one side and then scramble to the other, my feet skidding on the exercise mats. Despite my best efforts, the ribbon catches my elbow.

After I've wriggled free, the student helper speaks up in a bored tone. "Keep track of all your limbs. Don't just think about your core."

I bob my head. I thought I was doing that, but I'll give it a better shot.

I start tucking my arms closer to my body, but the next time he flicks the ribbon against my calf. Taking a deep breath, I prepare myself for another round.

It's all right. I'm just getting started.

As I dodge another sweep of the ribbon, a twinge of pain

jolts through my ankles. I stumble—and feel the ribbon snagging on my wrist.

In the next group over, Vim snorts. "Looks like someone's klutzy with both her mouth and her feet. I bet you'd be scared of humans if you ran into one with a weapon like that."

Embarrassment sweeps through me. I know it's flickered in my hair, because her eyebrows leap up.

Tansy has joined Vim and her brawny friend. She tsks her tongue mockingly. "Poor thing. You've upset her."

I paste a determined smile on my face. "I'm all right. I'm sure we can all learn how to survive."

The brawny woman frowns as if she's taking that comment as an insult too. I whirl back toward my student helper.

After several more dodges, a couple more flares of pain, and a few more snags of the whip, I welcome the chance to step aside and give Fen a turn. As she begins the dance of dodging, my gaze slides over the other students.

Yellow ribbons are swishing through the air all around the room. Gnash walks between them, pausing to observe one group.

The woman next to him pops her hip to the side and juts her chest out a little farther. The one who's scrambling to steer clear of the ribbon catches sight of him and leaps up rather than to the side—maybe because that makes her skirt swish with a glimpse of her panties.

He gives her a couple of tips, and she beams at him with a flirty tilt of her head. More whiffs of the ripened fruit flavor reach me.

The tiger shifter teacher has a lot of fans, whether because of his muscular power or because he's one of the school's highest authorities. When he moves on to the next group, I see one of the male students start preening rather than paying attention to the exercise.

With her lithe frame and flexibility, Fen has managed to evade all but one smack of the ribbon. But when our teacher prowls over to watch her, a look that's pure terror flashes across her face.

She hops to the side, ducks, jerks backward, and nearly trips over her own feet. She might have been able to recover, except in her anxiety, a dribble of water seeps down her arm.

Her sneakers slip on the sudden puddle, and she tumbles into the mat face-first with the ribbon slapped across her back. A kick of tabasco-sharp embarrassment hits me a moment after the impact.

One of Gloss's friends snickers. Her voice carries across the room in a false undertone. "There the drip goes piddling again."

I clench my hands against a spurt of anger, but Gnash ignores the comment. He waits until Fen has gotten back to her feet.

"You have to get a grip on that wishy-washy talent," he says, and stalks off without another word.

I touch her arm. "You were doing really well for most of the exercise."

Fen nods with a jerk, but shame still seeps out of her.

Once everyone's had their practice, the student helpers rejoin Gnash to report everyone's scores. The tiger shifter records the numbers before unzipping a duffle bag by his feet. "For the second weapon we'll study today, I've brought the real thing to show you. You won't want to get too close."

Using two steel rods, he lifts a mess of shimmering gray strands out of the bag.

As the glinting object unfurls in front of us, my heart lurches so hard I lose my breath.

It's a net. Like the one—the one that caught me—

Tansy's barely muffled guffaw brings me back to the present. She's staring at me. "She's a wimp after all. Terrified just looking at the thing."

I raise my hands to my head, and an orangey-yellow glow wavers across my forearms. A few of the other students giggle.

Swallowing hard, I breathe as evenly as I can. The glow of fear fades alongside the tension whirling inside me.

"What's the matter, Periwinkle?" Gloss asks in a crystal-smooth voice. "You can't get that worked up over a little silver and iron, or they'll catch you without even throwing the net on you."

A little silver and iron. As if those aren't the two substances most toxic to shadowkind.

I give myself a little shake. Even though my hair has stopped glowing, I can't totally shed the lingering wisps of terror.

"Not so tough now," the brawny woman jeers.

Do they think this is a joke? They have no idea what can happen to you if you're trapped in one of those nets.

"We need to watch out for those things—and learn how to escape them," I say as energetically as I can. "But I know we can survive the hunters if we're strong. All you have to do is listen to the lesson instead of trying to hook up with the teacher."

As soon as the words leave my mouth, I know I've made another blunder. A mix of anger and humiliation wafts toward me from all around the room like rancid salsa.

Gloss glances toward Gnash. "She's eager—maybe she should be the first to get a close look at the net."

Every particle of my body recoils, but the tiger shifter beckons me forward. The presence of the noxious metals nips at my skin.

As I walk up to the gleaming mass, my ankles throb. I

wobble, and Vim barks a laugh. "Look how shaky she is after all her big talk."

Tansy sneers. "There goes her hair again, like she's pissing herself with light."

My teeth jar against each other. I'll be fine. I have to be fine.

The thought feels more desperate than reassuring.

I stop a couple of steps from the net and hold myself rigidly still. More snickers bounce through the room.

I don't like this feeling. It's too much like the worst times —I can't let myself dwell on it—can't let myself get too upset.

I can't admit to the man who wanted me kicked out that I might not be able to handle this lesson.

Gnash speaks in a growl. "Once you're wrapped in one of these nets, you're stuck. If you see one, you hightail it in the opposite direction. If humans throw one at you, drop as low as you can and dash or roll at top speed. We'll practice with regular rope nets."

He nods for me to step back. As I retreat, my legs sway again.

The brawny woman strides past me, stomping her heel very purposefully on my toes. "Now who's the wimp?"

I never insulted her. I only wanted to help everyone.

But all I feel are the glares and the smirks. The mutters aimed my way. My pulse pounds in my head.

Gnash is just putting the metal net away when the peal of the bell signals the end of the class period. "We'll try the practice nets next session," he announces.

As we head for the door, my nerves scatter all over again.

To feel those bindings pressing against my skin—the coarse texture, the interlocking pattern—

I hurry down the hall, not thinking even of Fen. A

mocking call reverberates after me: "I don't know if you can run fast enough, weakling."

I dig my fingernails into my palms.

I just have to get away. Somewhere quiet and alone where I can simmer down.

A door up ahead shows darkness through the small window. The label above the frame calls it the Media Room.

With a renewed burst of speed, I push inside.

I stagger to a halt at the edge of a big dim room. Faint light emanates from screens behind glass booths along the edges of the space. A handful of beings are sprawled across sofas opposite the door, watching an image start to play on a larger projector screen.

"Mortals all over the country have been watching this show for years," one of the shadowkind tells the others in an eager voice.

Then the bouncy tune of a sitcom opening theme fills the air. *"When you reach the end of the day, well, it's another day over."*

The most stating-the-obvious of all possible lyrics. I freeze in place.

"And you can't forget all the things that you really should go for."

That painful half-rhyme. A whimper builds in my throat.

The sound hurls me back to the dank room that held cages blazing with light, to the small TV always buzzing and jangling off to the side.

His favorite show. Every day, that song. No matter what he was doing to us—

The cloying voice continues as if trying to win an award for triteness. *"But open your eyes, open your arms, and—"*

The horror rolls over me, too heavy for me to shove it away. Like the net, like when he caught me—

The whimper bursts out in what's closer to a wail. I

hurtle back into the hall and stumble into a chemical-smelling space that looks like a supply closet.

And the thick, dark agony I've tried to tamp down explodes out of me.

It sears through everything nearby as forcefully as my joyful glow did at the wedding. Terror and anguish and fury blare together into a deluge of misery.

Through the flood, I feel a yelp and a rasp of pain. A shudder and a sharp sting as if my darkness has sliced right through someone's essence.

I'm hurting them. I didn't mean to.

I'm sorry, so sorry.

I don't know how to stop it.

9

Jonah

When I step into the administration meeting room, Peri ducks her head where she's standing before the curved table. Her petite but curvy frame tenses just slightly, the way it always does when she sees me.

Because she's afraid of me.

Pretty much every shadowkind at the academy either fears me or resents me—or both. As soon as they find out my unique purpose here, as soon as they realize I'm one of the few humans with powers to rival their own, there's a shift in the way they look at me. Something hardens in their eyes, whether stiffening like steel or going distant and glassy.

With Peri, it's worse than most. Her fright isn't based on hearsay—she's experienced the snare of my sorcery firsthand.

And she hasn't switched to being angry about the assault on her mind like many beings do.

It's as if she's bracing herself, trying to shore up courage in case I inflict my magic on her again.

Unfortunately, today she has good reason to be scared, just not of me. Out of the six people who'll be deciding her fate, I'm probably the least of a threat.

As I take my spot behind the table, Albumin stalks in. The vampire positions himself at the far end, and the meeting can begin.

When Shanty clears her throat, I can't stop my gaze from darting to the empty seat beside her. The place where Rollick would sit if he'd joined us.

The demon who founded this school should weigh in on matters as serious as this. He's been away much longer than usual.

Pearl is his closest associate here, or at least the one least afraid of badgering him when she wants answers, and all she's been able to say is that he has "personal matters" to attend to. I hope Quinn, the human woman he's devoted to, is all right.

If it wasn't for her—well, for both of them, but mostly her—I'd have died at age three.

Of course, I can't say for sure that Rollick would have decided in Peri's favor even if he were here. Every expression around the table is solemn, even Pearl's, despite the succubus's usual bright energy.

Shanty fixes her solemn stare on Peri. "Periwinkle, do you know why you stand before us?"

Peri's head bobs lower in a nod. A soft glow wavers through her striking teal hair: flickers of a sickly yellow that matches her anxious stance and a deep maroon that might be shame.

Her voice comes out quiet and strained. "I hurt people.

Other shadowkind. I'm so sorry. I didn't mean to—I tried not to."

Toni speaks up in her usual crisp tone. "You don't deny it, then? The wave of dark energy that swept through the school came from you?"

Peri's mouth twists. Her pained expression looks so wrong on her sweet face. "I wouldn't lie. That's how it happens. If I get too happy, light bursts out of me. If I'm upset…"

Darkness.

We exchange glances around the admin table. None of us has ever seen a power quite like what Peri displayed this morning.

Shadowkind are at home in the darkness. It's where they can escape.

But something about the shadows that exploded out of this innocent-looking being scraped against the essence of those who were closest. One of the students described it as sandpaper wrenching over his skin, another as a deep searing as if she was burning.

And it was over in a matter of seconds. How much permanent damage could Peri do if her power kept going?

"You were upset," Pearl repeats in a softer voice than her wife's. "Can you tell us what happened to bring you to that point?"

Peri stares down at her hands, which she's twisted in front of her. "It was a lot of little things. I was in self-defense class and had trouble with the exercises. Some of my classmates poked fun at me, and others were annoyed. I saw a hunter net, and it reminded me—"

Her words hitch to a stop. My throat constricts at the anguish that's clear on her face.

"It reminded you of what?" I can't help prompting.

Her arms come up to hug herself. "I was caught in one

before. Obviously I got away. It shouldn't bother me. I tried to stay calm."

Toni frowns at Gnash. "You were teaching the class. You didn't notice that she was getting agitated?"

The tiger shifter scowls back at her. "The students always hassle each other. You know that's part of the training. I didn't see anything that looked like reason for concern."

"And yet here we are," Albumin says in a detached tone.

As Gnash aims his scowl at the vampire, Shanty taps the tabletop. "But her power didn't burst out in class. It happened a minute or two after dismissal, didn't it?"

Peri shoots her a tight little smile. "I tried to get away from the things that were bothering me. It—it didn't work well enough."

Al tsks his tongue. "Here only a few days and already terrorizing her fellow students."

Peri's head droops even lower.

My reply tumbles out of me. "She *has* only been here a few days. She's barely had a chance to learn how to control her powers. And we didn't realize they could harm shadowkind, or we'd have been taking more precautions to begin with. That's partly on us."

"We have to consider the safety of all the students," Toni says.

Pearl makes a dismissive sound. "Everyone was fine with a little time to recover—no permanent damage done."

"This time," Gnash growls.

Peri's shoulders hunch, and my throat constricts. I remember her coming into my classroom a couple of days ago, smiling with Fen, so pretty in her contentment that it was hard to drag my gaze away from her.

"She cares about her fellow students," I say. "I've seen her doing her best to support them. She's already formed a positive relationship with Fen."

Gnash lets out a faint snort. I know he doesn't think very highly of the naiad, but he doesn't argue with me.

Shanty studies Peri. "Would you be willing to attend daily one-on-one tutoring sessions to see if we can get your errant energies under control?"

Peri's head jerks up. "Yes, of course. Sign me up! If I didn't have to worry anymore… I promise, I don't *want* to hurt anyone."

I don't know how anyone at the table can doubt her sincerity.

But then, a sincere monster can still be a monster, whether they like it or not.

Gnash still looks disgruntled. "We'll need to discuss the situation further amongst ourselves. If you stay, it'd be with a severe warning. We won't tolerate more outbursts like this."

Peri nods frantically. "I understand."

Shanty motions to the door. "Please wait while we make our decision."

Peri hurries away, with a slight wobble to her gait that sets me on the alert. Was *she* injured?

She keeps going without incident, so maybe it was just a nervous twitch. She clearly hates the idea of being banished to the shadow realm.

It's hard for me to imagine her bright presence consigned to the endless darkness my shadowkind mentors have described. That place might have created her, but I can't say she belongs there.

The moment the door has closed, Gnash turns toward me. "You shouldn't be soft on her just because you feel guilty about dragging her here."

I wince inwardly. "That's not why I was defending her. You can see that she means well. She isn't trying to be a threat."

Toni rubs her temple. "In some ways, that could be

worse. If she can be this destructive even when she's trying her hardest *not* to be…"

All right, it's a little horrifying to think what Peri could do if she *wanted* to hurt someone.

Pearl swats her wife's arm. "We have to give her a real chance to master her powers. Lots of beings can't figure it out on their own."

"But lots can't smother a whole hallway in searing darkness in an instant." Shanty turns to Gnash. "What were your impressions of her in class?"

"She was clumsy but gave the exercise a good effort," Gnash admits. "More than some of them that've been here longer and should know to take the lessons seriously. And she showed spirit when the other students were hassling her. If it wasn't for the explosion of shadows, I'd say she has promise."

I give him a pointed look. "She still does. It's obvious she hasn't interacted with other shadowkind very much. She's still finding her footing, but she's very committed."

Shanty squares her shoulders. "All right. I think we should give her another chance, taking far greater precautions. And of course her badge will be updated to warn her classmates. We didn't start this school to abandon difficult cases at their first stumble. Any significant arguments?"

Albumin sighs but doesn't say anything. Toni dips her head in acceptance.

"Good." Shanty brushes her hands together. "Meeting adjourned. I'll let her know the verdict—and start her first one-on-one session. I should handle those personally."

I head out of the meeting room with tension still coursing through my body. It sends me toward the exercise room.

I change into my workout clothes quickly, stretch, and decide to start with the rowing machine. The rhythmic back and forth is weirdly relaxing at the same time as it kicks my ass.

That machine is also one of the least social options, which can be a plus. I keep a casual attitude walking through the exercise room, but I'm starkly aware of the glances that flick my way—and then avert, sometimes with a sidle farther away from me.

The shadowkind students and staff who come to work out their physical bodies chat with each other plenty. But I'm not only one of the rare humans in the mix—I'm one of the few we warn our students against in class.

My sorcery doesn't call attention to itself when I'm not tapping into it. I could if I wanted to, though, and that's all they need to know.

And even though I had my powers passed on to me by my sorcerer parents… the fact that *they* could wield sorcery means someone in my bloodline most likely murdered shadowkind to consume their essence, paying for the power with innocent lives.

I prefer not to think about that aspect of my distant history… but I doubt any shadowkind who's aware of how humans gain sorcerous skills ever forgets that fact.

I settle into the rhythm of the machine until the ache I was waiting for prickles through my muscles. Most shadowkind come into being with at least slightly superhuman strength. If one of my missions outside of school requires a physical fight rather than one of magic, I want some chance of holding my own.

The whir of the machine fills my head. I'm heading into minute twenty-three when someone drops a weight into its rack too abruptly.

The clatter jolts through my nerves. A memory flashes behind my eyes: a shadowkind creature crashing through a window and landing on the floor with a clacking of its vicious claws.

I flinch, and the handle slips from my fingers. It smacks into the head of the machine.

Forcing myself to inhale slowly, I slide over to retrieve the handle. Did anyone notice my lapse?

A surreptitious glance around suggests not. I try to lose myself in the rush of exertion again, but my mind can't quite detach.

Maybe it isn't just the instinctive reactions to my sorcery that set me apart. Maybe my past means I'm putting up barriers I'm not even aware of.

Because I know too vividly that not all shadowkind creatures are innocent.

It's been a long time since a horde of very literal monsters slaughtered my birth family and kidnapped me. It was only a brief fragment of my life that they kept me captive before Quinn and Rollick came to my rescue. I barely think about it anymore.

That doesn't mean the dreams have stopped, though.

I grit my teeth and push myself even faster.

When I came to the school, I told myself the students would adjust to my presence. That we'd find a way to accept and even welcome each other. After all, I grew up surrounded by shadowkind. I know plenty of them aren't like the brutal fiends that destroyed my first home, just as I'm not like the sorcerers who develop their talent by destroying other beings.

Somehow, six years into my tenure here, the harmony I imagined hasn't materialized.

At what point do I accept that it never will?

When my shirt is sticking to my back with sweat, I peel myself off the rowing machine. As I debate whether to move on to weights or the treadmill next, one of the shadowkind support staff slips out of the shadows a few steps away from me.

"I'm sorry to interrupt, Jonah. Rollick's sending along a being who's been disruptive at one of his clubs. You should oversee the transfer in case there's major resistance."

Here I am, back in the role of jailer.

That's what I signed up for. That's the one thing I can do for the school that no one else can.

So I force a smile. "Let me take a quick shower, and I'll meet the retrieval team at the car."

IO

Periwinkle

As we walk down the hall toward the gym, I cock my head, trying to wrap my mind around the rules Fen just explained to me. "So there are five hoops, but you only throw the ball in them when they're lit up. And you're supposed to use your powers to move the ball."

Fen nods. "If you can. Obviously not everyone has powers that would work. The most important rule is that you can *only* affect the ball, no tripping up the other players. And if you break the ball, that's not good either. It's another way to practice our control."

Control that I'm still feeling pretty shaky about, especially now that the school administration is watching me extra closely. And this game sounds like it requires a chalkboard full of equations.

I rub my forehead. "And *everyone* has to play morphball?"

Fen shoots me a sympathetic smile. "It's kind of the main

pastime around here, at least for beings who are into sporty stuff. If you can hold a top five position for a month, you get special rewards. Coach Brandish mostly lets the enthusiastic students play and swaps out a few of the rest of us from class to class so we get a little practice. But she always wants to see what the new students can do, so she'll definitely put you on."

I give myself a little shake. It's just a game—a game specifically designed for shadowkind. It could be a lot of fun!

Even if I'm not very good at it. I laugh. "I don't think making my hair glow is going to help propel the ball."

"That's okay. The best I can ever do is push a splash of water at it, and mostly I miss." Fen ducks her head with obvious embarrassment. "I'll cheer you on from the bleachers!"

I guess that's what I'll end up doing during most future morphball gym days too. No problem. I definitely know how to cheer.

I've been in the smaller workout rooms before, but not the full gymnasium. As we step through the door, my eyes widen taking in the immense space.

The walls must reach up the full two stories of the building. The white ceiling is crisscrossed with metal girders and lighting fixtures high above us, like a giant was practicing weaving with steel. The bleachers on either side have room to seat at least a hundred students.

On the other two walls, five hoops protrude from panes that I've gathered will beam light at random intervals. The panes form the approximate shape of a cross, three in a vertical column and one on either side of it, but the side ones can apparently travel up and down as well as glow. Because the rules weren't complicated enough already.

A large screen mounted near the stands shows a list of five students with their photos—the current morphball rankings. Most of them I recognize only vaguely, but Hail's coolly handsome face gazes out from the second spot.

That must be one more reason our fellow students fawn over him.

A stout woman with slim tusks protruding from her jaw marches over to us. Fen's voice squeaks. "Hi, Coach Brandish."

From what I've heard, the main gym instructor is a troll. Big, strong, and fierce. I draw myself up to my not particularly impressive full height and offer her a determined smile. "Hi!"

She looks me over. "So you're the new one. You play on the red side today. Fen, you can stick to the bleachers."

"Thank you, Coach Brandish!" My friend gives my arm an encouraging squeeze and darts off.

The coach ushers me to the far end of the court where four other players are waiting, wearing varying shades of red. She runs through the rules Fen already told me. I can already tell my main job will be avoiding getting in anyone else's way.

"You'll want to change that outfit," she adds.

I glance down at my typical flowered dress and track jacket. Not standard gym attire.

Closing my eyes, I blink in and out of the shadows, re-emerging in terry cloth shorts and a crimson tee to match my team.

They don't look particularly happy to have me joining them. One of them, a friend of Gloss's I think, wrinkles her nose.

The other side of the court doesn't look any friendlier. It appears we're going up against Hail along with the player ranked number four.

The chilly, elegant man watches the teams coming together with an air of bored assurance, but Number Four prowls across the polished floor, flexing his bulging muscles. "We're going to destroy all of you!"

The being standing next to Hail looks up from her examination of her fingernails. "The newbie won't be any trouble, that's for sure."

Hail simply offers a smile cold enough to provoke a shiver. He's too far away for me to taste any of his emotions, but I have a feeling they'd be equally sharp.

None of them have really gotten to know me yet. I smile back with a hasty wave.

Hail's smile tightens. Hmm. I lift my arms in an enthusiastic gesture. "We'll all play a great game!"

I might as well get started on the cheering, since that's my forte.

Coach Brandish claps her hands. "All right, we need one more for each team. Verve, it's been a while since I saw you push yourself—go to the blue team. And for red—"

A tall form that's all sinewy muscle leaps to his feet partway up the bleachers, his voice a familiar deep growl. "I'll play."

The chatter on the benches falls silent other than a couple of gasps. Even the coach looks taken aback.

My antisocial roommate scowls, tension rippling through his sculpted limbs. His buffed-bronze hair drifts forward to shadow his dark green eyes.

Coach Brandish finds her voice. "You have an exemption, Raze. Playing isn't necessary for your evaluation."

The huge being's gaze flicks over the court. Does it stop on me for an instant?

Does he think he needs to demonstrate how fearsome he is so I'll finally flee our shared room?

"I'm in the mood for a little competition," he mutters. "I'll play fair… and everyone else had better do that too."

His next glower is aimed very pointedly at the blue side of the court.

Hail scoops up the spongy white ball and spins it on his finger. "We don't need to break rules to win."

A brief whoop rises up at his comment, but for the most part our audience remains unnervingly quiet. Prickly-tart apprehension washes over me.

What do they think Raze is going to do?

Coach Brandish appears to trust him at least enough to give him a chance. She motions for him to join us on the court. His ropey limbs flicker briefly as he swaps the black Henley he was wearing for a scarlet tee.

The coach holds out her hands, and Hail tosses her the ball effortlessly. She raises her whistle to her lips. "First side to twenty-five points or whoever's ahead at the bell wins."

She blows the whistle and launches the ball into the air.

Three of the panels behind the blue team's hoops flare white. My teammates surge forward to snatch at the ball. The blue team rushes in too.

A gleaming shard of ice materializes in the air and knocks the ball straight into Hail's waiting hands.

The winter fae grins and sprints across the court, gliding most of the distance on more ice he's conjured beneath his feet. As the red team converges on him, he whips the ball over our heads to Number Four.

Three of our nets have lit up too. The beefy shadowkind hurls the ball with a warble of supernatural force. The net pings with the goal.

A digital scoreboard next to the list of top players gleams to life. Apparently that basket earned the blue team three points.

Frustration wafts off my teammates with pickley sourness. "Don't let them run right by you," one of them snaps at me. "Can you do anything useful?"

"Yay team?" I say hopefully. He rolls his eyes.

Gloss's friend snatches the ball out of the air with a thrum of energy. She darts toward the far end of the court, and I pelt after her in case I can assist my teammate.

Number Four barges into her way, and I leap into his. Or at least I try to.

Shoving my feet against the floor sends a flare of pain through my ankles. I stumble instead and sprawl on my belly.

Not my most graceful move ever.

"It shouldn't be hard to keep track of your feet when you're that close to the ground," someone taunts.

I bounce back up to sneers aimed my way—and Hail's icy stare just before he swivels toward the ball.

Who cares what he thinks? We can still win. "Let's go, red!"

Gloss's friend passes the ball to one of our other teammates, but Hail closes in on her, sending out a blast of wind. The chill ripples over me even where I'm hustling behind them.

The woman squeaks and flings the ball toward the nearest red shirt… which happens to be Raze.

My massive roommate grabs the ball, the white sphere tiny in his hands. He launches it at one of the glowing nets.

Which stops glowing a split-second before the ball smacks into it.

Gloss's friend mutters a curse under her breath and shoulders past me with a purposeful shove. "Maybe you should just stay on the floor."

"I wouldn't want to trip anyone," I point out helpfully.

A low snarl carries from Raze's direction with a sizzle of jalapeno-hot anger. I suppress a wince. He must be pissed off at my performance too.

The game goes back and forth several more times, with

four more goals for the blue team and only two for ours. They're up to twenty points, and I'm panting and sweating through my T-shirt. My feet throb with stings of pain that resonate up my calves.

What's so bad about hunter nets again? I think I'd rather play with those.

I only have to make it through this one game. I can keep giving it my best shot.

Next time I'll sit on the benches with Fen, who's belting out my name every time I manage to race to the other end of the court without tripping over my feet.

The smallest member of the blue team snatches the ball. He bounds across the wooden floor with longer strides than his slim frame should be capable of, propelled by his supernatural talents.

I scamper after him, but of course Raze gets there first. He shoves in front of the other player just as the smaller guy springs into the air.

The airy man was already hurling the ball toward one of the nets with a crackle of power. Electricity sizzles all around the white sphere.

A burst of stray sparks smacks into Raze's forehead.

My roommate staggers sideways with a howl of pain that's echoed by a surge of searing emotion. A gasp of sympathy jolts from my throat.

The ball bounces off the rim of the net. The guy who threw it—and, strangely, every other player—scrambles backward, away from both the ball and our injured classmate. Even Hail's nonchalant stance has gone rigid.

Right, because almost all the shadowkind in this school are compassion-challenged.

I hurry to Raze's side. The immense man clutches his face, shadowy essence leaking from splits in his flesh. He blinks, and just for an instant behind his splayed fingers, I catch a glimpse of eyes that aren't the green I saw before but pure, depthless black.

My throat constricts with worry, but I keep my voice soft and bright. "That looks painful, but we can make sure you're okay. We just need someone with healing powers to—"

He jerks his head away. "Leave me alone!" With a tremor of the air, he vanishes into the shadows.

My hands drop to my sides. I look around, wondering if Coach Brandish will intervene—either to get my roommate help or chide him for shedding his physical form.

The room is silent. Everyone is staring at me—both the other players and our audience on the bleachers.

They all look vaguely stricken, as if I've done something horrifying like puke worms or sprout pus-seeping boils.

I check my arms to confirm there aren't any seeping boils that I didn't notice, and Coach Brandish finally barges into the middle of the court. "All right, it's almost time for the bell. Let's call the game now. Zing, I'm docking two points for that foul."

My gaze slides back to the spot where Raze disappeared. I can't sense him nearby anymore.

Doesn't *anyone* care that he was wounded?

II

Periwinkle

S hanty sighs and leans back in her chair. She's keeping her expression neutral, but frustration emanates from her like cheddar sharp enough to bite.

"We won't get your powers under control if you can't bring them out to practice," she points out, reasonably enough.

I offer an apologetic smile and look around the small room the siren brought me to for our second one-on-one session. There's nothing between the beige walls except a few chairs and a narrow desk.

Apparently the walls contain shielding against shadowkind power—if I have an outburst, it shouldn't blast the rest of the school. I don't need to be worried.

But even thinking about provoking the kinds of emotions that've made me blaze with light or darkness in the past makes my body tense up.

I have so many awful associations with those moments. So many echoes of the pain I've caused.

"I'll keep trying my best," I say. "I've never made one of those blazes on purpose before, or even purposefully made my hair glow. But I'm sure there's a way!"

My optimistic remark only sets off another prickle of irritation, but Shanty doesn't show it on her face.

She points me toward the mirror hanging on one of the side walls. "Let's focus on the glow. Take yourself back to the classroom when you saw the hunter's net. Watch yourself for any visible reaction, and if you start to see one, focus on whatever sparked it until you've got a steady glow going."

I nod and push to my feet. My reflection stares back at me, uncertain but determined. My hair is its typical vibrant but not luminous turquoise.

Watching the blue-green strands for any trace of a glow, I picture the shiny net that Gnash displayed to our class. I dredge up the taunting comments my classmates made, the stings of pain that lingered in my feet.

Something deep inside me balks. I force myself to imagine the silver-and-iron strands smacking around me, burning my skin and pinning my limbs—

A faint flicker travels over my head: a yellowish glimmer of fear. My pulse thumps with a jolt of triumph.

And my pleased response to my success squashes any terror I managed to tap into. The glow blinks away as if it was never there.

When I glance over at Shanty, I can't tell if she even noticed it. She's still studying me with a slight frown, twisting a strand of her dark blue hair around her finger.

I take a deep breath. "I'm sorry. I really am trying. It doesn't seem to work well with only memories, but we'll figure out something."

The siren hums to herself. "Our time is almost up. We

can try incorporating some stimuli for you to respond to in the moment next time. Maybe videos of frightening things, or I can find ways of startling you. Is there anything you find particularly disturbing that I could include?"

It seems like a bad sign that my tutor is setting out to particularly disturb me. I guess it's easier to unsettle someone than delight them.

My mind trips back to the sitcom theme song that pushed me over the edge the other day, and my innards clench up.

No. That would be too much, too dangerous… and also too bizarre. How could I explain why it bothers me without getting into my whole horrible history?

If the school administrators knew what I did and how much harm I caused before, they'd banish me for sure.

I shrug. "Just the usual things? Scary creatures, people getting hurt…"

The one who caged me before used to hurt *me* to shock those emotions out of me… I don't want to recreate that kind of scenario either.

Shanty nods. "I'll give it some thought, and we'll see if we can make more progress tomorrow."

So much to look forward to. But if being distressed means I learn better control in the end, disturb me away!

I keep that hopeful thought in mind as I open the door, only for my heart to skip a beat. Jonah is standing in the hall outside.

My startled reaction must show on my face, because the sorcerer steps back with a bashful dip of his head. "Sorry. I just wondered how your sessions with Shanty have been going—I didn't mean to interrupt anything."

"It's all right," the siren calls. "Periwinkle's session is finished."

I let the door drift closed behind me, resisting the urge to hug myself. Why is Jonah keeping an eye on me? He defended me during the meeting—is he worried he made the wrong decision?

Nervous words tumble out of me. "It's only been a couple of sessions. I haven't made much progress yet. But we're going to try new approaches next time."

Jonah offers a small, crooked smile. "You don't need to justify anything to me. I know it can take a while to get a handle on supernatural powers."

I cock my head. "Why were you worrying about how I'm doing, then?"

Jonah rakes his hand through his thick black hair, looking twice as awkward as before. I find myself wanting him to smile properly—wide and relaxed, so it shines through his whole face.

He would look awfully handsome like that.

Okay, I probably shouldn't be thinking of the teachers here—let alone the administrative staff, let alone a *sorcerer*—that way.

But it's true.

"I wasn't worried," he says. "Not that you were making trouble. It was more that I wanted to be sure you're okay."

I blink at him. "Why wouldn't I be?"

I got to stay here at the academy, to keep trying... What else could I have asked for?

Jonah appears to grapple with his words for a moment. "You aren't like most of the students I compel here, Peri. You'd obviously have come to the school of your own accord if you'd known about it. You're always trying to help everyone... It must have felt awful when I pushed my sorcery on you. I'm sorry about that. I wish I never needed to use it at all."

"Oh." Anything else I might have said snags in my throat. His guilt over the situation and his concern for me waft off him like an over-salted stew, not totally palatable but oddly hearty at the same time.

Who knew that sorcerers might regret using their powers —that any of them would care how they affect the shadowkind they manipulate?

But then, Jonah's not at all like the only other sorcerer I've known.

I recover my tongue. "Thank you—for speaking up for me. For saying I should stay. I'm sure everything will go much better once I'm totally used to this place."

Jonah's shoulders ease down. A relaxed smile almost like I imagined touches his lips.

He really is enjoyable to look at.

"I'm sure it will too," he says. "I know some of the other students can be harsh, but— stick with the ones you can make friends with like Fen and don't let the others get under your skin."

I nod emphatically. "I'm not. They're just... scared, and angry, about a lot of things that mostly have nothing to do with me."

"I'd bet that's true about an awful lot of people. Peri— even whatever you experienced with the hunters—"

My stance stiffens automatically.

Jonah cuts himself off and shakes his head. "I don't want to bring back bad memories. But if you need to talk to someone—I grew up with beings who'd been through a lot of trauma at the hands of humans. Sometimes they come by the school. I could arrange a visit sooner."

My mind has stuck on one of the first things he mentioned. "You grew up with shadowkind?"

A short laugh escapes him. "It's not obvious? Yeah, I was basically raised by a few of them who had a little family together. My birth parents—I get my knack for magic from them—I lost them when I was little. The beings who adopted me wanted to make sure I didn't grow up seeing the shadowkind the way most sorcerers do. You could say it worked out."

It must have. My impressions of him rearrange themselves, and suddenly it's hard to find him frightening at all.

He only used his magic on me to bring me to a place where I could get help. He obviously doesn't want to hurt me.

A smile of my own curves my lips. "I think so. I guess... I could talk to you too, couldn't I? If I thought I needed to. Since you know a lot about shadowkind who've been through… difficult situations. And you're right here."

Jonah pauses for long enough that I start to think I've said something wrong. Then he beams back at me with a wash of happiness that's all plum-sweet. "I am. That would be totally okay. I'd always be happy to talk."

A tingle sweeps through my body that has nothing to do with any emotions I'm picking up from him. I'm not sure what to make of it, but I'm abruptly self-conscious that my hair is going to start glowing in some embarrassing color.

A hint of deeper color touches Jonah's brown cheeks. I catch a dash of something even sweeter and richer before he steps back. "Anyway, I should let you get to your other classes. I'll see you later, Peri."

I watch him stride off, the strange feeling still bubbling in my chest.

Is there something wrong with me that I wish I could see more of him right now? Just sit with him and ask all about his childhood, what his powers mean to him—everything?

Run my fingers through his hair… and over other parts of him too?

Maybe that would be okay to try. Another time. When I'm more sure of my emotional control.

With a new spring in my step, I head toward my dorm. A trio of beings chatting outside a classroom stop and look in my direction.

If we've had classes together, I don't remember their names, but one of the women nudges her friends with her elbow. "Look, it's that know-it-all newbie."

The other two women giggle, one with a hiss of her overlong tongue. "Got any tips for us, sssmartie pantsss?"

I let their mocking tone slide off me. They don't really know me. It's not me they're actually put off by.

"I'm not trying to bother anyone," I tell them. "I'm sorry if I upset you."

Even my apology sets off a flare of annoyance in the women. The first one sneers at me. "We're not *upset*. We just think a nitwit like you should figure out your place before you spout off at the rest of us."

The second woman giggles again. "In self-defence class, she was shaking like a dandelion in a breeze."

The third chimes in. "Telling us not to be scared of the assholes out there when she's terrified of all of us."

I frown. "I'm not afraid of you."

"No?" the first woman says.

Before the sound has finished leaving her lips, the second woman lunges forward. Her face transforms into a grotesque visage, all wrinkled purple-black skin, searing scarlet eyes, and vicious fangs she snaps inches from my face.

With a startled squeak, I stumble backward. The demon reverts to her human-esque form a moment later. She and her friends burst into laughter.

The third woman points at my head. "She's freaked out now. Like a living mood ring."

A prickle runs through my scalp. My hair is glowing.

All thought of my harassers flees my mind. I spin on my

heel and dash back to the room where I had my one-on-one training session.

"Shanty!" I say breathlessly as I burst in, but the chair behind the desk is empty. She's already gone.

My gaze latches on to the mirror. I hustle over just in time to see the yellowish sheen dwindling in my hair.

Can I make it brighter again?

I recall my jolt of panic when the demonic woman sprang at me, but the glow fades completely away.

I peer at my reflection for several more beats of my heart, resolve building inside me.

That woman helped me, even if she didn't realize. Any time people hassle me or embarrass me, it's a chance to practice.

I just have to keep turning my problems into gifts.

I2

Mirage

As I prance nimbly along the back of the wooden bench, my claws dig into the wood to steady my shrunken body. The sleek, furred form that's my natural state in the mortal realm moves through the world much more swiftly than my larger, human-like presence. I can leap and whirl and pounce in an instant.

I spring onto the patio stones of the reform building's inner courtyard, spin just for the sake of feeling the air ripple over my thick fur—and prick my ears at the sound of a cleared throat.

"Mirage, you know students are supposed to maintain an appropriate mortal appearance as much as possible."

I snort as much as my snout allows and shift into human-ish form.

Toni is facing me, her arms crossed over her chest—a typical pose for the school administrator who hassles me the most. She's tall for a human woman, putting her almost perfectly eye to eye with my average male height.

I cock my head and grin wide enough to show my fangs that linger even in this body. "Foxes are mortal creatures."

Up goes her eyebrow. "Not with five tails, they aren't."

I spread my hands in a gesture of innocence. "I can't help it if my animal form comes with bonus features."

"You can help whether you take it on." She frowns at me. "Your teachers report that you're still making partial shifts at random times. You know that isn't acceptable. Do you not *want* to make your education here work?"

Do I want to be banished to the mindless dull of the shadow realm instead, she means.

I give my head a vigorous shake. "I'll do better. All foxiness will stay inside. Scout's honor and never a bother!"

I give her an enthusiastic salute, but her frown doesn't budge. "You're getting low on chances, Mirage. If it matters to you, you'll follow the rules."

Rules are the dullest thing of all, I think but don't say. The need to challenge people, to break them out of their drudgery and invigorate their lives, is woven into my essence.

But I suppose I can do more of that without indulging in my fox self, as much as I enjoy it.

After Toni has stalked off, I make a few spins on two legs rather than four. This body is decently spry too.

I flip over the bench, whip around while balancing on one hand, and slink over behind another bench where two beings are deep in conversation. They look much too serious.

I can help with that.

I crouch low behind the bench, gathering myself. Then I bound over the back, right between the two of them, tumbling into a somersault on the other side.

The two beings jerk apart with a yelp. I give them a wave, and they burst into laughter. "Oh, it's just Mirage."

Pleased, I saunter on through the courtyard. At the far end, two other shadowkind sit at a small table. A gameboard lies between them, black and white pieces marching across the pattern of squares.

They're focused so intently on the game that they don't notice I've strolled nearby. A glimmer of mischievous inspiration passes through me.

I wiggle my fingers at my side. The board seems to stretch and curve as if it's forming a mountain in the middle.

The players freeze, gaping at their morphing toy. With another wiggle, I make the wooden surface appear to undulate like waves. The pieces whirl in a manic dance.

"What the fuck?" one of the beings says. The other's jaw looks like it's about to fall right off.

Suppressing a chuckle, I close my hand, dismissing my magic. All at once, the game looks like a regular board again.

As the players peer around them, I pretend to be fascinated by the flowers sprouting along the edge of the patio stones as if I had nothing to do with the prank.

A bright but gentle voice speaks from a couple of feet away. "Why do you do things like that?"

My head snaps up, a grin springing into place automatically. The shadowkind woman with the turquoise hair that sometimes glows is watching me, her head tilted as if she's curious rather than annoyed.

She has a pretty face. An intriguing body with lots of slopes and valleys to explore. There are certain special games it might be delightful to play with her.

"Do what things?" I ask, even though I can guess what she means. It's more entertaining to make people explain themselves.

She motions toward the table. "Surprising people. Startling them. You seem to do that a lot, but kind of randomly."

I let my grin widen. "It's fun. Gotta get all we can before we're shoved in a van!" Human language allows almost as much play as human bodies. The way words bounce together when they sound similar gives me a quiver of giddiness.

I have the urge to pop my fox ears out to add to the amusement, but I haven't forgotten Toni's recent warning. Maybe I can get away with that tomorrow.

The new shadowkind woman's smile has tightened a little around the edges. Almost as if she's getting sad.

"You don't seem like you're totally having fun," she says. "There's something else… Did someone hurt you? Do you need help?"

It's my turn to freeze in shock. What does she mean—how could she—?

Oh. She glows emotions, and she must pick up on them too. The way she's talked to our classmates—yes, I should have seen it.

What does she think she's seeing in *me*?

For a second, I can feel her peering under my skin, into a jumble of images that rise up at her attention. Stark lights and gleaming bars, burning metal, squeals and whimpers—

I cast off the fragments of memory with a twitch of my limbs and a buoyant laugh.

I *am* having fun. As long as I keep moving, nothing can catch up with me.

Why is she trying to trip me up, get me stuck?

I lift a shoulder in a partial shrug. "I'm thinking you should mind your own business. Sorry if you don't like a little play when it could make your day."

The fall of her pretty face brings a twinge of regret—another emotion I don't want gnawing at me.

"I didn't mean I don't like it," she says. "You're really good at brightening up class. I was just—"

I turn on my heel and amble away from her as if I can't

hear her speaking, adding a brief swish of a tail for good measure before I whisk it out of sight. Guilt pricks at me, but it isn't as if I owe her anything.

I meander around the courtyard again, doing flips to conjured applause. The smiles and giggles I get in return should set me at ease, but restlessness winds through my chest, propelling me onward, farther, faster.

I know where to go when I'm feeling that way.

I leave the courtyard and lope through the halls to the gym. This late in the afternoon, no classes are using it, but it's too early for the recreational morphball games my classmates sometimes set up. Perfect.

With a little shake, I transform my jeans and loose collared shirt into a tee and running shorts. Then I launch myself along the track formed by lines painted on the varnished floor.

You wouldn't think running in literal circles would be satisfying. Before I came to the academy, sometimes I'd work out this energy by racing through the streets of whatever city or town I found myself in, dodging mortals who'd flinch out of the way.

But the combination of exertion and predictability is strangely gratifying. I can slow down or—more often—push myself faster, and nothing will stand in my way.

I circle around the track, each iteration a little faster, a little more burn in my legs. The sensation will disappear as soon as I slip into the shadows, but it's exhilarating while it lasts.

On my sixteenth circuit, another student pokes his head into the room. He looks so big and dopey that I chuckle to myself.

He walks over to examine the metal crate that holds the sports balls. A picture sparks in my mind, bringing a sly smile to my lips.

As I come around the next bend, I curl my fingers—and nudge my power against the latch on the crate's lid so it pops free.

The front of the crate swings open. Balls tumble out over the unsuspecting shadowkind, bonking him in the head and chest.

I expect him to simply sway and then laugh like I've just started to. But apparently he's not all that steady in his human body.

He staggers to one side and the other amid the bouncing balls. One trips him right over. He falls with a smack of his head against the floor and an accompanying cry of pain.

Coach Brandish materializes out of the shadows with a fierce expression. "Mirage! Why would you attack Cliff?"

I hesitate as she rushes over to help him to his feet. "I didn't mean to hurt him. It was just a little trick."

"A trick that did hurt him." She lets out a huff, glancing back over her shoulder at me. "I'm reporting this incident to the administration. They won't be happy about it."

Her threatening tone raises my hackles. I shed the discomfort with a chiding click of my tongue. "Our great leaders shouldn't hate."

She points toward the doorway. "Go to your dorm bedroom. *Now.*"

When I waver, she takes a step toward me, an eerie sheen lighting in her eyes. "I said go. You can take yourself there or I'll have Jonah compel you."

A shiver ripples down my spine at the memory of the sorcerer's magic. I duck into the hall.

At least I can get a little more of a run in.

I jog toward my dorm, seeing if I can outpace the sinking sensation in my gut.

13

Periwinkle

As we leave our Mortal Culture class, Fen gives a little shudder. "I don't know how humans can enjoy listening to music like *that*. It gives me a headache."

I laugh, a little of the rhythm still resonating through my bones. "It had a good beat. I guess you're not much of a dancer?"

She giggles in return. "That's fair to say."

"Maybe you just haven't found the right music yet. There's lots that's more floaty and less thumpy."

Fen makes a skeptical sound. "We'll see. I'll be happy if I can master *walking* without ending up dripping."

At the junction of the halls, I swerve toward the cafeteria, but my friend touches my arm to halt me. "I'm sorry—I almost forgot. I've got a meeting with my study buddy."

I blink at her. "Study buddy?"

Her smile turns sheepish. "That's what the teachers like to call it. After you've been at the school a little while and they know your strengths and weaknesses, they'll pair you with another being who's farther along in their studies as a mentorship thing. You'll probably get assigned one in a few weeks."

The thought perks me up. I haven't really hit it off with anyone except Fen since I arrived at the academy. An assigned friend is better than none at all.

I lean in to give her a quick hug. "That's all right. Have fun!"

Fen brightens so much that I walk the rest of the way to the cafeteria feeling as if I've earned top marks. There's someone at the school I've brought a little happiness to.

I have to keep working on spreading that happiness farther. It's hard when most of the students interpret every gesture in the most negative way, but I'll figure it out.

I enter the cafeteria buoyed by my resolve and stall in my tracks just inside the door.

The large room is decked out in much fancier trappings than usual. Stark white tablecloths cover the round tables, laid with crystal wine glasses and silky napkins. Subdued instrumental music flows through the space. As I watch, a being dressed in a formal suit brings a plate to one of the seated students.

This must be a type of human meal the teachers want us to practice. I have no idea what the rules are for anything this elaborate.

It feels like there must be a *lot* of rules.

At a huff and a waft of sour exasperation from behind me, I turn my head. One of my dormmates, a female shadowkind who's among Gloss's friends, glides over and catches my elbow. "You don't have a clue, do you? Come on, you'd better stick with me or we'll all be humiliated by association."

My skin prickles at the insult, but it sounds like she's actually going to give me a little guidance. I follow her to a table where a few other women are already sitting.

Seeing Gloss, my legs balk. But her friend is dipping her head in answer to the elegant shadowkind's piercing glance. "We could make sure she isn't too much of an *embarrassment*."

Is she really so concerned that the teachers will think badly of my dormmates if I mess up? Only faint emotions emanate off her, but what I catch is brittle and prickly like cheddar crisps.

A small smile curves Gloss's lips. She nods her head in acceptance. "Good thinking, Fleet." As I seat myself, her cool gaze lingers on me as if she's already finding me wanting.

The only emotion I taste from her is the faintest whiff of resigned satisfaction, like champagne on the verge of going flat.

"I didn't come here to watch shadowkind act like boars," she says evenly. "I assume you've never eaten at an upscale restaurant before?"

I shake my head.

Gloss rests her slender hand against her pointed chin. "First, of course, you'll need to order. It's important that you catch the waiter's attention with the right utensil. Pick up the larger fork and wave it high in the air in a circular motion."

Gamely, I select the larger of the two forks at my place setting—why would we need both? Are they magically enhanced with different features?—and swivel it in the air over my head.

Gloss's instructions appear to work, because another being in a suit trots over before I've made more than a few rotations. "Would you like the filet mignon or the linguine al limon, madam?"

I don't know what either of those things taste like. In my momentary hesitation, Gloss's friend Tansy jumps in. "You should get the linguine. The rest of us will have the filet mignon, but it'd be too much for you to handle, I think."

The other women around the table nod, so I do too, with a smile at the shadowkind playing waiter.

As he hurries off, Fleet motions to the bottle of wine the others have poured from. "Are you going to have something to drink? You need to stand up and bow to your glass before you pour, or it'll look like you don't appreciate the fine foods we've been provided with."

I've never enjoyed the bitter tang of alcohol, but it seems sampling it is an important part of the customs. I stand and dip low over my glass before I fill it halfway.

Giggles carry from a couple of the nearby tables. People are still having fun despite all the strict rules. Hopefully the food will taste good.

"Oh!" another of the women pipes up. "We forgot to tell her how to handle the napkin. Before you set it on your lap, you need to pull it carefully over your hair to show that you don't have anything unsavory on you."

Humans spend a lot of time worrying about what's on top of their heads. I run the soft cloth over the top of my hair and along the waves that course down my back and shoulders.

Just as I'm spreading the square of fabric on my lap, three waiters arrive with two plates each. They set them in front of us—mine with a heap of long, flat noodles with a pale sauce, the others with thick rounds of meat and a cluster of glazed vegetables.

Tansy flicks her fork toward my plate. "The linguine is simple. You raise one end of a noodle to your mouth and suck the rest in as quickly as possible. The louder you are about it, the more it shows you're enjoying the food. *We* have to fiddle around with knives and try to carve our steaks properly."

She sighs as if this will be a tricky process.

My dish certainly sounds easier. I poke at the noodles with my fork to find an end, spear it, and raise it to my lips. With a deep slurp, I suction it into my mouth.

It's delicious, a little sour but also creamy. As I chew, a vibe of merriment colors the air, more fruit punch than wine. Gloss and her friends grin at each other as they pop delicate morsels of meat into their mouths.

I offer a smile of my own and snag a second noodle. I've just finished sucking it between my lips when a full laugh breaks out at the table next to ours.

I glance over, curious to find out what the joke might be… and realize all the beings sitting there are watching *me*. Some of them are chuckling, others covering their mouths as if horrified.

As I stare back at them, more guffaws break out across the cafeteria. Shadowkind at seats all around us are pointing my way and vibrating with hilarity.

My lips part in shock, and giggles burst out of Fleet. She claps her hand over her mouth, but when my head whips around, all the other women except Gloss appear to be fighting their own laughter.

Gloss merely arches her eyebrows at me with the same cool smile she gave me when I arrived at the table. "Thank you so much for that fantastic demonstration of ridiculousness."

A blush scorches my cheeks. The renewed wave of snickers tells me my hair must have lit up with the emotion, but I'm already too embarrassed to care.

I thought—they acted like they were going to help me, however begrudgingly.

They tricked me, used their knowledge to manipulate me.

Just like—

A queasier emotion brings me to my feet. I shove away from the table and power-walk to the cafeteria door.

It doesn't matter if I'm messing up my fine dining practice even more. I need to get away from the taunts and hostility faster this time and simmer down before I come to a boil.

A louder swell of laughter chases me out the door. My feet fly down the hall, around one bend and then another. I breathe as steadily as I can alongside the rhythm of my steps.

If I can just get to my bedroom… There's nothing that'll stir up more emotions in there. Even after I tried to help him on the morphball court yesterday, my roommate is pretending I'm not around unless I force the issue.

To my relief, the dorm's common area is empty. Everyone else is still at lunch. I should be completely alone.

With a quiver of hope, I shove open the door to my bedroom—and freeze.

The sight and smells smack into me simultaneously. Brownish-red smears slash across the walls. The air stinks like rotting meat. Lumps of something that looks unnervingly gristly lie strewn across the floor.

A few deep gouges rake across the mattresses, ripping through the blankets amid the carnage.

The little bit of lunch I ate lurches up my throat. I clamp my mouth shut against a groan and scramble backward.

My shoulders slam into the door that swung shut in my stupor.

The image blurs, flashes of memory assaulting me. Torn limbs. Spurting blood. The shrieks and the groans, and the pain—oh, the pain, lancing through me again and again with every wound—

With a force so intense the air ripples, Raze snaps out of the shadows. My body tenses instinctively, but before the question of whether he had anything to do with this has time to fully form in my mind, his bewildered expression knocks it out of me.

His lips draw back from his gleaming teeth. "What's this supposed to be? Why would you do it?"

His tone is so accusing that I flinch. I open my mouth to protest that I didn't, but all that comes out is a whimper.

I didn't do *this*, but I did other things. So many other things.

I'm never going to fix them all.

Oh, no.

As the wave of despair sweeps over me, Raze snarls and lunges back into the shadows. I grope toward the bed, but there's no security in the savaged, stained sheets.

It's coming back. It's going to happen again, even though I got away.

I jack-knife over with a cry, and the horror blasts out of me.

Searing darkness. Vicious misery.

Figures crumple and voices squeal, and all I can do is clutch my knees against the sensation of losing all grip on myself. Clutch my knees and count.

One, two, three, four, five, six…

And on.

And on.

So many more hurts added to the tally in my head.

14

Periwinkle

I don't resent the cage-like room. If anything, I'm grateful for it.

As long as I'm in here, pinned by the piercing lights that reflect off the shiny walls, I can't harm anyone.

The academy's administration already forgave me once, and I screwed up even worse just a couple of days later. Maybe I'm not safe for the human world, no matter what I do.

Maybe I came into existence with powers too erratic to be controlled… or maybe my crimes before I came here broke something that can't be fixed.

A voice crackles from a speaker mounted somewhere I can't see. The intoned syllables carry a current of sorcery that winds through my essence.

Follow me to the meeting room. Don't move except to walk where I lead.

As the commands take hold, a door opens in front of me. Squinting against the stinging light, I hurry toward the gentler glow outside.

It's only after I step into the hall that I recognize Jonah as my escort. He motions me down the narrow, pale gray corridor, his expression tight.

I keep pace, my stomach knotting at the thought that he's angry with me. But just before he pushes open the door at the end of the hall, he glances over. "I'm sorry about this. It's a mandatory safety precaution. I know you wouldn't try to hurt anyone."

I swallow thickly. At least *someone* believes that no matter how badly I've bungled things. "I understand."

We step into the dwindling daylight of the late afternoon. The building where I was held is a squat beige cube set apart from the two much larger stucco buildings that hold the two divisions of the academy side by side.

As the dry desert air prickles in my nose, we go through the back entrance of the sprawling reform building. It's only a short trek down that hallway to a meeting room I'm too familiar with.

The other five administrators are already poised behind the kidney-shaped table, their faces as grim as Jonah's or worse. Even Pearl's blond curls look deflated.

A vibe of disappointment and uneasiness wafts through the air from all around me, sour as curdled milk.

Jonah leaves me in the center of the room to take his spot at the end of the table. All six pairs of eyes study me.

Gnash speaks first, his voice a low growl. "You were already on thin ice, and now this. You've barely been at the academy for a week, and you've hurt several students."

I can't give up. Pushing through my doubts, I lift my chin. "I'm learning a lot. There've just been... incidents I didn't avoid fast enough. I'll get better at it."

Jonah raps his hand against the tabletop. "We have to take into account the behavior of the other students toward Peri. You all saw what they did to her room. We've heard what happened at lunch."

Toni shakes her head with a swish of her dark bob. "Embarrassment and vandalism aren't the same as an outright physical attack. And the students Periwinkle hurt weren't even the ones who harassed her."

Shanty's mouth twists into a slanted line. "And when you're out among humans, you need to be prepared to face situations that upset you. Mortals can be cruel and selfish. If even more of them start hunting us… Lashing out puts all our survival in danger."

My head droops. "I tried so hard to stop it, I promise."

"That's part of the problem," Pearl says softly. "Your powers are out of control—our control and yours. If you're not getting a better grip on them even when you'd really like to… I'm not sure what we can teach you."

I suspect the outcome of this meeting is already decided, but I make a last-ditch attempt, putting on my best winning smile. "I'll keep practicing—more one-on-one sessions. I'll stay in the confinement building as long as you want so I *can't* hurt anyone."

Al speaks up in his flat tone. "You can hardly practice if there's no one around to provoke you. How would we know that we wouldn't see the exact same result as soon as you returned to regular classes?"

A very good question I wish I had the answer to.

Gnash stands up and glowers at me. "In light of all recent events and your inability to control your powers, the only choice we can make for the security of the academy and the shadowkind community at large is—"

The whoosh of the door opening cuts him off. A casually commanding voice rings out. "You started without me."

I stare at the shadowkind man who strolls inside, but that must be okay, because all the administrators are staring at him too.

He isn't especially impressive to look at, with polished features that are handsome enough but a body that's not quite as tall or bulky as Gnash's. All the same, my skin quivers with the aura of power he emanates.

Whatever kind of being he is, he's one I'd give a wide berth. If I had the choice.

The new arrival has just reached the chair at the middle of the table when Shanty finds her voice. "Rollick. I didn't realize you'd decided to join us."

So this is the mysterious founder of the school, the one who wanted to give all shadowkind a chance to adapt to the mortal world. I peer at him more closely, as if his tawny hair and gleaming teeth will give me a clue about how he's going to handle my case.

I can't catch any emotions trickling off him. Either he's very good at moderating his internal reactions or he's very calm about what's going on.

That makes one of us.

He sinks into his chair in a laidback pose and folds his hands over his stomach. His dispassionate gaze takes in his colleagues. "I had an inspiration but wanted to make sure everything was in order before I proposed it. And I spoke to the other involved parties first. I assumed the one in confinement was the least urgent."

His attention slides to me with a hint of what might be… amusement? Pearl did hint that he has an odd sense of humor.

Gnash clears his throat. "I'm not sure there's anything more to discuss. This being admits she can't control her powers. She's inflicted wounds on several students. Keeping her here endangers all her classmates, so we have to move to banishment."

I knew that was where he was going before Rollick interrupted him, but my heart lurches anyway. Another protest rises in my throat.

"Hmm." Rollick continues studying my face, directing his answer at me. "From what I've gathered from my staff's reports, you would prefer *not* to harm anyone, and you've expressed ample dedication to getting a grip on your powers. Is that right, Peri?"

The fact that he uses my preferred nickname sets me slightly more at ease. I square my shoulders, demonstrating my dedication as well as I can while standing here. "Yes, that's absolutely right."

"And you're also very concerned about staying out of the shadow realm."

I dip my head. "Yes, um, sir. I wouldn't mind going back for a little while! But I don't absorb much emotion in the shadows... I can't get enough nourishment without coming to the mortal realm."

"It sounds like you have a strong motivation, then. Excellent." Rollick looks around at his colleagues. "In that case, I have a unique proposition."

Pearl arches her eyebrow. "What are you up to now, Your Demon-ness?"

Rollick's lips twitch with a smile at her irreverent tone. Okay, he might wield enough power that he could disintegrate me with a snap of his fingers, but I don't think he's a bad guy.

He leans farther back in his chair. "We've had reports of strange shadowkind activity up north. Lesser beings acting in unusually destructive ways... The few associates I've already sent to investigate have failed to return—or in one case, returned so injured I hesitate to send him again."

Toni frowns. "You've mentioned this before. How does it relate to Peri's situation?"

Rollick's smile grows. "We have a few beings here at the school with potent powers but behavior so erratic they pose a threat to the other students. As an alternative to banishment, I suggest that they might benefit from some hands-on learning. They'll investigate the strange occurrences as a team and, if possible, eliminate the problem. If they succeed, we have proof that they can corral their impulses when the stakes are high enough."

And if we fail, we… disappear? Or possibly even die?

Not my preferred outcome, but I can't say it's any worse than being banished to the shadow realm to starve.

At least this way, I still have a chance to make things right.

"I'll do it!" I pipe up before anyone needs to ask. "I'll take up whatever mission you want if it means I might get to stay here in the mortal realm."

Rollick beams at me. "Excellent. Your three classmates felt the same way. We can get started almost immediately."

Al's near-translucent skin has somehow paled more. "You're going to send a group of unpredictable, destructive shadowkind off on their own—"

"To deal with an unpredictable, destructive problem," Rollick says. "It seems fitting. I have other concerns that prevent me from delving in for a sustained period myself."

He swivels. "And they won't be alone. Jonah, I'd like you to accompany this 'team' as their commanding officer, so to speak."

Jonah's mouth opens and closes again before he finds his voice. "Me?"

Rollick's tone turns droll. "Who better? In a case like this, your sorcery may prove invaluable, both for tackling the unknown threat… and keeping our wayward students in line as need be. Unless you don't feel up to the task."

Jonah looks queasy, with a pang of defiance that hits me like a spicy dumpling. He sits up straighter in his chair. "Of course I can handle it. Who are the other students?"

Rollick gets up. "Three troublemakers who've been on the verge of banishment for ages—and who've been making a particular nuisance of themselves lately. I think they should make an interesting squad."

He saunters over to the door and calls into the hallway. "You can come in now."

The three figures stalk through the doorway one by one. My heart drops—and then plummets even farther.

First is Mirage, with a flash of his fangs through his grin like he's thinking of snapping at me again. Even when he comes to a stop, he keeps shifting on his feet as if he can't stay still.

Next comes Raze, who I last saw accusing me of defiling our dorm room. The massive shadowkind stares at me and then jerks his gaze away, his sinewy shoulders hunching.

Last to enter, with nonchalant strides as if the mission we're about to be sent on means nothing to him, is Hail. The chill that follows the winter fae thickens when he sets eyes on me.

His lips draw back in a sneer. "You're sending the pipsqueak with us? This is a joke."

"No one's laughing," Rollick says smoothly. "You can figure out how to work together—and how to work your powers without them going haywire—or you can take a one-way trip to the shadow realm. If you've changed your mind, feel free to say so now."

The men remain stubbornly silent. My hands clench at my sides, but I keep my mouth shut too.

I can fulfill this mission. I'll prove I can do more good than harm.

As long as the men on my team don't demolish me first.

15

Periwinkle

The silence in the administration room lingers, as if Rollick is waiting out the rest of us to see who'll break it first. I'm not ashamed to pipe up in the hopes of ending the uncomfortable tension.

"Where are we going, and how are we getting there?"

The demon smiles. "Excellent enthusiasm. I'll give you a thorough briefing before you leave."

"Briefing with plenty of grief-ing," Mirage says in his singsong voice. There's a swish as his tail appears and promptly vanishes again.

Toni narrows her eyes at the fox shifter. "You need to keep all those inhuman appendages under wraps when you're away from the academy. We have to stop these shadowkind creatures from catching the attention of mortals, not add to the problem."

He offers her a jerky salute, as if he's trying to be playful but can't quite pull off his usual irreverence. "And if I mess up again, I'm really in a mess. Mess*age* received loud and clear."

How exactly did he mess up in the first place? I haven't seen Mirage get into any significant trouble here at the school. But then, he could say the same about me.

Hail scoffs. He's put on a bored expression, but the uneasiness wafting off him tastes bitter as wasabi. "This whole group is a mess. If you want me to prove something, let me do it myself. These duds will only drag me down."

Raze lets out a growl, tension rippling through his ropey muscles. "If we're here because we're duds, I think that means you're one too."

They're all agitated, upset. That's the opposite of our assignment.

With a bright if cautious smile, I hold up my hands. "Hey, we're not duds, any of us, or Rollick wouldn't think we can handle this problem. It's incredibly generous that he's giving us another chance instead of banishing us. We'll find those weirdo shadowkind and figure out what's up with them, no problem."

Raze's fierce expression softens. Maybe he's not still pissed off at me over our gore-splattered room.

Hail shakes his head, but he doesn't outright argue. Despite his dismissive attitude, the bitter flavor of his emotions turns milder.

Mirage shivers and then cracks his knuckles. "Weirdo shadowkind. Takes some to know some, huh?" His chuckle still sounds a bit tight but more honestly amused than before.

Satisfied, I turn back to the table to find all the administrators studying... me. I'm not sure how to read some of their expressions, but Gnash is definitely suspicious and Pearl is pleased. Rollick has a gleam in his eyes I'd call sly if that made sense.

Al simply looks bemused. "Well, Rollick, your choices might not be quite as inexplicable as they first appeared."

"Thank you for the vote of confidence, Albumin." Rollick claps his hands for our full attention. "You'll be supplied with phones within the hour, at which point you'll head out. I've pulled all the details I have into a comprehensive report that I'll send to your devices. The unfortunate fact is that we don't *have* a tremendous number of details at this point."

Raze frowns. "You said the other beings who've gone to investigate didn't come back or returned injured. If we run into trouble where we're going, what should we do?"

The demon's eyebrows arch. "I'd imagine *you're* more than a match for anything you might find out there if it comes to a physical fight. The sightings have come from a fairly desolate area of northeastern Canada, where few beings of both the shadow and the human kind make their home. Jonah will have contact information for associates of mine in nearby cities, but they wouldn't be able to provide immediate support."

If the problem is happening out in the wilderness, it's no wonder information is scarce. There could be all kinds of things going on up there that no one's witnessed.

I keep my chin high. We do have a combination of impressive powers. I don't know how much I can help, but I'll be able to pick up on the emotions of any humans or shadowkind we encounter. That'll be handy for judging threats.

There'll also be fewer people around who I could hurt if I have an outburst. It all works in our favor… except for the whole walking into unknown danger part.

"I'm sure we can look after ourselves well enough to get a

handle on the situation," Jonah says. His voice stays calm, but I taste an undercurrent of anxiety with a metallic tang.

He's not even shadowkind, and he's getting stuck watching over four of us who've done enough harm to nearly get kicked out of the academy. I guess he can work his sorcery if we get too unruly, but from what I've seen so far, he wouldn't enjoy having to enforce order with his magic.

That's why Rollick is sending him, though. He's the only one who *could* control us if we're acting out—other than by tackling us with physical force.

I'll take mind control over being shredded to a pulp, thank you.

Rollick nods to Jonah. "The five of you will fly up in one of my jets, and I'll have a camper van waiting for you—large enough that you can use it as a base of operations. It'll be stocked with plenty of food and other supplies. The more you can steer clear of the human settlements up there, the better. They've already gotten more glimpses of shadowkind than I like."

Hail grimaces. "Is this really a test or just another type of banishment? Or a punishment, having to deal with them?" He flicks his fingers toward the rest of us.

"What about us having to deal with you?" Raze snarls.

Mirage laughs and whips himself around in a graceful twirl. "The games are already beginning."

Shanty stands with a scrape of her chair legs loud enough that all three of the men go still and silent.

She eyes each of them with a stern expression. "I'm only going to remind you once. Rollick *is* making a very generous offer, but it's limited to one chance. You're going to have to figure out how to work together rather than tearing each other's heads off, or you'll all be banished."

I swallow thickly. I'd like to vote for heads staying on.

Rollick rubs his hands together. "I'm going to arrange

your vehicle and that briefing. I can see you four had better stay in here and practice your 'getting along'."

As he saunters out, another shadowkind appears at the doorway. She murmurs to Pearl, who leans over to speak with her colleagues.

Shanty turns to me. "You have a friend who's noticed your absence and asked permission to say goodbye. Would you like to reassure her that you're not banished from this plane of existence just yet?"

My heart leaps with a pang of affection. "Fen?" The siren inclines her head. "Yes, please and thank you."

As she ushers me to the doorway, Hail lets out a haughty sigh that I ignore. Where's his fan club gone? Do they even know he nearly got banished?

Do Raze and Mirage have any friends? I've never seen Raze talk to… anyone, really. People like to laugh at Mirage's antics, but I'm not sure I've noticed him having an actual conversation either.

Should that make me sad or scared?

Shanty stays with me in the hall. In a matter of minutes, Fen comes hustling toward us. Her face brightens when she sees me.

I open my arms, and she accepts the hug, even though she has to lean over me with our height difference.

When she steps back, her fingers are dripping a murky puddle onto the floor. "I was so worried when I heard they put you in isolation."

I pat her reassuringly before she needs to go on. "It's okay. I'm not being banished. I'm doing like an extra credit project to hone my self-control, so I'll be able to fit in better when I get back."

That seems like a reasonable way of framing the mission. I glance at Shanty, and she gives me a shrug of casual approval.

"That's great!" Fen beams. "I'll miss you, but it won't be so bad if I know you'll be back."

I give her arm another squeeze. "Don't let the harsher beings get you down. I'll see you soon."

I hope.

16

Raze

In the shadows in the back of the camper van, I barely notice the movement of the vehicle. From the way the rest of my "team" rocks where they're sitting on the padded seats, the road must be bumpy. My patch of darkness remains peacefully still.

Which is good, because I can't say there's anything peaceful inside me. How the fuck did I get roped into this insane mission?

Because it was either that or banishment. Because as much as I hate the damage I've done in the mortal realm, I can't eat shadows.

Some sadistic quirk of shadowkind nature makes some of us reliant on what only this realm can provide. My basilisk stomach craves fresh raw meat.

The hardest part is learning how to stop my deadly anger from seeping from my eyes and skin when I'm not on a hunt.

What excuse do the others have for being on the verge of banishment?

I peer at the figures on the seats. Hail's expression is a picture of perfect cool. Ice crystals dance above his outstretched hand—he's looking out the window rather than at the fragments as they consolidate into a sculpture of a miniature mountain range.

Show-off.

I think the winter fae *likes* hurting people. He never looks away when Gloss and the other beings who follow at his heels harass our fellow students. He didn't hesitate to insult Periwinkle the second he saw her in the administration room.

If he dislikes so much about this place, why does it matter to him to stay? Does he think he'll ever graduate if he's treating mortal beings like garbage too?

He must have agreed to Rollick's deal for some reason, even though it involves working with the rest of us.

At the front where he's driving, Jonah switches on the radio. Mirage was already swaying even when the van wasn't, but he smiles now, adding a bounce of his slender leg and a click of claws that glint from his fingertips for brief instants.

I've never known what to make of the fox shifter. Does he enjoy flouting the rules? He seems happy when people laugh at his bizarre behavior, but it's obviously gotten him into a lot of trouble as well.

As I watch, he starts drumming his palms against the seat while tapping one foot. Hail glances across the van, his eyes narrowed. "Can't you sit still?"

Mirage grins wider. "Where's the fun in that?"

The fae man lets out a huff and turns farther toward the window as if he wants to pretend he's not even in the same vehicle as us.

I'd gladly punt him out the window if that wouldn't end our mission before it's really started.

Periwinkle has kept quiet for most of the ride so far. Her eyes brighten at Mirage's seated dance, in a way that twists me up for reasons I can't explain.

"I like music too," she says. "Anything with a good beat makes it easier to keep your spirits up."

Mirage hums vaguely, his head veering back and forth with the rhythm. "We're going to need our spirits ever so high for this puzzle we have to puzzle out."

Periwinkle swipes her hand through the waves of her turquoise hair, looking a bit awkward as if she's not sure how to reply. I wouldn't know either.

Looking at her reminds me of the other aspects of the mortal realm I'd miss. I don't need beautiful sights to survive, but there's something amazing about taking in stunning landscapes and artful creations that don't exist in our home world. Seeing all the things that still exist undamaged, no matter how badly I've screwed up.

Periwinkle's human-like form is definitely pretty. All those vibrant colors that match the warmth I've seen her offer our fellow beings.

I wonder what her actual shadowkind form looks like.

As if she senses my attention on her, her gaze veers toward the slanting shadow I'm lurking in. A hint of tension grips her posture.

She vanishes, leaping into the shadows herself.

My heart sinks. She felt me staring—I must have made her uncomfortable.

Then a ripple of distinctive energy moves toward me through the darkness along the edges of the van. Somehow, even merged with the shadows, this being gives the impression of light.

Periwinkle comes to a stop near enough to give me

a concrete sense of where she is but not so close that our energies touch. Her soft voice sounds clearer when we're on the same plane. "Hi. Um. Is it okay if I talk to you? If you want to be left alone, I won't bother you."

The fact that she's being so careful about my feelings twists me up even more. "You're not bothering me."

Her voice instantly turns cheerier. "Oh, good! I wanted to tell you I'm so sorry for how this all turned out. I promise I didn't vandalize our room—I never would have ruined anything that didn't belong to me... or anything that *did* belong to me, really—"

"I know," I break in, unable to keep the gruffness from my voice. "A few minutes after I left, I heard the beings who did it laughing about the 'prank.' I'm sorry I yelled at you. I shouldn't have assumed you were trying to get me kicked out."

When has my unexpected roommate done anything out of malice? How could I have thought she'd do that?

Periwinkle pauses. "No one's been very nice to you at the school, have they? You haven't had an easy time."

My shame burns with a flare of guilt and horror. "I haven't given everyone else an easy time. I don't blame them for keeping their distance."

Would I really blame *her* if she had wanted to provoke me so I'd break the rules and be cast out?

But even now, when she could take my statement as an excuse to leave, she eases closer to me in the shadow. A gentle warmth spreads through my essence like it might if she took my hand. "It's scary when you don't mean to hurt anyone but you do anyway, isn't it? But I don't think that means you deserve to be lonely."

How can she sound as if she knows how it feels firsthand? I'm not even sure what she's doing here with the bunch of us delinquents. Is it just because some students have taken offense to things she's said?

Maybe Gloss complained, and the administration decided to side with her.

The truth tumbles out of me before I can think better of it. "I don't want to hurt you too."

Periwinkle simply remains next to me, emanating her natural warmth and brightness. "I don't think you will. Maybe we can help each other figure things out!"

I'm not prepared for the rush of hope that hits me with those words. For how much I want them to be true.

For how much it matters to me that she'd even suggest it.

I shouldn't be surprised. Not after she stayed in our dorm room despite my efforts at intimidation. Not when she ran to me when I got smacked by that burst of electrical power during the morphball game.

She's making this offer to me, not to Hail or Mirage. She came into the shadows to clear the air between us and confirm I don't see her as an enemy.

Is it possible she's right that we could help each other?

I should grunt and say we're better off looking after ourselves. I *mean* to say that.

But her warmth has melted enough of my defenses that what slips out instead is, "I'd like that."

"Good!" Periwinkle whirls around and pops back into the physical plane, standing in the middle of the van.

She looks down at her flowered dress and track jacket and cocks her head. "If we're secret agents tracking down villainous shadowkind, we'll need to be tough. Time for a wardrobe change!"

In a blink, she reappears in a new set of clothing she's imagined onto her short, curvy figure. Tight jeans with a couple of rips cling to her rounded hips. She's swapped the blue jacket with its rainbow stripes for a black leather one.

She hasn't completely abandoned her usual color scheme, though. A neon-pink flower beams from the chest of her otherwise black tee.

Periwinkle grins and strikes a pose like a TV police officer cornering a bad guy. Hail rolls his eyes in apparent disdain. Mirage lets out a bark of a laugh.

I simply peer up at her, fond amusement tingling through my essence like the warmth of her presence did moments ago.

A chillier jab follows, piercing my center as if I've been run through by one of Hail's ice sculptures.

This woman might be the sweetest being I've ever known. All the rebellious clothes in the world won't be enough to protect her from whatever dangers we're hurtling off to face.

Will I be?

17

Periwinkle

I hop out of the van and spread my arms in the crisply cool morning air. It rushes into my lungs in a deep gulp.

This isn't the kind of environment I'm drawn to. I can't see any buildings or people in any direction, only the winding road with tall trees on either side. There are no emotions to absorb except for the currently subdued feelings of the men I'm working with.

But there's something refreshing about the solitude that I'm not sure I've appreciated before. No need to worry about how I'll be affected by my surroundings. I can take in what makes the mortal world special with no pressure at all.

The men have spread out along the sides of the road in what's becoming our typical approach at each stop. There's not much I can contribute other than confirming that I'm not picking up worrisome emotional energy nearby. And moral support.

"Let's find those weirdo shadowkind!" I declare, planting my hands on my hips with a warble of my new leather jacket. "They don't stand a chance against us."

The men go on searching for the strange beings Rollick told us about.

Well, I guess it's mostly Raze doing the searching. He prowls along the treeline with his lips parted, inhaling every scent that drifts on the breeze. A forked tongue darts past his lips.

Apparently basilisks—which as far as I've determined are giant lizards?—have a good sense of smell.

So do foxes, but I don't know how seriously Mirage is taking our mission. As soon as we stopped, he shifted into his shadowkind form and now is bounding between the tree trunks with whirls and flips, swishing his five bushy tails.

Raze shoots a frown Mirage's way, but I don't mind seeing the fox shifter cavort around. When we're cooped up in the van for a long stretch, he starts giving off a vibe of painful restlessness that makes me think of cheek-puckeringly sour grapefruit.

I'm sure if he notices something strange out here, he'll say so. In the meantime, we get an acrobatic show.

Would Hail's powers help him pick up on any unusual shadowkind nearby? He's ambling along the edge of the forest too, in the opposite direction from Raze.

The fae in movies have those pointy ears. Maybe he's got super hearing.

He stops and tips his pale face to the beaming sun. Something in his expression softens from its usual icy sharpness.

I catch a trace of butterscotch pudding awe that brings a smile to my lips. "It's gorgeous out here, isn't it?"

Hail's eyes snap to me, his features hardening all over again with a much pricklier emotion that I barely taste before it's gone. "Of course you'd be thinking about the view. I still can't see why we got stuck with a cream puff."

I would protest that cream puffs are delicious and delightful, and also shaped very differently than I am even if some parts of me are on the round side, but just then Raze lets out a grunt of apprehension.

Jonah takes a step closer. "What?"

The massive, sinewy man turns his head where he's standing about thirty feet down the road. His tongue flicks farther over his lips.

He tenses. "Some kind of creature passed this way—not like anything I've smelled before. There's something about the scent that … doesn't seem totally right."

Hail snorts. "Not totally right. I'm sure that description will have Rollick applauding our work."

Jonah shoots the winter fae a glower of warning before turning back to Raze. "Can you follow the trail?"

The basilisk shifter stalks farther along the shoulder. "It's faint, but I think whatever it came from started following the road here. The scent gets stronger when I walk this way."

"Let's see if we can catch up." Jonah motions the rest of us into the van. "Raze, you sit up front with the window open. Let me know if I drive too fast for you to pick up the scent."

I scramble into the back and nab the spot on the bench closest to the driver's seat. A rumble spreads through the cushions when Jonah starts the engine.

As he drives, Raze tips his head out the open window like an incredibly over-sized Doberman. His eyes narrow against the rushing air. "It's still getting stronger."

When we reach a crossroad, we stop so Raze can quickly survey the area. He strides with a purposeful intensity that's hard not to watch, his muscles flexing beneath his tan skin.

He points to the left. "That way."

We've only been zooming in that direction for another minute or two when a shriek shatters the quiet of the wilderness.

Jonah mutters a curse and presses his foot to the gas. The van roars forward.

We all sit braced and staring out the windshield, even Hail's icy detachment shattered. As we come up on a small cluster of buildings beside the country road, frightened shouts carry from deeper in the human settlement.

Jonah jerks the wheel to careen onto the even narrower side road. Outside a low brick building, several humans have scattered around a table laid with a checkered cloth and several plates of food.

They were having a breakfast picnic, croissants and scrambled eggs tragically abandoned. Now they're backing away from a dark shape I only catch a glimpse of amid the nearby shrubs.

Jonah brings the van to a rasping halt on the gravel shoulder of the road and leaps out, but Raze throws open the passenger door even faster. He lunges past the panicked people toward the creature in the shrubs.

I dash after him, my pulse skittering with the memory of him falling during the morphball game. He was fine then, but we don't know what this creature can do.

As I run past the humans, my new leather jacket flapping at my sides, their fear washes over me like a deluge of pickle juice. Then a more potent wallop smacks me from up ahead... from the unknown being crashing through the bushes.

"Stop!" The cry bursts out of me before I even think about it, but Raze listens. He skids to a halt a couple of strides short of the shrubs, his claws already extended from his fingertips.

I hold out my hands in a calming gesture both for him and the being shuddering a few feet away. "It doesn't want to attack anyone. It's not feeling aggressive, only scared."

The other men come to a halt behind me.

"Mirage," Jonah says. "You can alter perceptions—can you make these people forget they saw this thing—and us?"

"Faster than a fox fleeing a hound!" Mirage replies cheerfully.

I focus all my attention on the strange creature in the bushes. I can only make out some tufts of fur, the edge of what might be a wing, the lash of what I assume is a tail. It's not terribly large, only the size of a standard poodle, but the humans wouldn't have known what to make of it.

I keep my voice as soothing as I can. "Hey there. We won't hurt you. We just want to find out what's going on. We'll make sure those people don't yell at you anymore."

Thankfully, whatever Mirage is doing allows me to keep my promise. No more yelps or hollers split the air. Door hinges squeak—I think he's persuaded the humans to go into the building.

The sour flavor of terror starts to recede.

"Very good," I murmur. "We're going to come around the bushes so we can see you better. I promise we'll give you lots of space."

Hail scoffs under his breath. "This is ridiculous."

"Let her try," Jonah says, quiet but firm.

I move first, backing up a few steps and then easing through a gap between the decorative bushes. The shadowkind creature gives off a brief quiver of renewed anxiety, but it stays huddled next to its temporary shelter rather than bolting.

I've never seen a being like it before, but lesser creatures do come in a wide range of appearances. This one gives me the impression of a bedraggled cat that's ballooned far beyond its ideal size, with crooked ears, one useless leathery wing, and not just a tail but two slim appendages whipping back and forth from its belly.

The men follow me, hanging even farther back. The creature starts to cringe away.

I hold out a hand toward it beseechingly. "You're safe. We're only going to look at you. See, we're staying all the way over here."

It relaxes slightly. Mirage lets out a low chuckle. "Beating the beast with sweetness."

At the edge of my vision, Jonah sends a smile my way. "Thank you, Peri. You're doing great."

Hail takes on a bored tone. "What the fuck *is* that thing?"

The moment he's asked, the answer changes—because the creature does. All at once, its legs shoot up, its chest expanding, the wing vanishing into its side and a ring of spines jutting out in its place. It surges up and out to nearly my own size.

I can't help flinching backward with a shiver of surprise. "I didn't think lesser beings could change their forms."

Jonah's brow has furrowed. "They normally can't. I've never seen one do that before."

Raze's voice comes out uncertain even in its gruffness. "Neither have I. It's definitely what I smelled before—and its scent just changed too."

Even Hail sounds a bit taken aback. "It hardly looks *dangerous*, in any case."

Nope. Now the thing looks like a bedraggled, swollen, spiky bulldog on stilts—incredibly weird, but wobbly as a newborn foal.

"We don't know that *this* creature caused any problems,"

Jonah says. "There could be something much bigger going on. I'm going to ask it to show us the rift it came through."

I'm confused about how he thinks asking is going to work until a string of sorcerous syllables tumbles off his tongue. The hairs on the back of my neck rise even though the command isn't aimed at me.

But this is one of the reasons Rollick sent Jonah with us. There isn't any other way we could convince the creature to lead us to the place where it emerged from the shadow realm.

The creature gives its body a dog-like shake—and nearly topples over on its side. A seal-like *arf* escapes its mouth.

Jonah frowns and repeats his sorcerous command with more emphasis. The creature shudders, but then it turns away from the village and trots off toward the trees.

We follow much closer now that it's being compelled, just a few feet behind it. I only get vague impressions of the creature's current emotions—a little discomfort mingling with a flicker of relief to be heading someplace familiar. The sorcery doesn't appear to have bothered it.

It sets off through the woods in a straight line, I suppose going directly toward the rift. Its spikes rake against the sides of the trees.

There's no way we could follow it in the van.

Hail sucks a breath through his teeth. "This rift had better not be a hundred miles away."

Raze scowls. "We didn't drive very far after I caught the scent. It could be close."

"Or we could roam all across the world," Mirage puts in with a laugh.

Jonah's tone goes dry. "I don't think we need to—"

It happens in a split-second. One instant, the creature is swaying along like it already was, seemingly free of distress.

The next, a vicious fury hurtles out of it like a charred but bloody steak thrown in my face.

"Watch out!" I yelp.

The creature whips around, its body blasting outward into a mass of clawed limbs and horned tentacles, most of which are slicing through the air toward—

Hail flings out his hand. A wallop of frigid air surges off him.

The cold front slams into the creature and knocks it right off its feet. Its dark gray flesh turns blue, its skin and scales frosting over.

It tips over and hits a tree with a solid thunk, limbs as rigid as a statue. A few of the brand-new tentacles snap off and thud to the ground.

He froze it solid.

The fae stares at the results of his hasty reaction. His alabaster skin looks even paler than usual. "I—I wasn't trying to *kill* it."

He's too startled to suppress the waft of fetid-gruel horror that rolls off him.

Not only was he not trying—it bothers him a lot that he did this.

Hail might be a jerk, but a twinge of sympathy quivers through me. I give him a grateful smile. "You protected us. It was going to hurt us, and you made sure it didn't. You moved so fast—it was amazing."

His dark blue gaze veers toward me. Then his jaw tightens.

He makes a harsher scoffing sound than before. "As long as teacher boy doesn't dock points off our assignment for going overboard, I suppose it's all right."

I can tell he's squashing the uneasiness, not recovered from it.

Jonah swipes his hand through his rumpled hair, peering at the creature in its enlarged, especially monstrous form. "That… is not something I want to run into unprepared again. Peri's right, Hail. You did what was necessary in the moment. I should have made my command clearer so it had no room to turn on us."

Raze's expression has shadowed. "It didn't seem like it would attack."

I shake my head. "It wouldn't have, before. It just… changed. A lot, all at once."

We stand there in a moment of unsettled silence. Mirage breaks it with a flip through the air to the frozen beast's side and a chorus of illusionary oohs and aahs.

He points off through the trees in the direction the strange creature was heading, fragments of sunlight glowing off his golden-brown face. "At least we know where our journey should take us next. Let's enjoy our sense of direction!"

18

Jonah

I can't say I've ever been a fan of camping. My enjoyment drops considerably when I'm also wrangling a team of belligerent shadowkind.

As I heat my canned pasta over the kerosene stove, missing the much more appealing dinner everyone will be having back at the academy, Raze comes striding out of the woods by the short lane where we parked. He's empty-handed, his light brown skin unmarked, but there's a feral quality to his gaze even with the green contacts covering his supernaturally dark irises.

Hail apparently picks up on his vibe too. The lanky fae pushes himself off the birch he's been leaning against and makes a face.

"You stink of death. If you have to go hunt, can't you clean yourself up properly afterward?"

The basilisk shifter glowers at him. "I have to *eat*, unlike some."

Mirage springs between them, leaping and diving through the shadows with flashes of one or another of his bushy tails. "Track them down. Pounce so hard. They don't stand a chance!"

As he continues his pantomime of the imagined hunt, the other shadowkind men take a step back. Hail rolls his eyes. "You're just insane."

"There's nothing wrong with a little madness," Mirage says cheerfully, and rolls to sprawl on his back with his arms folded behind his head.

The winter fae returns his attention to Raze. "Isn't there a stream around you could douse yourself in? If dipping into the shadows isn't enough to clean you off, maybe mortal substances will."

I suspect he's making up his entire complaint. Even if fae noses are stronger than human, there *shouldn't* be any trace left of physical material after Raze moves through the shadows. From what I know of the basilisk shifter, that's the first thing he'd have done after tearing into his prey.

Restraining a sigh, I open my mouth. "Hail, we have—"

Raze beats me to the punch, bristling with annoyance. "If you're so concerned about killing, you shouldn't have frozen that creature we were following today."

The twitch of Hail's expression confirms how much the accidental murder bothers him. His lips draw back in a sneer. "At least I'm not a savage, rending beasts limb from limb. How you think you're going to integrate with humans when you're exactly the monster they think shadowkind are—"

I scramble to my feet. "*Enough*. All of you. It's been a long day, and we're doing what we each need to get by."

Hail aims his sneer at me. "Oh, fabulous advice from our

incredible leader. What have you contributed to this mission so far? I don't remember receiving any expert guidance."

I'd like to take some guidance and shove it up the arrogant prick's ass, but that definitely isn't what Rollick sent me along for. "I'm offering you it right now. Simmer down, or the mission won't go anywhere."

Raze shoots me a wounded look. "I wasn't going to hurt him. He shouldn't be lashing out at people if he can't take a little criticism."

You can criticize him all you want when we're not in the middle of the woods trying to track down the source of the wackiest shadowkind I've ever seen, I want to say, but I can only imagine how Hail would react to my seemingly taking the other guy's side.

Mirage simply kicks his legs in the air and laughs with delight, as if we're putting on a show for his entertainment.

I hold out my hands placatingly, cursing Rollick for giving me this assignment—and myself for not having a better idea how to handle these clashing personalities. The demon expected more from me than this.

"I'm not accusing anyone of anything," I say evenly. "I'd just like to see tempers reined in rather than unleashed. You don't have to sing 'Kumbaya,' but you need to at least tolerate each other's presence."

Peri emerges from the back of the van. She sets her hands on her hips, which draws my gaze to the same area. Her impressive curves are accentuated by the tight jeans and fitted leather jacket she's traded her usual outfit for.

"Hail was protecting us," she tells Raze in a brightly insistent voice. "That's what matters the most."

She aims her gaze at Hail next. "If you don't like how someone smells after they're making sure they don't starve, give them a little more space, and problem solved!"

She walks over to Mirage and peers down at him. "And

it's better to have fun when everyone else is in on the joke instead of upset. Just so you know."

Despite her cheery approach, the men all look stunned. At least it shuts them up.

Peri has some kind of magic to her, even if most of her fellow students haven't recognized that yet.

In the abrupt quiet, I motion to the van. "I'm the only one who needs to sleep, so I'm taking one of the two benches. I think you should all give yourself some distance wherever you go in the shadows overnight. Hail, stick to the east side of the road. Raze, stick to the west."

Hail's lip curls. "You trust us not to abandon you, captain?"

I ignore his mocking tone. "I trust that you know that I can call you back if it comes to that. And if you run, that's an automatic fail. If you wanted to get banished, you could have saved us the trouble and told Rollick back at academy."

The winter fae grimaces, but he knows I'm right. He stalks off around the other side of the van. Raze frowns and vanishes into the shadows amid the trees.

Mirage peers at me with mischief glinting in his eyes. "What about me? Where do I fit in?"

I can't stop my voice from coming out dry. "I guess you could hang out on top of the van? I get the feeling you'd like having a wider view."

Mirage laughs and jumps up, transforming into his fox shape as he does. He bounds from the ground to the hood and onto the roof with a patter of his paws.

I inhale slowly, hoping none of them could tell how rattled I was. Hoping my precaution will be enough to prevent further squabbling in the middle of the night.

I've been driving most of the day as we try to narrow down where the unnerving shadowkind was heading. I need my rest if I want to avoid guiding us straight into a ditch tomorrow.

As I lift the little pot off the miniature stove, Peri hunkers down next to me. She considers my meal as I stir it. I catch a slight wrinkling of her nose that she quickly hides. "Is that good?"

I guffaw. "Not really. But it's easy, and it'll hit the spot. We're not out here for fine dining."

Well, I'm not, anyway. Who knows what kind of satisfaction Peri's been getting from the miasma of emotions that've been flowing between our group.

She sits back on her hands, gazing into the darkness of the woods while I gulp down my pasta. I can't stop my own gaze from lingering on her.

It's not just her pretty face and her softly curvy figure, though both of those *are* plenty enticing. There's a looseness to her stance that I haven't seen before, as if she's released some tension I hadn't realized was gripping her.

She's been trapped from the moment I dragged her into the cage with my sorcery, hasn't she? Even at the academy, as much as she's wanted to learn to control her powers, she was hemmed in by the rules and the hostility of her classmates.

I'm sorry that she was forced onto this dangerous quest, but I'm glad she got an escape from those restrictions. Maybe the experience will make it easier for her to adapt to the academy's boundaries once we go back.

Assuming we fulfill Rollick's mission without the entire team falling apart.

Peri looks over at me and gives me one of her sunny smiles. My heart skips a beat despite my best intentions.

It's hard to comprehend that a being made of shadows could contain so much light. So much it can overflow to the point of burning.

Right now, the glow she gives off is only metaphorical, in

the warmth of her expression and her voice. "You know, a lot of people boss everyone else around to make themselves feel good. Superior, I guess. But you really do it because you want the rest of us to be happier and safer. I think that'll make the difference, even if they don't always want to listen. So keep at it." She grins.

My voice locks in my throat. I shouldn't be surprised—of course she can pick up on my emotions just as well as anyone else's. I've seen her try to reassure people about their insecurities time and time again.

But I'm not sure I've ever felt quite as seen as right now, with those bright blue eyes shining back at me.

They stir other emotions that every professional ethic balks against. When she reaches over to grasp my hand in a gesture of solidarity, I force myself to let go as soon as I've given her fingers a quick squeeze to show I appreciate her kindness.

The warmth of her touch seeps over my skin, kindling a deeper heat.

"Thank you," I say, keeping my voice totally calm. "I hope you're right."

"I know it's made a difference to me." She gets to her feet. "If the guys are sticking to the shadows, I'll try one of those bench-beds. I want to see what sleeping in a room on wheels is like."

I let out a casual chuckle. "It's all yours."

But as she walks back to the van, I can't help wondering how much sleep I'll be able to get after all, with her lying right there across from me.

19

Periwinkle

My eyes twitch open. A mishmash of clashing flavors wobbles through my nerves like someone's upending a buffet table over me.

I sit up, peering through the darkness. Faint moonlight seeps through the camper van's windows, highlighting Jonah's sleeping form tucked under his blanket.

The sight of his black hair lying rumpled against the small pillow brings a twinge of affection into my chest that's not totally familiar. I have the urge to reach over and smooth the strands back from his face.

It's not as if he minds his hair getting in his eyes when they're closed anyway.

I don't want to wake him up, and another splatter of strange emotion hits me at the same time. Definitely not from Jonah—it's reaching me from too much of a distance.

We're alone in the van. None of our shadowkind companions have snuck in to shelter in the shadows.

Have Raze and Hail gotten into another argument? I'm not sure how much I can intervene, but talking them down this evening seemed to help a little.

Time for my one-person cheer squad to come to the rescue.

I slip through the shadows along the tiny gap at the edge of the doorframe and re-materialize on the dirt track outside. The chilly night air wisps against my skin. Crickets chirp in the thicker darkness of the woods.

I can't pick up on any signs of trouble with my other senses—no snapped words or grunts of combat. Only another spurt of emotion that's too muddled to decipher.

I'm not tasting any hostility in the impressions, at least. I don't think I need to fear my imminent demise.

Watching for any evidence to the contrary, I venture into the forest in the direction the pulses of emotion are emanating from. I'll get a better idea what's going on, and if I think I need backup, I'll call for the others then.

It turns out I don't need to call. I've taken less than ten steps before a lean figure topped with bright red hair emerges from the shadows by my side.

Mirage cocks his head, gazing down at me. He keeps his voice hushed, though his usual lively energy still ripples through it. "Where are you off to, our little rainbow?"

A trace of a blush touches my cheeks at the reference to my glowing hair and the various embarrassing emotions it's put on display. "I'm noticing unusual feelings from something—or more than one thing—out this way. I thought I'd take a closer look."

He clicks his tongue, mock chiding. "All by yourself."

I shrug. "I didn't want to bother the rest of you if I didn't need to. You could go back to the van."

A grin stretches across Mirage's face. "Exploring is much more interesting. If there's trouble, I can outfox it for you."

Another pang of affection fills me, even though the fox shifter has been irritable with me before. "You really don't need to, but if you want to come along, I'm happy to have company."

"It's settled, then. Mirage and Periwinkle, back in a twinkle." He winks at me with a brief swish of his five bushy tails before they vanish back into his human-esque body.

The rhyme comes with a brief flicker of satisfaction like fresh cherry pie. "You like playing with words a lot, don't you?"

"I like playing with all things. Why not have fun wherever you can?" He hops over a fallen log with a swift flip before landing. Then he stops, maybe realizing I can't leap over quite so nimbly, and offers his hand to help me clamber over.

His grasp is unexpectedly steady. I kind of wish I didn't have to let go.

I walk on more cautiously as I wait for another of those strange sensations. For maybe a minute, nothing comes, and I start to think it's gone and we should go back.

Then another flare wriggles through my nerves from closer by.

I point up ahead. "Still this way."

Mirage bounds along beside me. "You're not worried about what it could be?"

I consider the question. "A little. But not very much. It doesn't feel *bad*, only… confused."

"Confused people—and shadowkind—do bad things."

"But sometimes they do good things too. Or they need help so that they can. If we ignore them, we'd never find out."

He lapses into a short silence. "You like to unravel mysteries!"

He sounds so delighted with his revelation that I hate to correct him. "Sort of. I just… like to understand everyone. There are so many different feelings, and they don't always make sense. When I start sorting them out, a lot of the time that seems to make the other being happier too. So we all win."

I hesitate before glancing up at him. "Like… you always look like you're having fun on the outside. Like you're happy. But sometimes I can tell you're actually sad or even scared. You don't have to pretend, you know. You need to recognize what's wrong to make it better."

Mirage tenses with a flash of his fangs. "*I* don't need any help. It's all playing around."

His voice is sharp, but the flare of emotion that prickles over my skin is more anxious than angry. I've stuck my foot in it again.

Let's see if for once I can retrieve that foot from my mouth before it ends up right down my throat.

I dip my head apologetically. "I'm sorry. I'm realizing that a lot of beings don't like it when I mention how they feel. If it's easier for you focusing on having fun, I won't bother you about it."

Mirage opens his mouth and closes it again. An expression of consternation crosses his face. He gives his body a little shake, his fox ears shimmering into existence through his ruddy hair.

"I don't want to talk about it," he says.

I give him a sympathetic smile. "I don't know your reasons, but there are things I don't like talking about either. I have to remember that more when it comes to everyone else."

His gaze darts to me, something shifting behind his

bright brown gaze. "*You* aren't the trouble, Rainbow. The trouble's in here." He touches the side of his head and then the front of his chest. "I like how you are—when you're not asking about those things. You want everyone to be happy."

A spark of joy lights in my chest. "Yes. Yes, I do."

"Your powers made problems, but never on purpose."

"I wish the only thing I ever did was make people happy."

Mirage hums. "Sometimes playing makes problems too, even though it should all be fun. I don't…"

He halts with another waft of discomfort, tart as a kumquat.

"It's okay," I say softly. "Whatever's happened, I'm sorry it happened to you. But I'm glad you're walking with me whether you tell me or not."

He doesn't say anything. He just reaches out and clasps my hand. Warmth blooms over my skin from where our palms touch, and my smile turns giddy.

Then I feel the topsy-turvy emotions in a sudden jolt from just ahead.

I drop my voice to a whisper. "I think we've almost found… whatever it is."

We creep along even more carefully. Mirage lifts his feet in an exaggerated pantomime and grins at me. Thankfully he refrains from adding a laugh track.

The trees thin around a small clearing, and I catch a glimpse of a hunched form between the trunks.

I stop where I have a full view, studying the creature. It stands on tall legs like a giraffe's but twice as spindly, ridged plates jutting across its belly and a thick tongue lolling from its crooked beak.

It raises that beak toward the leaves of the nearest tree but can't seem to bite any off. A shudder of frustration runs through it, followed by another punch of tangled emotions.

The poor thing. Maybe it would like some mac and cheese or a triple chocolate cake? Those always put me in a good mood… not that I have either on hand.

As I try to decipher the scrambled impressions, the creature's entire body spasms. Its legs plummet to half their previous height; its beak juts farther into a pointed, furred snout.

Talk about a makeover.

My breath catches in my throat. "It's another of those strange changing shadowkind."

I spoke at a murmur, but the creature's new form must come with keener ears. Its head snaps toward me. With a thin shriek, it crashes into the underbrush on the other side of the clearing.

Mirage springs forward. "I'll catch it!" He flickers into fox form and then into the shadows in a blink.

I hustle after both him and the creature, but after the walk, my physical legs are ready to stage a rebellion. When I push them to a run, twinges of pain reverberate from my ankles.

Wincing, I slip into the swath of darkness along the edge of the clearing. But even when I throw myself forward as quickly as I can, the space ahead feels empty.

Mirage and the strange shadowkind have already outpaced me. I don't know if they continued in the same direction or veered off somewhere.

I stop, surrounded by unfamiliar trees and bushes. The chill of the breeze penetrates the shadows.

With a shiver, I return to physical form. My awareness of the mortal world is clearer when I can use my senses fully.

I can't see, hear, or smell any trace of my hiking companion or the creature we were tracking, though. If Mirage caught the beast, he'd call for me to join him, wouldn't he?

Turning around, I recognize none of my surroundings. Which direction did I come from? Every stretch of trees and underbrush looks the same.

How do I get back to the van from here?

This is why I like cities. They have signs.

I should have laid down a path like that fairy tale with the two children. Shiny stones, not bread crumbs—bread crumbs are only good for the birds.

I walk a little way in the direction I think will take me back to the clearing where we spotted the creature, but it's just trees, trees, and more trees. I've only gotten more lost.

It was important to find that shadowkind. It might help us figure out where the beings like it are coming from. But I can't help anyone if I pull an accidental disappearing act.

What will Jonah think if he wakes up and I'm gone? Will Raze be angry? Will Hail call me useless?

I hug myself and peer around me. A sallow yellow glow tints the nearby trunks. My hair is glowing with my growing fear.

If Mirage hasn't caught the creature by now, I'm not sure he will. He really shouldn't be following it on his own after the last one attacked us out of the blue.

Assuming he didn't simply ditch me.

No. I don't believe that. I can still feel the comforting pressure of his hand around mine.

I lift my voice to carry. "Mirage? Mirage, where are you? I couldn't keep up. Mirage!"

For several beats of my heart, all I get is the dark glower of the gloomy forest. Then a fox head pops from between two bushes.

Mirage transforms into human-esque form as he bounds out. He grasps the sides of my arms. "Are you all right?"

He looks so concerned that my pulse flutters. I want to

lean into him, but I'm afraid he'll pull back rather than gather me closer.

Instead, I recover my smile. "I was too slow and I got lost, but I'm sure we can find our way now that I've found you."

Mirage hums. "That shifty being was too quick even for me. Following its trail was already hard before I heard you calling. Maybe Raze can track it tomorrow."

"That's a good plan."

Mirage turns me so we're facing in the same direction, tucking one hand around my elbow. "My nose is good enough to follow *our* trail. I'll get us back before anyone wails!" He pauses. "If you'll count on me for that too."

I beam at him. "Of course. Thank you—for coming, and for leading the way."

As Mirage smiles back at me, a wash of emotion streams off him like nothing I've sensed from the fox shifter before: sweet and warm but poignant, like pork belly drizzled with salted caramel.

Even when I've gotten lost in the woods, I can do something right... whatever exactly that was.

20

Periwinkle

As the sky starts to darken with the end of our second day on the road, Jonah pulls the van onto the shoulder. I peer through the window across the rocky landscape with its cover of evergreens, waiting for Raze to arrive.

We've been winding through the back roads all day, periodically checking in with our best tracker. Raze has gamely followed the scent of the patchwork creature Mirage and I spotted last night, and we've stuck as close to him as we can within the van.

It takes several minutes for him to emerge from the shadows. He gives his broad shoulders a shake, his impressive muscles rippling across his arms. "The trail just kept going to the northeast. I've passed a few other scents that have a similar quality, but they're even older, so faint I'm not sure I could stay on them very far."

Jonah sighs and peers at the sky. "I don't know how much point there is in continuing to follow even this creature. It might be roaming at random."

"An excellent pep talk from the man in charge," Hail drawls.

I jump in. "It was worth trying. We didn't have any other new leads. But Jonah, you must need to rest after so much driving." His fatigue trickles off him like a thin, salty soup.

Jonah shoots me a grateful smile. "I'm doing all right, but I'm not sure how much longer I can keep it up. We'd better find a place to camp out for the night and start tomorrow fresh."

Mirage spins around and launches himself into a tight flip against the van's inner wall. "Time to get out of this tin can!"

"Let me see where a good spot would be. We don't want local police deciding we're suspicious and interfering with our mission."

Jonah consults his map and drives until we reach an overgrown lane that leads to a rusty gate. It looks like it's been an eon or so since anyone's opened it. The padlock securing the chain is more rust than metal.

I thought the basilisk shifter was loping alongside us, but there's no sign of him. My forehead furrows. "What happened to Raze?"

As Hail hops out of the van, his voice takes on a disdainful note. "He's probably off tearing the mortal wildlife into bloody pieces."

Right. Raze needs to feed to keep up his energy—and he can't absorb the nutrition he needs simply by hanging around beings with emotions.

My powers might be confusing, but they're a lot more convenient.

I grab the camping stove and help Jonah set it up on a

patch of gravel. By the time he's cooked his canned dinner and eaten most of it, Raze still hasn't returned.

Can I blame him if he'd rather not face Hail's snarky remarks?

The thought that he thinks his team would be more cruel than welcoming sends a pang of sadness through me.

"I'm going to make sure Raze is okay," I announce.

Hail snorts, which for once I can understand. Anything that could make Raze not-okay would pulverize me in an instant.

But that's only when it comes to physical defense.

Jonah simply nods. "Stay on the alert for odd creatures. We don't know when we might cross paths with another one that turns aggressive on a dime."

I can't follow scents the way Raze and Mirage can, but my emotional awareness gets more sensitive when I'm familiar with another being. Like recognizing a person when they're too far away to see their face, just by the way they walk.

I clamber up a low slope dotted with lumps of granite, and an impression I know is Raze creeps into my mind. He's sated and feeling both satisfied and a little ashamed of that.

The conflicted emotions make my heart hurt more.

I pick up my pace, hurrying through the brush as quickly as my short and unpredictably wobbly legs will safely take me. Falling on my head and needing him to come to *my* rescue isn't the plan.

I can tell Raze has heard me coming before I see him. One crunch of a twig underfoot sets off a pepper-sharp twang of alarm that fades just as quickly.

He can probably smell that it's me. I hope my scent is at least a little pleasing.

It would really suck if he's smelling dead fish or gym socks whenever I'm around.

I've only made it a short distance farther before the basilisk shifter comes to me. He marches between the trees and stops when we're in view of each other.

His voice still has a hint of a growl, but it's mostly confused. "What are you doing, Periwinkle?"

I smile at him. "Looking for you. It didn't seem fair, after all the work you've done on your own today, that you'd have to spend the whole night alone too."

His expression stays puzzled, his stance rigid. "I'm fine on my own. I prefer it."

I tip my head to the side. I'm picking up frustration and defiance but also a whiff of longing. Definitely nothing that feels content.

Liar, liar, pants on fire.

I raise my eyebrows. "I don't think that's true, not completely. I don't have to even talk if you don't want me to. What if I just sit with you and we can see if that's better than staying by yourself?"

Raze scowls, but something softens in his eyes at the same time. "Well, come on then, Glowbug."

Despite his grumpy tone, something lights up inside me at the nickname. It sounds more fond than dismissive. As if he likes the fact that I glow, just like Mirage suggested he appreciates my rainbow of colors.

It'd be nice if my mood-ring tendencies came with a few benefits.

The basilisk shifter tramps back across the slope, and I hustle behind him. He glances back to check on me just as a spike of pain radiates up one ankle.

I stumble. Raze is there unexpectedly fast, grasping my elbow to steady me.

He peers at me with sudden solemnness. "You're not clumsy. You've been injured."

Darn those predator instincts.

An uneasy flush spreads under my skin. I force another smile. "It was a long time ago. No big deal. It doesn't matter anymore."

I don't want to dredge up those awful memories.

Raze's thumb skims over my arm in a gentle arc. He echoes what I said to him just minutes ago: "I don't think that's true."

My throat tightens up. He's the only one who's ever noticed.

That doesn't mean I'm going to bawl all over him. I shrug with a light laugh. "I had a bad run-in with a cruel human. He hurt me, and some of the wounds left lingering effects. It was a good lesson in what to watch out for. And in getting creative about staying on my feet. I learned a lot!"

Raze doesn't look impressed by my studiousness. His lips draw back from his teeth, which extend into the razor sharp edges that come with his basilisk form. "What man? Where is he now?"

I can only answer honestly. "I don't know. I'd rather think about the much nicer people I can hang out with. All right?"

Raze expels a growl followed by a long, slow breath. Then, before I have time to react, he scoops me up into his arms as if I weigh no more than a feather pillow.

Tucking me against his broad chest, he strides onward.

The feel of his sculpted, heated muscles against my side sends all sorts of tingles through my body. Not the effect I'd imagine he intended to provoke. A flare of need sparks between my legs.

The few times I dabbled in physical merging in the past, I didn't really know those other shadowkind. Just a quick romp with someone who caught my eye and had the same impulse.

How much better might it be with someone I've come to care for? Who cares about me?

Could that be the missing ingredient that makes humans jump on each other so avidly?

I shouldn't let my mind wander in that direction. Raze is only stopping me from slowing him down, not propositioning me.

"It's okay," I protest. "I don't mind walking."

He lets out a decisive huff. "*I* mind."

Something inside me wilts despite my best efforts. "I'm sorry I'm slow. I—"

Raze stops and gazes down at me, his mouth gone taut. "No. I mind you hurting when you're only trying to help me."

Oh. I stare back at him for a thump of my heart. He starts walking again, and I let myself relax in his careful embrace.

He doesn't go much farther, just to a small clearing where a ridge of protruding rock sticks out like a bench. Raze lowers me gingerly onto one end and then sits down at the other, a few feet away. As if he assumes I wouldn't want him any closer than that.

He might have good predatory instincts, but his attraction radar is way off.

Or maybe he *has* picked up on my reactions and he's trying to discourage me because I'm not his type?

I push those muddled thoughts out of my head and focus on the man sitting next to me. I came here for his benefit, not my own.

Since I promised him he didn't have to talk to me, I peer through the forest into the thickening dusk. The crickets are out again, chirping away like birds of the night, and a half-full moon has risen to cast its silvery light over us. The breeze licks through my hair, cool but not uncomfortably cold.

Raze speaks without warning, his voice low and a little hoarse. "You're always so… nice to me."

I glance over at him with another twinge through my heart. "Why wouldn't I be nice to you?"

He's looking at the ground rather than at me, his mouth twisted in a grimace. "I wasn't very kind to *you* when you first came into the dorm."

"You don't need to worry about that. I could tell you weren't actually angry at me. You didn't mean me any harm."

A choked sound lurches out of him. "I *never* mean any harm. It just… happens. You don't know how many people I've hurt, how many beings… If I don't stay totally in control, my powers can spill right out of me."

My stomach knots. "I know how that feels."

Raze shakes his head. "It can't be the same. I'm a basilisk. I put on contacts to act as shields, but if I get upset, my true eyes can sear through them—and kill anything I look at. Poison seeps right out of my skin. Everything I see, everything I touch…"

He glares down at his hands. "I didn't want anything like that to happen to you. I want it even less now that I know how sweet you are."

He called me sweet. My pulse flutters despite the grimness of the rest of his words.

I scoot a little closer. "You've never hurt me at all. I'm not afraid of you."

"You should be. Everyone else is. Everyone knows what can happen if they're in the wrong place at the wrong time."

I dare to push myself even closer and set my hand on his arm. He twitches at the contact but doesn't pull away.

"You carried me," I point out. "Nothing bad happened."

"I made sure I was totally calm and that there was nothing around that would startle me. And it was only for a few minutes. It was better than leaving you in pain."

I trace the bulges of his muscles, unable to resist my

fascination with his powerful body. At my touch, a quiver of emotion races into my veins from Raze, hot and heady as pecan pie straight out of the oven.

That definitely doesn't feel like disinterest. I think he's still trying to protect me—from himself.

I tip my head to gaze up at him. "You know, you didn't just save me from pain. Having you hold me like that felt *good*."

Raze gapes down at me as if he can't believe what I just said, but a starker rush of his desire washes over me.

I take the chance and bob up on my knees so I can press my lips to his.

Raze's chest hitches, and then he's clutching me to him, his fingers twining with my hair, his mouth scorching as it devours mine. Every inch of my body blazes with a joyful glow.

Some of it tingles from my scalp into my hair. After a moment, a pinkish haze seeps through my closed eyelids.

Raze will be able to see it too. Know how happy he's making me. How much I want this.

No shame prickles through me with that knowledge. All I can do is keep kissing him with all my eagerness, my pulse skipping giddily.

This incredible man, so compassionate and selfless. He's been so very lonely. I can taste it on him.

But I light him up too. I've proven that not everyone will want to run away from him.

Raze's lips crash against mine once more. The kiss has barely begun before he wrenches himself backward.

"It's not you," he rasps hastily. "That was— I wanted it. More than I should have. We shouldn't do that again. If I get caught up, I can't make sure you stay safe."

I can see we still have a long way to go.

I give his arm a gentle poke. "What if I'd rather have this deliciousness than safety?"

Raze lets out a strangled groan. "Peri…"

"All right, all right." I beam up at him. "Come back to the van with me then. Everyone will want to see that you're okay. You can keep me safe even while I sleep."

21

Fragments of ice spin above my palm in a controlled whirl. I focus on them rather than the rumble of the van, my "teammates" sitting around me, and the forested hills looming outside the windows.

If we were back at the school, I'd conjure a form that provides an obvious challenge: a feat of visible intricacy that would have my audience gasping in awe. But I don't give a fuck about impressing the screw-up fox, the pipsqueak, the bloodthirsty brute, or the brownnosing prick at the wheel.

So I settle on something just for myself. Still a challenge but a hidden one—a challenge that'll keep me occupied and away from the thoughts niggling at the edges of my mind.

At a nudge of my will, the particles spiral closer together. Bit by bit, they meld into larger pieces of the structure.

The sculpture trembles with a bump of the van over a

pothole, but my concentration holds the bits in place. More and more frozen crystals condense into the larger whole.

When it's finished, the final creation looks like a lump on my hand—a mountain crag dotted with ripples of forest and a snowy cap, with a waterfall tumbling to a pool at the base. Only I know that behind that waterfall lies a network of caves full of all sorts of beings bustling around, sharing meals, playing music, or sprawled in relaxation.

A short, pudgy figure slides over on the bench. The cream puff peers at my creation and smiles at me. "Your sculptures always look so real. Is that a place you've actually been?"

Only in distant daydreams. I curl my fingers and disintegrate the sculpted ice into a sprinkling of snow. "I don't need to see something to conjure it. Some of us have an imagination."

I've kept my tone disdainful, but Periwinkle's smile doesn't budge. "You must have a very good one. Can you stop them from melting, or do they always only last a little while?"

I think of the immense ice structures that fill my dorm room, turning it into an enclave of hopes still out of reach. "They last as long as I want them to. *My* powers aren't so shaky."

If she picks up on the jab at her pathetic glow, she gives no sign. "You could make a whole collection of them. Put on a show like humans do—in a gallery! I bet all kinds of beings, shadowkind and human, would like to look at your art."

The earnest admiration in her voice and the picture she's drawn of me gathering all those beings together wash over me like a warm breeze. For a second, the chilly words I'd like to say melt in my chest. I have the absurd urge to keep listening to her.

What the fuck is wrong with me?

What's wrong with *her* that she's showering me with supposed kindness when I've given her nothing but cold shoulders? Does nothing faze her at all?

My confusion wakes up my temper with a sharper edge. "Put on a performance for mortals? What idiot would want to do that? Other than you, obviously."

Periwinkle doesn't so much as flinch, but the lean figure sitting on the other side of the van snaps his head around. The fox shifter's lips draw back from his fangs.

"It takes one to know one," he says in a singsong voice like a mortal child's taunt, but his bright eyes glitter with an unexpected warning.

Since when is he the pipsqueak's bodyguard?

I narrow my eyes at Mirage. "Spoken like another idiot."

His grin turns fiercer. "We can battle it out for the top spot. How many tails do you have?"

Before I can decide how I'm supposed to answer that, Periwinkle holds out her hands. "Hey. No one's an idiot here. We're figuring out how to be a team." She meets my gaze. "If I'm being too pushy, you can just tell me. I'll listen."

How is it that my irritation simmers down with that one gentle remark? Suddenly I'm remembering her telling me how amazing I was for freezing the shadowkind beast that attacked us.

I grit my teeth. It doesn't make sense that she has any effect on me.

Especially when I can't seem to affect *her* at all.

Mirage lets out a little huff, but he leans back in his seat as if mollified. I consider tossing another barb at him to show I'm not so easily tamed, but right then the van grinds to a stop.

Up front, our sorcerer babysitter rolls down the window. "Have you found something?"

The carnivore who's acting as our tracker has materialized on the side of the road.

Raze nods in a jerk. "I caught another trail. It smells like there are a few of those odd creatures together. They traveled beside the road but then veered into the deeper wilderness. You'll only get farther away from them if you keep driving."

Jonah grimaces, but he cuts the engine. "We'd better continue on foot, then. If we can catch up with them or find out where they were going, we'll need all our skills."

Will we? Does the sorcerer expect me to lock them in ice like I did the first one?

I don't think the poor beast deserved it. It wasn't acting remotely aggressive until its sudden turnabout.

Something else is going on with these shadowkind. Rollick told us to investigate, not to slaughter them.

Jonah swivels in his seat to peer back at us. "All right, everyone out. We're going on a hike."

I pull my lips back in a sneer. Fragile mortal boy who can only stand alongside us because of his foul magic. Any of us, even the pipsqueak, could crush him if we moved too fast for him to speak a sorcerous command. But he thinks he should get to order us around.

"Of course, oh fearless leader," I say with all possible sarcasm.

Jonah frowns at me. His reply comes out flat. "Then get going, Hail. If you want to be finished with this mission sooner rather than later, the important thing is finding these beings."

It's particularly annoying that he has a point. I keep my sneer in place and wait for Periwinkle and Mirage to step out the back doors before I deign to follow.

At least the fresh, piney breeze outside revitalizes me after the stuffiness of the van. We set off between the trees, Raze leading the way with his basilisk tongue periodically flicking from his hulking, otherwise human-esque form.

A chipmunk chitters from a tree branch overhead, and a couple of sparrows flutter by, but there's no sign of humans. Just untamed wilderness, all that guileless life completely free. The best of the mortal realm laid out before us.

Only the knowledge of the confrontation that might lie ahead stops me from enjoying it.

We tramp across a couple of miles of uneven ground with the brush tugging at our legs. Then the terrain slopes upward. Rough knobs of rock protrude from the soil amid the trees and shrubs.

The effort of climbing sends an achy but not unpleasant sensation through the muscles in my legs. Physical bodies have so many unexpected quirks.

We're halfway up the hillside when Raze leans forward and inhales deeply. "The smell is thickening quickly. I think they might be—"

Before he can finish the sentence, a dozen dark shapes hurtle over the crest of the hill toward us.

The shadowkind creatures lunge into our midst, jagged teeth snapping here, bladed claws slashing there. They leap and thrash so wildly I can't make out more than glimpses of fur and feathers and scales.

I stumble backward and manage to knock aside one creature's snapping jaws with a swift thrust of my arm. Raze roars and throws himself at the densest cluster of them, shifting into his immense lizard-like form as he does.

His maw closes around one beast's neck with a crack of its spine and a gush of smoky essence. His pitch-black eyes sear into another being so viciously it squeals and spasms.

I dodge a third creature, this one the size of a wolf but covered in coarse hide like a elephant. It throws itself at me sideways, quills jutting from its skin, and all I can do to keep myself from getting impaled is hurl a blast of ice at it.

Even through my jolt of fear, I don't want to kill it. None of this makes *sense*. Why would these beings suddenly group together to attack us?

But in the chaos of the moment, the bolt of frigid energy hits the creature not just in the legs but in its lower torso too. It keels over, eyes glazing.

I've stopped its heart.

Guilt clogs my throat. I take another step back, my gaze darting over the battle.

Raze is tearing into another of the beasts, one as large as a tiger. Jonah is shouting out words in his sorcerous language that set my skin creeping. I can't see that any of the shadowkind in the onslaught are responding to his commands.

What provoked their rage? I've had to put up with these dopes for days, and even I'm not that pissed off.

We have to be missing something.

The atmosphere of the forest resonates through me, reminding me that I'm a creature of the wilderness myself. I focus all my senses on the rampaging beasts.

What's driving them? Is there a threat they're reacting to?

What I see leaves me colder than before. There's just… nothing.

I can't pick up any actual fury in the creatures' violence. No impression of instincts kicking in, no signals of panic or protective agitation.

All my own instincts about wild places tell me this is a totally mindless frenzy.

To my right, Mirage springs in front of Periwinkle to pounce on a ferret-sized beast that hurled itself at her. Raze rips open yet another being among the several smoking bodies already littering the hillside.

The few remaining creatures seem to recognize that the tables have turned, though I still don't observe any signs of distress. They simply wheel in tandem and sprint up the hill the way they came.

Raze halts over the corpse he just savaged and shifts back into humanlike form, his chest heaving.

Jonah glances around. "Is everyone all right? Any injuries?"

"A few scratches," Raze rumbles. "Nothing that won't heal quickly."

My bewilderment comes out in rancor. "We're all fine. But what the fuck happened there? Aren't you supposed to be wielding your vast powers to harness the demented beasts, sorcerer boy?"

Jonah cuts his gaze toward me with a twist of his mouth. He isn't happy with the results of this battle either, even if we "won."

He drags in a rough breath before answering. "I tried. My sorcery wouldn't catch hold."

Periwinkle's forehead furrows. "Is it because they're the strange kind of shadowkind? But you were able to control that one before."

"I was. It did take more effort than usual, but it wasn't impossible." Jonah's expression darkens. "The only cases I've ever come across where sorcery was completely ineffective… it was because another sorcerer had already imposed control."

Ah. So we can blame more humans for this mess? What a shocking surprise.

Mirage has bounded up the slope and is peering over the crest. "They ran east. Should we follow them?"

Jonah's revelation and everything I know about the patterns of the natural world collide into a knot of certainty at the base of my throat. "If we want to get to the source of the problem, we need to follow their trail backward and find out where they came from."

And which mortal asshole pointed them in our direction.

22

Periwinkle

Night is falling through the forest. The trees have turned to silhouettes, the sky to slate gray. The lumpy ground keeps making its best attempts at tripping me.

At least I can feel the dips and ridges through the shadows. Needing extra guidance, Jonah aims the beam of his keychain penlight at the terrain just ahead of him.

Mirage and Hail merged with the shadows ages ago, and Raze only flickers out occasionally to give us glimpses of the trail to follow, but the sorcerer has to rely on his two legs. It doesn't seem fair to leave him tramping onward as if he's alone.

Unfortunately, my feet and ankles have joined the conspiracy against me. The pangs shooting up from them are sharpening by the minute. We've been backtracking the trail of that violent pack of shadowkind for hours.

The pain stirs memories I don't want: noxious metals pressed into my skin, muttered words weaving right into my mind.

Jonah said the creatures that attacked us were probably controlled by another sorcerer. A sorcerer who sent shadowkind rampaging through the forest.

Not exactly a gesture of friendship.

Sorcerers are dangerous. Sorcerers push and cut and *hurt*…

I breathe as evenly as I can, hoping Jonah will take my silence for fatigue. I don't want to talk about the other emotions conducting a dance-off inside me.

Of course, I don't always get a say about what shows.

As we pass through a small clearing, Jonah veers closer. "Are you picking up on any unnerving impressions?"

My gaze darts to him. "No. Why would you think so?"

"I just noticed—your hair's been flickering with a bit of that glow it gets when you're feeling something strongly. An orange-y color that looks uneasy to me. But maybe I'm misinterpreting."

He's not, but I don't want to tell him that. I also don't want to lie.

I could take a page from Mirage's book and turn the situation into a joke.

I summon a laugh. "It's great being a walking mood ring. Always blaring what's going on inside whether I want to or not. The forest is pretty spooky when it's getting dark, don't you think?"

I'd rather he assumes it's the atmosphere that's unsettled me.

Jonah echoes my laugh. "You can say that again. Maybe we should head back… but we might not find a lead this good again."

"You're the only one of us who *needs* sleep," I remind him. "It should be up to you."

He smiles tightly. "I can keep going. Rollick is counting on us."

I'm not paying enough attention, and my next step brings my foot into a hollow at a bad angle. The searing ache that lances up my calf has me biting my lip against a gasp. The orange glow flares bright enough for me to see it.

Soon I'll be a mood torch. As much as I hate to abandon Jonah, it's getting too hard to hide my discomfort.

"My physical body is getting tired," I say as an excuse. "I'm going to slip into the shadows to give it a break."

And to rest my throbbing legs.

Jonah nods without any sign of distress. But then, he'd never make me feel guilty for looking after myself, and he's good at keeping his own emotions simmered down.

Maybe I should ask him to give me some lessons alongside Shanty's… if we ever get back to the academy.

I hop into the nearest patch of darkness and ripple onward with all bodily sensations dispelled. In the shadows, I'm more clearly aware of Raze following the trail ahead of us, Mirage bounding among the trees to my left, Hail's presence flowing along at a more measured rhythm to my right.

The sky is completely black when Raze pops out of the shadows and stays corporeal. He speaks in a hushed voice. "I think we've got something."

I leap to his side and find myself at the edge of a larger clearing. Jonah points his light where Raze indicated.

A log cabin squats by the trees at the far end of the clearing. The structure stands only one story tall and maybe twenty feet across, with a wooden shed beside it.

Moss creeps across both buildings' walls and roofs, and no light glints through the single dingy window. Jonah peers at it, braced as if for an attack. The other men materialize around us.

"I smell a human as well as shadowkind," Raze says. "Just one. Male. Not very fresh. No one's here right now—probably not for hours."

Jonah frowns at the main structure. "It looks like a hunting cabin—meant for stays of only a few days. Did the shadowkind creatures hang around here or just pass by?"

Raze stalks along the edges of the clearing, his reptilian tongue flicking over his lips. I gaze down at the ground and notice the imprint of a boot sole in the dirt.

Not too long but wide. Like the person who made it was short and stout like that cabin.

An image of a man who fit that description wavers up from the depths of my mind. My pulse stutters with a fresh prickle of pain through my ankles.

Running away flailing suddenly feels like a good plan.

I squeeze my hands at my sides. I'm fine. Raze just said no one's here.

And whoever was here before, it obviously couldn't have been *that* man.

Raze returns with a grim expression. "As far as I can tell, the shadowkind creatures here recently came from different directions. The faintest trails are scattered. The most recent trail is all of them together, heading in the direction where they ran into us."

Hail's voice is flat and cold. "So the sorcerer gathered them here and sent them off on a hunt."

Jonah grimaces. "Let's take a closer look and see what else we can find."

As we walk to the cabin, his light glints off tiny shapes amid the scruffy grass. Mirage ducks down. "Stars on the ground to match the sky!"

His fingers brush them, and he recoils with a wince. "Stars that burn. They're silver and iron."

I peer at the trampled earth. Ringlets of pale gray metal shine amid the grass—few enough that I can barely pick up on their repelling quality.

My forehead furrows. "They look almost like…"

My voice trails off with a smack of panic that makes flailing feel even more appealing.

Hail finishes for me. "Links from one of those hunter nets."

My heart is suddenly pounding twice as fast. A prickling sensation spreads all over my skin. Echoes of interlocking links searing into my limbs and face…

I drag in a steadying breath, but the air flows shakily into my lungs. My legs stiffen under me.

My voice comes out in a thin chirp. "I can stay out here! Someone should keep watch, right? I'll shout if I see anything."

Jonah shoots me a concerned look, but I manage to smile at him. He beckons to Raze. "Come on. We'll need that keen sense of smell to investigate."

All four of the men push into the cabin.

I take a couple of steps back from the scattered links and reach for the exercises Shanty started to teach me. Picture somewhere calming. The park in that city—

A crackle amid the underbrush makes my pulse lurch. He could be coming, storming in to capture us all. We have to—

I shut my eyes against the blare of panic.

No. What's happening here has nothing to do with my past. I need to get a grip on myself and help with this mission.

The thought has only just passed through my head when Mirage bursts out of the cabin clutching a few metal objects in his arms. "Look what we found!"

They don't gleam as brightly in the dim moonlight as the bits of netting did in Jonah's penlight beam, but I can make out their shapes well enough. He's holding a tarnished, scuffed medal, a small trophy cup with a dent in the side, and a figurine that I think is an award, the head knocked right off.

My mind blanks. All I can see is the display case in that basement room, the memorabilia the man who caged me kept of his "defeated enemies."

A wail careens from my mouth. He's found me again— he's going to trap me and haul me away and—

The horror explodes out of me in a wave of darkness thicker than the night.

Mirage yelps. There's a shout from somewhere behind him. Distress and pain, reverberating into me from all of them—

A few firm words cut through the cacophony in my head. I yank back the agonized energy pouring out of me, reining it in by some means I didn't know I had.

Then I'm standing there, trembling and panting, staring at Jonah—who just gave me a sorcerous command to stop.

I didn't rein myself in, not really. He did.

I only catch a glimpse of his fraught expression where he's standing in the cabin doorway before he's focusing on the other men. "Is everyone okay? If you need to enter the shadows to recover, we can sort out the rest after."

Mirage is lying on the ground just a few steps away from me, the trinkets he was holding strewn on the ground, his arms wrapped around his stomach. Little puffs of essence drift up from his body, but he inhales raggedly and opens his eyes.

"It hit hard, but not too deep," he says. His gaze flicks to me with a knitting of his brow.

Hail is leaning against the cabin's outer wall, one hand

clutching the side of his face. His pale cheek looks scraped raw, more essence trickling off it. He stares at me, but he's on his feet, so Jonah must decide he's not on the verge of kicking the bucket.

And Raze... Raze crouches on the ground in front of Jonah. As I watch, he shifts from basilisk to humanoid form. A few patches of the tan skin on his arms give off whisps of essence.

Only Jonah looks uninjured. He was the farthest back—he must have gotten me under control before the worst effects of my outburst reached him.

My throat closes up so tightly it takes several seconds before I can pry it open enough to speak. "I'm so sorry. I didn't mean—I got scared—the emotions overwhelmed me."

My voice breaks with a hitch.

I wrench my gaze to Jonah. "Thank you for interrupting the outburst. I didn't know how to stop it on my own."

He offers a tentative smile, but the other three men are all staring at me. Shame tingles through my hair, casting a reddish-orange glow into the air around me.

Hail, for all his impenetrable cool, winces.

When it's clear my latest emission isn't going to hurt him, he seems to feel the need to recover his honor with a caustic remark. "How the fuck does a pipsqueak like you fling out a power like that?"

Raze doesn't say anything, but his jaw works. I can feel how taken aback he is in the salty-bitter torrent of emotion coursing off him.

I told him we'd protect each other, and then I hurt him.

I take another step back, my eyes filling with tears. The urge grips me to spring into the shadows and flee, as far away from here as I can get.

If I move fast, Jonah might not be able to stop me. I could go all the way around the world, never set foot within a thousand miles of the academy again, be ever so careful how I ease in and out of the mortal world.

It would be better for them too, wouldn't it?

At my next backward step, Jonah speaks up in a quiet, steady voice. "Peri, it's going to be okay. You're not in trouble. You didn't do that on purpose."

I swipe at the first tear that trickles down my cheek. What does that matter when I injured my supposed team anyway?

He keeps talking in the same soothing tone. "Something upset you—it set you off. That might be the key to figuring out what we're dealing with here. Stay with us, and let's work it out."

He can't know that what upset me was something from years and years ago, nothing that's really here. Just a few vague similarities...

But what if this sorcerer *is* similar to my former captor? Maybe they have a club of evilness?

Is it possible what I know about that awful man could be useful in finding this one?

Mirage has rolled onto his feet. He studies me with his bright eyes, his mouth slanted. "You *didn't* mean to hurt us, did you, Rainbow?"

A choked sound escapes me. "No. Of course not. I never do."

Hail's eyebrows shoot up to the fringe of his pale hair. "How often have you exploded like that?"

Raze's eyes widen even more. "That was like—right before we were threatened with banishment. You were upset about our dorm room. There was a surge of darkness..."

I have to answer the question in his voice. "Yes. That was me. That's why I'm here."

Hail blinks, looking at me as if he's never seen me before.

Jonah breaks in, setting a reassuring hand on my arm. "You can help us finish this mission, Peri. Tell us what bothered you."

Deep down, a lot of me still wants to escape their bewildered gazes and vanish into the woods. But every memory of past pain summons a growing determination to make sure it doesn't happen again.

How can I say I want to make up for my past crimes if I don't do everything possible to end this new threat?

I consider Jonah's face, tasting the emotions simmering beneath his controlled surface. Watching for a lie. "Are you going to tell Rollick that I lost control?"

If I'm going to be banished as soon as we go back to the school... I don't know if it'll change my decision, but I'd like to be prepared.

Jonah shakes his head. "You didn't do any significant harm. And now we know my sorcery can rein in your power, at least if I catch you early in an outburst. That makes you less of a threat, not more."

Is he going to follow me around every day back at the academy, reminding me to chill out?

Actually, that idea gives me a thrill I'm not sure he'd appreciate.

I rub my hand across my face again and square my shoulders. "Okay. I'm not sure how much I can help, but a few things here... They remind me of a sorcerer I knew before."

23

Mirage

Peri isn't meant to look sad. Even though my body is still prickling, whiffs of essence shedding from my skin as it knits back together—even though she sent out the blast that scored my flesh—the sight of her drooped head has me bristling on her behalf.

Something here reminded her of someone who *hurt* her.

Flickers of the past—blazing lights, glinting metal—dart through my head. My voice sharpens. "What did that sorcerer do? We should string him up, shoot him down."

Raze's growl echoes my mood. "If the man who's responsible for turning those creatures savage is the one who attacked you before—"

Peri shakes her head quickly. She lifts her chin, girding her stance even more in the leather jacket and ripped jeans that can't disguise the softness of her body. "Whoever is messing around with the shadowkind here, it can't be the same man. He—he didn't live anywhere near here. He wouldn't have gone off somewhere with hardly any people around."

Our own sorcerer gazes at her steadily. "It sounds like you knew him well. And obviously they aren't good memories. Will you tell us what happened?"

Peri's jaw wobbles. I have the urge to shout out, "Stop!" To conjure bright and sparkly images around us that will make her giggle and grin rather than tremble on the verge of tears.

I want to understand, but I know how those kinds of memories can scrape at you too. Leave you raw on the inside where no one can see but the stinging never ends.

Before I can finish grappling with the impulse, Peri speaks in a voice gone unusually flat. "He had me caged for a little while. It was very painful and scary. I try not to think about it, because if I get too caught up…" She motions to us with an apologetic grimace.

Hail lets out a huff where he's standing stiffly straight by the cabin, his cheek no longer wisping essence. "So you go around blasting burning shadows all over the place? Why haven't they banished you already?"

Raze spins on him. "She's obviously *trying* to avoid it."

Hail's voice turns even more disdainful, though his dark gaze lingers on Peri more avidly than I like. "Trying and failing plenty." His attention shifts to Jonah. "And no one warned us what the pipsqueak is capable of."

Our sorcerer frowns at him. "Her badge was updated while we were at the academy to show she'd harmed shadowkind. I haven't informed the rest of the team of every damaging thing *you've* ever done. If you want us all to have a full accounting, I don't think you'd come out ahead, Hail. So maybe keep the judgments to yourself."

The winter fae's mouth tightens, but he does shut up.

All the same, Peri has deflated again. Looking at her now, it's hard to imagine all that searing power burst from this gentle being.

But it did. I've never felt anything like that.

There's so much I don't know about her.

Why wouldn't there be? Every time our conversations got remotely intense, I leapt to divert them like a rabbit fleeing a wolf.

Peri exhales shakily. "It doesn't seem right that our powers should break out of us when we don't intend them to, does it? I want to control them better."

She pauses, and a starker sheen of tears forms in her bright eyes. "I want to be part of the team. I want to help track down *this* sorcerer and stop him. But if the rest of you don't feel safe with me around anymore… I won't make you stick with me."

An ache expands through my entire body. If she doesn't pitch in, Rollick and the other administrators will pitch her *out*—out of the academy, out of the entire mortal realm.

"*I* want to keep working with you," I say quickly. "You keep us on our toes. I like the excitement!"

Hail glowers at me, but I'm being honest. Peri's softness made me nervous. How could she accept a being like me with so much mischief and chaos in my nature?

But it turns out she's got some chaos of her own. Maybe that's why she's never seemed rattled no matter what I'm doing around her.

What *other* powers will she show off next? She might beat this awful sorcerer all by herself—and I'll happily watch.

Raze nods, stepping closer to Peri with a protective air that inexplicably makes me want to slip closer too. It's not as if I could defend her better than he can with all that muscly strength.

She also needs someone to keep her spirits up and put a

smile on her face, doesn't she? I can do better at that than Mr. Doom and Gloom.

The lizard man bares his teeth at Hail. "We've all made mistakes and had trouble controlling our powers. That's why we got sent on this mission. You've been complaining that Peri isn't powerful enough—don't start complaining that she can do *too* much."

"I'd rather her not be powerful in a way that can fuck us up," Hail mutters, but without much energy to the words. He considers Peri again. "I don't suppose you can decide to blast people who deserve it? *That* might be useful."

A shiver runs through Peri's body. Even if she can lash out like that, I don't think she likes the idea.

"I don't know how to control the power either way," she says quietly. "Not preventing it when it starts to happen on its own or making it happen when it isn't already. But I'm working on getting there."

Hail hums. "We'll have to see, then."

Jonah claps his hands together. "Yes. We'll see if this team can hold together, but we'd better *all* do our best to make that happen. Now why don't we take a closer look at this cabin?"

His tone gentles when he turns to Peri. "Do you think you'll be okay to go inside and look around? What was it that set off your emotions?"

She appears to steady herself. "There was a footprint—I thought it looked around the right size to match the sorcerer I knew. But that doesn't tell us a lot. He was short but wide —a lot of mortals are shaped that way."

She points toward the cabin. "And the metal on the ground—links from a hunter's net—he used those, but so do all the hunters and probably lots of sorcerers too. The worst part..."

Her gaze drops to the scattered objects I carried out of

the cabin, their dingy sides glinting faintly on the ground. "The medal and the trophy and all that… He had a display case full of those kinds of things. He stole them from… from people he didn't like and wanted to punish. They reminded me so vividly I panicked."

Someone should send that man straight to jail, no passing Go.

I scoop up the trinkets I found intriguing and tuck them out of her view. "My fault for being hasty."

Peri shakes her head. "You were excited because you thought you'd found something useful. Maybe you did. Do they have names or other information about who owned them?"

I plop on the ground and lay out my three bits of loot.

The disc on a ribbon only says, "Valedictorian" with no other words. The cup-like one and the little statue have wooden bases with a bar of metal attached. The bars look like they used to have some words etched into them, but they've been scratched up so much it's impossible to make out more than a few random letters.

Jonah glances at Peri. "The sorcerer you knew—did he damage the mementos he held on to like this?"

Peri frowns. "Most of them were dinged up, but I'm pretty sure they still had the names on them. He wanted to remember who they'd come from. Where did you find them, Mirage?"

"The cabin has a trap door going to a basement. Sneaky low-down sorcerer." I flick out my claws briefly. "They were lying on the floor near a table. Not much else down there."

"You didn't take a very thorough look the first time," Jonah points out.

Peri straightens up. "Let's do that now."

Hail eyes her. His voice sounds both wary and amused.

"Are you sure you won't be jumping at shadows, Cream Puff?"

She meets his eyes steadily, her usual perky tone returning. "I've calmed down. I know we're not dealing with the same sorcerer who captured me. If I'm staying on the team, I'm doing everything I can to get to the bottom of the problem."

She marches into the cabin ahead of the rest of us, showing none of the nerves that held her back earlier. I bound after her, wondering what she'll make of the space that seemed drab to me.

The main room of the cabin holds a wood-burning stove, a sink, and a tiny table with a single chair. The other half of the main room is totally empty. You'd expect to find a bed there. Maybe the sorcerer only has one, so he brings it away when he leaves?

The trap door lies open. Peri's stance tenses, but she heads down the rickety stairs without hesitating.

She stops at the bottom. "The sorcerer I knew kept the beings he trapped in his basement. It makes sense. Easier to keep us out of view from other humans when he was living in a city. Easier to set up protections against escaping. But there are no cages or protections down here. Not even nets."

Jonah descends after her with the gleam of his artificial light. He scans the walls. "It's like whoever was using the place cleared it out and left."

Hail grimaces. "Did the sorcerer realize we were coming?"

The basilisk shakes his head. "The smells around here are too faint. He must have left before we were attacked, and we weren't even heading in this direction then." He pauses. "Maybe he moves around a lot. That's a better strategy for a predator who doesn't want to be turned into prey."

"He's not going to get any choice about that!" Peri

declares, but the faint bluish glow that's formed in her hair gives me the impression of disappointment.

Jonah sighs. "Well, I can't see anything that would tell us where he went next. I'd better get in touch with Rollick and let him know about this development."

Pulling out his phone, he clambers back up the stairs. The rest of us follow.

As Jonah taps text messages onto the phone's screen, Peri meanders along the edge of the clearing as if looking for more clues. The determination on her face tugs at me to join her.

I extend three of my tails as I do, swirling them in a playful spiral, but she hardly seems to notice, let alone give me the laugh I wanted. She just shoots me a small smile and continues her search.

Tension ripples through my chest. When she's talked to me, she's always tried to understand me. To make room for whatever ugly feelings I'm holding in that even I don't want to face.

What if she needs the same thing now? To know that *she* isn't alone in being haunted by memories?

Would acknowledging a little of my own history be so terrible if it makes her feel a lot better?

My throat constricts, but I push the words past it. "I was trapped by humans once too. Kept in a cell. Hurt. And—"

No, I don't want to even think about the rest of it. My tails snap in a tighter whirl behind me.

Peri stops and focuses on me, her pretty eyes so wide I'd like to dive into them. "That's awful. No wonder you'd rather be having fun and playing around now."

Just like that, most of my discomfort melts away. She *does* understand—we both have our own kinds of chaos.

I want to wrap my arms around her and bury my face in

her hair, tumble around in a giddy embrace, but even I can tell this isn't a good place for *that* kind of fun.

Instead, I simply lean in and give her a quick peck on her temple. "You deserve all the fun too. Whatever happened before, it doesn't matter."

Her smile comes back, a little warmer this time.

Before I can decide what else to say, Raze's voice carries from the other side of the cabin. "I followed the sorcerer's scent a little farther."

Peri and I hustle over just as the lizard man points off to the east. "About a mile from here, there's a road and a spot where a large vehicle was parked recently. His trail ended there. He must have driven away. I can't tell which direction to keep following."

He grimaces, but Jonah claps him on the shoulder. "It was a longshot anyway. I'll take pictures of the cabin in case there's something we didn't realize the significance of. Then Rollick wants us back at the school so we can give him our full report—and decide what to do next."

24

Periwinkle

When Jonah wraps up his account of our mission so far, the administrative staff study the rest of us. I can't call most of their gazes friendly, though Pearl is smiling in her usual encouraging way and Rollick simply looks thoughtful.

The demon rubs his chin. "It seems your collaboration has kept you all in one piece and revealed more information than my past investigations turned up. I'll call that a win. Why don't you return to classes for a couple of days before you head north again? Take a breather from each other."

Gnash jerks his head around. "Rollick—do you really think—"

The school's founder cuts him off with a mild look that nonetheless makes the hairs on the back of my arms stand up. There's no missing the demon's aura of power.

"Why shouldn't they have a quick break and continue their education?" he asks. "If you have specific concerns about their performance, you've gotten plenty of time to question them."

Throughout Jonah's report, the tiger shifter and his colleagues have been lobbing questions at us like balls in a batting cage. I swallow thickly, afraid they've somehow figured out that I lost control again even though we avoided mentioning that one fact.

It's Toni who speaks up, in a more even tone than Gnash's. "They were on the verge of banishment. They haven't proven that they can mingle with their classmates safely, even if they've survived the last few days without killing each other."

Hail makes a sour face as if he thinks he should get top marks just for refraining from murdering us, but Rollick hums. "A fair point. We have an obvious short-term solution. Jonah, perhaps you could give a sorcerous command to each of our delinquents to ensure they don't do anything harmful with their powers over the next forty-eight hours?"

My pulse hitches at the thought of more sorcery wriggling into my brain. I smile to cover my urge to protest.

I'd rather be brainwashed than hurt even more beings.

Jonah hesitates before answering. "I'll have to give the exact command some thought to make sure it works properly, and I'd probably need to repeat the commands tomorrow to ensure they hold." He glances at the rest of us. "As long as my team will accept that?"

Mirage pipes up first with an energetic shrug. "Better than being stuffed in a cage!"

Raze grunts and nods in agreement, though he's scowling.

Hail lets out a long-suffering sigh, but I can tell from the tart prickle of emotion wafting off him that he's more uneasy than resigned. "Whatever you feel you need to do before we continue this charade."

All the gazes at the table shift to me.

I push my smile wider. "Of course. It'll be easier for me to concentrate if I know my powers shouldn't go haywire."

Rollick claps his hands. "It's settled. Once you've gotten Jonah's orders, the five of you can resume your normal class schedule. I'll see you off again in two days."

A COUPLE of hours later with a new sorcerous command buzzing around my brain, I head into the cafeteria for lunch and get two slim arms flung around me.

"You're back!" Fen hugs me tightly and steps back as quickly as she leapt in. "I didn't even realize. Are you okay? Is the special assignment over?"

We're not supposed to talk about our investigations in any detail, but I can answer vaguely. "Not yet. We did find out a little, but not everything Rollick wants to know. How have you been doing?"

Fen ushers me to a temporary counter at one end of the room, where various other beings are lining up to request their food. The bright colors and plasticky furnishings remind me of the fast food restaurants I've flitted through in the human world. The air smells of greasy, salty goodness.

My friend peers at the list of meal options hanging over the counter and then turns back to me with a smile. "It hasn't been as fun without you to talk to, but I've been all right. I made it through a whole day without dribbling any water at all."

A chilly voice speaks up from behind us. "*Such* an accomplishment. The drip managed not to piddle."

Fen cringes. As if on cue, a few droplets patter off her fingers onto the floor.

I turn around to face Gloss and her friends as they break into tinkling laughter. No emotions drift off the elegant being at all—it means nothing to her to deal out casual cruelty.

Gloss won't care about my opinions on her attitude, so I aim for peace. "Why don't we all focus on getting some tasty food? It looks like there's plenty of it."

At my hopeful smile, Gloss's friends snicker harder. She shakes her head. "Yes, I can see why you'd want to avoid anyone focusing on *you*. What on earth are you wearing now? You look like a human gangster reject."

My skin prickles with self-consciousness. I hadn't even thought about my change in clothing—I'm wearing the leather jacket and ripped jeans that I switched to while on the mission.

It seems pointless to swap them for my old dress and track jacket combo now that Gloss has already seen me. That'll only make her feel she was right.

I'm about to turn around and simply ignore her when another cool voice carries from farther down the line.

"You should give the cream puff a little credit, Gloss. She's trying to broaden her horizons rather than sticking to the same old, same old."

My gaze snaps to Hail's dark eyes where the lean, pale fae has ambled over behind Gloss's pack. His mouth is set in a slanted smile; I can't tell whether he was mocking her or me.

Maybe both?

Whatever the case, Gloss obviously takes it as a personal criticism. Her jaw tightens, but she manages to return his smile. "I suppose even hopeless cases should get points for trying."

I turn back toward the counter. Fen raises an eyebrow at me but doesn't remark on Hail's intervention in front of his usual fan club.

When we get to the servers, I ask for a barbeque chicken burger and fries. The spicy scent that wafts from the tray I'm handed makes me giddy. Fen and I head toward the other tables.

A few feet from the nearest one, the floor turns abruptly slippery beneath my shoes.

My feet skid and swerve with a twinge of my ankles. The tray wobbles in my hands, and my fizzy drink tumbles onto the floor.

Fen snatches my shoulder and helps me catch my balance before I lose my food as well. Dark liquid streaks across the floor from my cup.

One of the school staff materializes from the shadows with a wrinkling of his nose. "I'll clean it up. Go on."

Striding by with her own food, Gloss tsks her tongue. "Such a klutz."

My hair flickers with a ruddy glow of both anger and embarrassment. I think she has wintry powers like Hail does. She was punishing me for what *he* said.

Maybe Rollick should add logic classes to the curriculum.

I have better things to think about. The burger tastes just as delicious as it smelled. For several minutes, I listen to Fen fill me in on the latest drama she's seen and heard around the school and put our bully out of my mind.

As we're leaving the cafeteria, Fen brightens. "Oh, there's a book I wanted to show you—it's got amazing pictures from all over the mortal world. We'll probably be sitting on the sidelines for the morphball game today. I'll run and get it from my room. Meet you at the gym?"

"Sounds good!" I set off with a spring in my step.

I only make it around one turn in the hall before Gloss catches up with me, on her own. I don't know how she moves so fast with those mincing steps.

She whirls on me with a flash of her amber eyes, her voice pitched low and outright frigid. "I don't know what charms you tried to work on Hail, but he'd never be remotely interested in a wimp like you. If he's been the slightest bit nice, it's only because he had no one better to pay attention to."

Her words cut straight through me. I wasn't looking to get any particular attention from Hail, but I still want to curl up in a ball against her hostility.

"I didn't try to do anything with him," I say. "If he wants to be with you, go be with him."

She makes a scoffing sound, her anger only sharpening. "You've been putting on your cluelessly sweet act from the second you got here. I know it's only because you're the weakest being here. I doubt you'll even come back the next time Rollick sends you away, and no one will miss you, not even the drip."

She glides off without a backward glance.

My muscles clench up instinctively with a tremor of my nerves. Even if Jonah's sorcery will stop me from blaring out harmful energy, I'd rather not test the limits of his command.

I close my eyes and see the glitter of silver and iron chain links on the ground, the gleam of battered trophies through glass.

My next breath comes shaky, but a strange sense of calm settles over me.

I might not be able to prove much, but I *know* I'm not weak. I survived a man much crueler than Gloss could imagine.

Compared to that sorcerer, she's the wimp.

The reminder carries me the rest of the way to the gym. I grin at Fen when she hustles in with her book and "Oooh" over the pictures of places she'd like us to visit together. But all the while my stomach stays knotted.

No matter what I do, some people in this place are always going to hate me, and I don't even understand why.

25

Periwinkle

The academy doesn't have much in common with human farms, but the plain, boxy structure set back from the two main buildings is doing a reasonable impression of a barn. As I walk over to it through the dry desert wind, my skin prickles as if I'm engaging in illicit agricultural activities.

I'm allowed to be here. It's still on the school grounds. And I couldn't do much damage to the dusty earth, wizened shrubs, or craggy mountains rising in the distance even if I wasn't under sorcerous command.

But it's the first time I've left the reform building on my own. Is a teacher going to appear wagging a disapproving finger at me?

I make it to the sort-of barn's door without any chiding. The hinges squeak as I slip inside.

The far wall stretches up two storeys to the building's

high ceiling. When I glance over, Jonah has already paused where he's clinging to handholds two thirds of the way up.

What Shanty told me is a rock-climbing wall looks like a kindergartener's version of stone. Brightly colored holds jut out in a variety of creative shapes.

I'm not sure why anyone practices climbing rocks in a big artificial box when there are actual mountains in sight, but I guess it saves a couple of hours' driving.

And I'm glad Jonah isn't a couple of hours from the school right now.

"Peri," he calls as I walk to the padded mats at the base of the climbing wall. "I thought I was going to see you in an hour. Is something wrong?"

Before I can answer, he's already clambering down. He took off his shirt for the climb, and a sheen of sweat gleams off his warm brown skin. His muscles flex with his movements.

A flicker of heat passes through me. How would his skin taste if I licked him?

A question I probably shouldn't ask out loud.

When he's close enough to the ground that I don't have to yell, I clasp my hands together in front of me. "Shanty said you'd be out here. I wanted to see you before the group meeting—to talk to you about something privately. I'm sorry I interrupted."

"It's all right." Jonah's feet hit the ground. He reaches for a small towel to blot the perspiration on his face and chest. I don't sense any emotion from him other than a faint flicker of self-consciousness.

Doesn't he know how delicious he is to look at?

In any case, he honestly doesn't seem upset. He peers at me from beneath the black waves of his hair, concern turning his eyes even darker. "What did you want to talk about?"

A flare of my own self-consciousness washes over me. I look down at my hands.

"I thought you might be the best person to ask since you've had a lot of experience with mortal beings *and* shadowkind… and you've always been nice to me, so you won't laugh… Why is anyone mean to anyone else? I've seen it from humans and from shadowkind. It doesn't make sense. They don't even usually feel good while they're doing it, not the way real happiness tastes."

Jonah blinks at me, looking lost. Maybe it's too big a question for anyone.

But he *doesn't* laugh, and I think the other administrators might have. Hail and Mirage definitely would—though with Mirage, not in a malicious way. Raze might think I was criticizing him. Fen wouldn't have any answers.

So the strangely considerate sorcerer is my only chance at figuring it out. The uncertainty has been gnawing at me since Gloss's insults yesterday.

Jonah delays his response by turning to put on his shirt, which is a shame, because it covers my view of his sculpted torso. His chest is still very nice to look at with the fabric overtop, but not quite as vividly so.

I decide it's better not to mention those thoughts to him either.

When he faces me again, his mouth has gone crooked. "That's a tough one, Peri. I don't know how much thought shadowkind usually give that subject, but human beings have been grappling with it for hundreds—probably thousands— of years."

I grimace. "So, no one knows?"

Jonah shrugs. "I don't think you *can* know exactly, because everyone has different reasons. But in my experience, cruelty is mostly about feeling in control. Some people don't know how to feel the better kinds of happiness, but they can figure out how to make someone else feel worse. So they settle for a smaller satisfaction, knowing that at least they're not the worst off around."

"Oh." I know from the soft tingle of my hair that it's shimmering my sadness at the idea. "That's awful. For everyone."

A hint of a smile touches Jonah's lips. "You just want everyone to be as happy as possible, don't you?"

I spread my arms. "Why wouldn't I? If everyone lived that way, maybe no one would be so sour they want to smear their unpleasant feelings all over everyone else."

"Life is pretty complicated. For mortals, because of all the pressures and responsibilities that go into navigating our society. For shadowkind, because you weren't made to be part of this world and your instincts often clash with what's acceptable here. Sometimes things just can't help but be tangled up."

I study him, focusing on his face now. "It's been tangled for you, hasn't it? Because you've lived around shadowkind so much, but you *are* human. How did you start feeling like you fit in at the school? Or with the shadowkind who raised you?"

Jonah's smile fades. "To be totally honest, I can't say I feel like I fit in even *now*. It's a tricky balance, leading classes and using my sorcery to rein in the shadowkind who need it without being seen as an enemy."

A twinge of guilt ripples through my gut with the knowledge that I saw him that way at first. "Then how do you stay happy?"

"Well, I do have a few beings on staff I know understand me, and students here and there who appreciate what I'm doing. And I take a lot of strength from the good memories from my past."

He motions to the climbing wall. "Back home, growing

up with my shadowkind 'family,' I was always climbing trees in the forest around the house. This is the closest I can get to that feeling here."

I gaze up at the wall with its handholds, wondering how it would feel to haul my pudgier and much shorter body up that expanse.

Jonah's voice softens. "You've already helped people even in the short time you've been at the academy, Peri. I know some of the other students have been hard on you, but that doesn't mean you've done anything wrong. I can see how hard you work at looking out for everyone around you. You've kept up a positive attitude through so much. It means a lot to me that you trust me after the horrible experience you had with that other sorcerer."

His reassurance lights a joyful glow inside me. I think it might be glinting out of my hair in cheerful yellow, but I don't mind him seeing that.

"You've looked out for me too," I say. "I know you're not at all like that man. You want us to be as happy as we can be, just like I do."

Jonah's smile comes back, setting off an even brighter flare of warmth all the way through my body. "That's true. I'd really like to see you find a place where you can feel free, without having to worry about your powers going wild."

This conversation makes me think I could. What do Gloss or Hail or any of them know?

As long as I keep my goals in mind, I *have* to find a way to reach them.

I turn toward the wall, coasting on my momentary elation. "I want to try climbing. It looked exciting, being all the way up there."

I'm already reaching for the nearest handholds above before Jonah can respond. As I place my feet against a couple of lower holds, he makes a restrained sound of warning. "The wall's for everyone, but it can be a little tricky to keep your balance if you're not used to climbing. Take it slow, and watch out for any shifts in the holds. Some of the ones higher up rotate for an extra challenge."

"I'm good!" I keep clambering onward, my spirits rising with each short distance I heft myself.

At first I move slowly, remembering Jonah's cautions. But the climb is easier than I expected. I push myself a little faster, delighting in the extra thrill of the effort radiating through my muscles.

I'm shooting all the way to the top.

"Peri…" Jonah says in a worried tone, and at the same moment, the handhold I've just grasped whirls in my fingers.

My hand slips off. My balance wobbles, and I tumble right off the wall.

For a second, all I'm aware of is the air whooshing through my hair and the lurch of my pulse. A yelp breaks from my throat.

Then my body smacks into a pair of muscular arms that reached out to catch me.

I find myself gazing sheepishly into Jonah's eyes. "Thank you. And sorry. I got too confident—and I should have just jumped into the shadows when I fell."

Jonah exhales shakily and offers me a bemused grin. He's so close that his gorgeous face makes my pulse skip again even though I'm perfectly secure now. "I can imagine it's hard to think logically when you're in freefall. I'm glad I could jump in there in time."

My hand rises to his cheek as if of its own accord, following the chiseled angles of his cheekbone down to his jaw. "You look after me in lots of different ways."

Something shifts in Jonah's expression, with a waft of emotion that's as tantalizingly sweet and heady as a Black Forest cake. It sparks a pang between my legs.

His head dips closer to mine, and for a second I think he's going to bring our lips together in an embrace as delectable as the one I shared with Raze.

I might have closed the last short distance if Jonah didn't tense a second later. He sets me down on the mat and backs up.

His face has flushed, but he's managed to rein in most of the mouth-watering emotion. "I should get back to the school. I'll see you there in a half hour to reinforce everyone's commands."

He strides out of the building before I can say another word.

I stare after him, my own emotions scattered. Was he upset? Why?

Does he have some objection to cakey deliciousness?

I push myself after him—and a massive, sinewy figure emerges from the shadows by the door.

Raze peers at me and then turns his head in the direction Jonah went, his muscular frame emanating aggression. "What does *he* think he's doing with you?"

26

Peri halts in her tracks at my growled words. When I glance at her, her eyes have widened.

A chill washes through the animosity stewing inside me. Did I sound like I want to hurt *her*?

I don't even want to hurt Jonah. Not really.

Only a little bit, nothing fatal.

Peri's voice is unusually tentative, but not as frightened as I feared. "We were only talking. He didn't do anything to me. You don't have to worry—he's always been kind."

I can't hold back another growl. My nerves are too on-edge, adrenaline racing through my veins from the hunt I'm returning from. The lingering flavor of raw flesh in my mouth brings out my most savage impulses.

I should have gone straight back to the school to cool down, but a cry I recognized as Peri's caught my ears when I was passing the building. I had to dash over.

And when I peered through the shadows around the doorway—

"He was *holding* you. He looked like he wanted to do a lot more than talk."

My hackles rise, remembering the starved expression on the sorcerer's face. As if he was seconds away from pushing her up against the wall and rutting into her. If he hadn't let go of her...

Another trickle of cold cuts through my anger. What would I have done? Aimed my deadly basilisk sight at one of our teachers?

There'd have been no more second chances for me then.

Peri is still studying me. Now she looks puzzled. "I slipped and he caught me so I didn't get hurt. Would it be a problem if he wanted something more?"

It shouldn't be. I still can't trust myself. All it takes is one bad moment—

I spin around. "No. It doesn't matter. I shouldn't have said anything."

As I leap into the shadows, Peri calls out my name. Ignoring her, I hurtle toward the academy's reform building.

The trouble is, I've got nowhere to go except my dorm bedroom. Which is also Peri's bedroom. And naturally my glowy roommate isn't willing to let our conversation end there.

I crouch in the darkness next to my bed, balling my shadowy presence as tight as I can and willing the niggling nips of anger away. It's only a few minutes before Peri walks in.

She turns toward me with her hands on her ample hips. The set of her mouth is determined, but her voice comes out soft. "Something's bothering you, and it has to do with me. I think we should talk about it until we work it out. Otherwise it'll keep upsetting you."

Is there any chance she'll give up if I simply don't respond? She's got too much stubbornness mixed in with the sweetness.

Maybe I should slink off the school grounds again, go someplace she can't find me and where I won't run into anyone else either. If the staff realize I've been roaming for longer than my allotted hunting session, I could get in trouble, but—

Peri takes a step closer. "Please, Raze. I don't want you to be upset with me."

Her plea cuts straight through my resistance. My entire being shudders at the thought of her regretting the mistakes that are actually mine.

I can't run off and leave her feeling guilty over something that's not at all her fault.

Reluctantly, I push myself back into physical form. I solidify my body in a sitting position on the edge of the bed, my hands clenched on my lap. "I'm not upset with you."

Peri's brow knits. "What are you upset about, then? I told you, Jonah was only helping me. Whatever else could happen with him, I know he wouldn't put me in danger."

Even after that night in the forest, she doesn't see. I grope for the right words, but eloquence has never been my strong point.

I can't help sounding gruff. "I don't want anything else to happen with him. *I* want you."

Understanding dawns on Peri's pretty face. "You're jealous."

I grimace, but there is no more accurate word. "Yes."

"But… You said you didn't think we should be kissing any more."

Shame prickles through me. I look down at my hands. "I didn't say I wasn't selfish. You *are* in danger when you're around me. But I still… If you're going to be with anyone… I wish it could be me."

There's a pause. Then Peri sinks down onto the edge of the mattress, close enough to rest her hand on my arm.

My entire body jolts with the awareness of her presence and the electric desire it stirs inside me. I don't dare look at her.

"It could be you," she says, with her unshakeable brightness. "I don't think I'm in *that* much danger."

My fists squeeze even tighter. "You don't know. I thought it would be fine before—that I would never— But I was wrong. There's too much poison in me."

Peri strokes her thumb up and down my arm. "Why don't you tell me what happened before, and I can decide."

A lump clogs my throat.

But why shouldn't she know? If I tell her, she might recoil in horror—and that would be a good thing. She'll leave me alone so I don't have to worry about doing her any harm.

I close my eyes. "I used to live among humans some of the time. I liked being around people, hearing them talk, seeing the things they'd do. What they could make. There was this woman who'd sit by the town's river to paint, and I'd watch her, and we started talking to each other… I wanted to be with her all the time."

Peri's stroking thumb stills. Is *she* at all jealous?

Is it wrong that part of me wants her to be?

The image of Caroline's dark hair and pale eyes swims up from the back of my mind. I force myself to go on.

"One night, we came back to her house and saw someone had broken in. They'd smashed one of her windows, thrown her things around, stolen stuff. I got so angry that I hadn't been able to protect her… my powers surged up before I could stop them. She was holding my hand—my poison shot right into her from my skin. It only took a second, and she collapsed. She *died*."

"Raze." Peri's voice shakes.

Instead of pulling away like anyone sensible would, she pushes herself up on her knees and wraps her arms right around me.

Her chin tucks over my shoulder, her bare cheek against my neck, with no fear of what might seep out of me now. "I'm so sorry. That must have been awful."

"I was awful," I mutter. "I lost my head. I ran around the neighborhood and murdered at least a dozen more people with my sight and my touch thinking one of them was the burglar, wanting to punish *someone*—but it was my fault. I'm lucky the staff here gave me a chance to reform instead of banishing me right away."

"They must have been able to tell that's not who you are. You had a bad reaction in a horrible situation. Anyone would have gotten overwhelmed."

"Most beings wouldn't have killed all those people because of it."

"You wouldn't again." Peri turns my face toward her so I have to meet her gaze. Her bright blue eyes shimmer with so much compassion my gut aches. "You probably never cared about anyone that much before—you didn't know you'd be set off like that. You've never gone on another rampage, have you?"

My mouth twists. "Only because I'm so careful. I've hurt a few of the other beings here accidentally when my temper got away from me."

"You must be getting good at staying calm. Hail kept picking on you during the mission, and you didn't hurt him. You didn't hurt Jonah even though you were upset just now."

"I still could. Part of me wanted to."

"Then it shows even more control that you didn't, not

even a little." Peri cups my cheek, the tenderness of her touch tingling through my skin. "I think you've been doing amazing after what was a terrible accident. And you couldn't hurt me as badly or as quickly as you did her, could you? I'm shadowkind, not mortal."

"I could still hurt you a lot—and if I couldn't stop it in time—"

"I'm not scared."

She leans in to brush her lips against my cheek.

My pulse stutters. For a second, I sit there frozen.

I want her so badly, a fire sears from my heart to my groin.

She knows how much damage I've done to people I care about, and she still wants *me*.

How can I push her away, right into the arms of whoever else will welcome her? If I refuse her, she *should* find someone who'll adore her the way she deserves.

But that someone should be *me*. I have to show her how much I mean that.

I swivel toward her, scooping her up and claiming her mouth like I did the other night.

Peri's hum of approval urges me on. She tastes and smells so sweet—she feels so soft in my arms. The joyful thrill of holding her close resonates through my being.

Caroline never knew what I really was, what beast lurks inside me. Peri recognizes every piece of me and welcomes me in spite of it.

She deserves all the affection in the world. Every kindness, every pleasure.

Maybe I can be careful but still have her.

I settle her on my lap without breaking the kiss. Peri slips one hand around my neck while the other teases into my hair. The brush of her fingertips sets off sparks through my scalp.

Now that I've released my desire, I want everything. I kiss her again and again, drinking in every eager noise she makes. Reveling in the heady pink sheen that lights in her hair.

Beneath her bubble-gum sweetness, I pick up a deeper, darker scent, as vast and breathtaking as the ocean. How can I do anything but dive right in?

I trail my lips along her jaw, down her neck, over her shoulder. Her shaky breaths and the squirm of her ass against my groin have my dick aching.

"You taste so good, Glowbug." With one arm looped around her waist, I bring my other hand to her breast. The swell of it through the fabric of her shirt fits perfectly in my large palm.

I stroke my fingers over the peak and earn myself a whimper. Peri dapples kisses along my neck, swaying into my caresses.

When I tug at her jacket, she doesn't hesitate to peel it off and toss it aside. Her gaze locks with mine as I ease my fingers under the hem of her shirt. The glow in her hair turns ruddier when I flick my thumb over her hardened nipple.

Peri bites her lip, which makes me want to kiss her again. Her eyelids flutter lower.

Then she sets her hand on my wrist, stopping me but stroking the skin to prevent the gesture from feeling like a total rejection.

"Raze," she murmurs, so breathless my cock gets twice as hard, "if we're doing this... does that mean you expect me to only be with you?"

I hesitate, a fresh chill dousing some of my hunger. "Do you want to be with someone else?"

Her smile is so brilliantly fond it melts away the momentary ice. "I'm very happy doing this with you. I just —I never thought about needing to put restrictions on having this kind of fun. But I guess humans do. And what we're doing… it feels like more than having fun. *I* don't want to hurt *you*. So I should make sure what I'm agreeing to."

I open my mouth and close it again. I want to tell her yes, that she's mine and mine alone for the rest of all time. If I made the demand, I think she'd smile again and say that's perfectly fine.

But not because that's what *she* wants. Only to avoid hurting me. Because this beautiful being always puts everyone else's feelings ahead of her own.

If I'm being honest with myself, she was looking at Jonah nearly as avidly as he was looking at her. Maybe there are others who've caught her eye.

She'd give up every other possible lover if I asked her to, without even thinking about what would make her happiest. That's not keeping her safe. That's putting her in chains.

I'd be as bad as the monster who trapped her with his sorcery.

The internal battle tangles me up inside. I bow my face close to Peri's, breathing in her tempting scent, soaking in the warmth of her.

"You always want everyone to be happy. I couldn't say I really care about you if I tried to cut off *your* happiness. If you want to get close with someone else… would you just tell me first? So I know and I'm not surprised? I might need to take some space for myself, but that's my problem. I don't want to get startled and lash out."

Peri's face has fallen. "If it would make you upset, I don't need to—"

I cut her off with a kiss, as tender as I'm capable of. "It's not about whether you need it. Knowing you're holding yourself back from everything you'd want… that would make me more upset. I would never lock you in a cage."

27

Periwinkle

I would never lock you in a cage.

Raze's words sweep through me, sparking glimmers of elation. How could he think he puts me in danger when he understands me that well, cares that much about making me feel cherished?

I run my fingers along his powerful jaw, reveling in the strength that emanates all through the body I'm pressed against. "Right here, right now, I only want you."

His mouth crashes into mine with a needy rumble that sets all of me alight. It might be more than just my hair glowing now, but I don't feel awkward about it.

I'm his Glowbug. He likes me just as I am.

A tremor ripples through my nerves at the brightness expanding all through me, but with each kiss and each caress, any trace of anxiety melts. This doesn't feel like the manic happiness that's burst out of me before in a chaotic blaze. The affection we're sharing and the pleasure it provokes stay wrapped close around my heart, focused just on the two of us.

It's a more selfish kind of joy than when I'm lighting happiness in strangers, but that doesn't make it wrong.

I yank at Raze's T-shirt, and he pulls it off. The sight of the sinewy sculpted expanse beneath makes me even giddier. I trace my fingers over his chest, grinning at his groan.

He dips his head again to chart a teasing path along my neck, with the gentlest graze of his teeth and little flicks of his tongue. His voice comes out in a husky murmur that sends a fresh jolt of desire straight between my legs.

"I'm going to make you feel so good, Glowbug. We'll take it slow so there's no pain at all."

He pauses, nuzzling my shoulder. "You've done this before?"

There's no accusation in the question. I tease my fingers through his thick hair and give him another kiss. "Yes. A few times. But this is already better. I didn't really know them. I've never… I've never felt close to anyone in all the different ways you can. I was always moving around and exploring too much, and then…"

The thought of the basement and the cages cuts off my voice. Raze growls as if he can scare those memories into submission and captures my mouth even more tenderly than before.

We peel off my shirt together, and it occurs to me that I can shed my jeans as quickly as thinking it. When I blink into the shadows and back in an instant, returning fully nude, Raze gives an awed chuckle.

He slides his hand up my thigh. As he strokes his fingers tentatively over the aching spot between my legs, a moan shudders out of me. I yank his mouth back to mine.

It does feel incredible—even better when I know how

much this moment matters to him. When it matters to me beyond the momentary pleasure too.

I want to do this with Raze over and over. I want to cuddle next to him in the courtyard and talk about what we're learning in our classes and join him on his hunts to taste the thrill of his feeding.

It's true that he isn't the only one I've started to get close to in the ways that run deeper than colliding bodies. I've never had a friend like Fen before. I've never started to recognize the patterns of joy and pain in another being the way I do now with Jonah and Mirage and even Hail, a little.

I've stumbled into a new dimension of happiness and connection that I only had a vague idea of from depictions in TV shows and fleeting observations of humans. All because I got dragged here to this school.

Even with all the rules and the beings who've picked on me, this place is the opposite of a cage. It's given me more than I've given up.

And now I get to experience a bodily bliss I didn't even know was possible. Raze slips a finger right inside me, and the pulse of pleasure has my head sagging backward. When my grip on his shoulders tightens, he gives another approving rumble.

It feels so good, but I crave even more. His matching eagerness washes over me like sparkling lemonade and peach pie.

I reach down his massive body to rub the bulge behind the pants he hasn't yet removed. Raze's groan reverberates into me with a carnal need as rich as toffee pudding.

He eases another finger inside me. Each pulse of them deeper sends another rush of pleasure up from my core.

"I don't know if you're ready yet," he mutters.

I yank at the waist of his pants. "I am. So ready. Please." I'm going to disintegrate from wanting so much.

Humans have to make this moment so much more complicated, but shadowkind don't get pregnant or sick. We can follow this bliss as far as it'll take us without a single worry.

With a ragged breath, Raze kicks off his pants. When he eases the head of his erection against me, I shiver in delight.

I lift my legs instinctively, and he slides right into the place where I'm slick with need.

Another groan tumbles from Raze's lips. They seek out mine for kiss after wild kiss as our bodies rock to meet each other. With each thrust, he surges deeper, until I'm as full as I've ever been, so full I can't imagine ever feeling empty again.

This is how it should always be. I don't have to meld with anyone else unless it's just as fulfilling as this moment.

I hold him close and buck with him until pleasure radiates through every particle of my being. Until it peaks and crashes over me in a deluge that leaves me crying out and clutching him.

Until Raze bows over me with a cry of his own and nestles me tight in his arms like he'll never let go.

Maybe nothing else matters. Maybe this means everything can be all right.

THE JOY of my interlude with Raze carries me through two afternoon classes, but by the end of a physical training session under Gnash's scowling instruction, my feet and ankles twinge with every step.

I don't want to complain to Fen, so I walk slowly down the hall with a sigh to suggest I'm just tired. Which I am.

"We've got an hour before dinner," she says, bouncing with an energy I don't normally see from her. "Let's go to the media room. I want to see if they have that movie we talked about in Mortal Culture class."

The thought of walking into the dim room where the TV triggered my awful memories just days ago makes my gut knot. I take a deep breath.

At least I'll be able to sit and rest my legs. And I have Jonah's sorcery wrapped through my mind to hold back the worst of my powers. It would probably be good to face that spot and prove that it doesn't have to bother me.

I smile at her. "Sounds like a plan!"

When we get to the media room, a few other beings have a different movie playing on the large screen. The roar of a car chase brings Fen and me over to the sofa.

One of the shadowkind motions for us to join them, and we end up sitting leaned against the sofa, watching as humans chase each other what seems like all the way around the world.

I'm pretty sure their argument could be fixed if they just talked to each other for more than five seconds, but at least they're having fun.

With each passing minute, the frenetic thud of my heart smooths out. I *am* okay. It was an unlucky coincidence that I stumbled in here when the worst possible thing I could see was playing, after I was already upset.

I surreptitiously massage my ankles, hoping the lingering pain will have vanished by dinnertime. When we get up after the ending credits, I feel a little steadier.

Fen shakes her head with a giggle. "Humans like to imagine getting very mad at each other, don't they? I guess it gives them an excuse to drive fast and see lots of different places."

I have to laugh too. "It seems that way. I think some of them get mad a lot for real, but it's less exciting in their regular lives. Maybe they like thinking they might get an adventure out of it."

When we walk into the cafeteria, Fen claps her hands. "Oooh, we're doing a buffet tonight. They always make those around themes. I wonder what region the food's from today."

A long serving table holds a dozen dishes covered by plastic lids to hold in the heat. Fen directs me to pick up a plate at one end, and we move from dish to dish with the line of fellow students, serving ourselves with massive spoons.

Fen puts a heap of yellow rice mixed with bits of chicken on her plate. "I think this is Indian. So many spices. Sometimes it makes my eyes water, but that's better than my fingers dripping."

I follow her lead, taking a little of everything. The savory scents swirling in the air make my stomach gurgle in anticipation. There's a thick green curry with chunks of fried cheese, a mix of golden cauliflower and potatoes, goat meat in a brownish sauce and chicken in one that's more orange.

Then Fen lifts the next lid, and the waft of the spicy smell makes my stomach tilt queasily.

The dish beneath is filled with chicken legs and thighs that shine vivid red. Like the pieces my captor would carry around in tin-foil wrapping; like the stain that'd coat his fingers and blaze on his tongue when he indulged in his favorite takeout.

The peppery smell would drift through the basement the whole night. Would waft off his breath when he'd lean close to the cage to poke at me—

My hands wobble. My laden plate slips through my fingers and smashes on the floor.

Fen jerks around. "Peri?"

"What the fuck are you doing?" the shadowkind behind me mutters.

My gut is lurching like the cars in that movie now. I

wrench my gaze away from the familiar dish, but images of the past keep ricocheting through my head alongside the smell filling my lungs.

"I'm sorry. I'm sorry." I bend down to gather the pieces of the broken plate.

A sharper pang shoots up from my feet. My breath hitches, and I have to close my eyes for a second to squeeze back the tears.

Is it always going to be like this? I can be having the most wonderful day ever, and one wrong thing throws me totally off course.

How can I predict everything that'll throw me back into the memories I've spent so long running away from?

"It's okay," Fen is saying, dashing over with another plate to help me collect the mess. "We can clean it up so fast."

But it's not okay. No one else freaked out because of a totally unoffensive food.

I smile and thank her and carry my ruined meal over to the trash can as if it's no big deal. But the whole time a knife of doubt digs into the center of me.

What if *I'm* broken, as permanently as that plate? What if I can never get better?

And if that's true, how can I be sure I won't drag everyone I care about down with me?

28

Periwinkle

T he camper van is loud and the benches kind of lumpy, but I have to grin as Jonah drives us away from the private jet on the landing strip, back into the farther reaches of northern Canada.

We've got our mission ahead of us, unsettling as it is. No confusing classmates are going to trip me up or laugh at me.

Through the steady rumble of the engine, I gaze out at the wild beauty beyond the window. Majestic forest ripples over the rocky hills.

Raze has decided to stay in physical form for the trip, sitting next to me with his arm tucked around my waist. He wafts fond devotion like French toast drizzled with the perfect amount of syrup.

Almost as comforting is the tickle of sorcerous protection wriggling through my brain. Jonah isn't restraining our powers now that we're away from the academy again, since that would defeat the purpose of testing us with this mission, and he needs plenty of energy to sway any strange creatures we encounter. But he did give us each a basic command not to listen to any other sorcery.

"It might not hold if this sorcerer hits you hard with his own orders," Jonah warned us, "but it'll hopefully buy you time to get away if you need to."

We don't know what we'll find on our second expedition. We don't know what the sorcerer will do if we track him down or why the shadowkind he's directed morph so strangely. But at least now we're more prepared.

Jonah calls to us from the driver's seat. "We're coming up on the first town Rollick suggested. Peri and Hail, get ready to interact with the locals."

Raze frowns, but he can't deny that he and Mirage would have a harder time blending in. Partly because of his massive form, and partly because none of us really trust Mirage not to whip out his ears or tails in view of humans.

The fewer that know shadowkind exist, the fewer there are to freak out about it.

I look down at my leather jacket, close my eyes, and flicker in and out of the shadows in a blink. My new attire includes a cloth hood on the jacket that I pull up in case my hair starts to glow.

Hail sighs as if this is all too much work for him. He adjusts the sleeves of his collared shirt to ensure they cover the stark blue veins that stand out against his pale skin.

A few minutes later, Jonah parks the van by a small clearing with a couple of benches, neither currently occupied. He twists in his seat. "The three of us will walk into town. Raze and Mirage, you can roam around and stretch your legs, but steer clear of humans for now, all right?"

Mirage springs into a handstand and then flips back onto

his feet with a flash of a grin. "Lots of space for the human race."

Hail rolls his eyes, but he gets out of the van.

Raze hesitates and leans in to give me a quick kiss. "Be careful out there."

I squeeze his arm reassuringly. "We're just going to chat people up. But if there's trouble, I'll shout loud enough that you can hear."

When we clamber out, Hail's dark gaze is fixed on me with unusual intensity. He jerks it away and strides toward the road. "The town is this way?"

I glance over at Jonah for his answer and find that he's also watching me and Raze with a tightness to his mouth I can't read. A quiver of emotion passes by me too quickly for me to really taste it.

A prickle of self-consciousness makes me duck my head. Is it really so odd that Raze would care about me?

I guess they're not used to seeing him even touch any of the other shadowkind, let alone kiss them.

Jonah jerks his attention to Hail with a nod. "Yes, it's just over the bridge. There's a convenience store and a café I thought we could stop in to grab lunch. We want to talk with the locals casually, but do your best to find out if they've seen unusual people coming through or if there've been any 'animal' attacks lately."

Hail ends up hanging back to let our sorcerer take the lead. The winter fae slips his hands into the pockets of his slacks in a careless pose, but I catch a whiff of tartly metallic anxiety.

I push my shorter legs faster to keep pace. "I'm sure it'll be fine. You're good at talking to people. Everyone at the school wants to hang out with you."

Hail's head ticks toward me with a scattered burst of emotion he quickly stifles. "I didn't ask for your advice," he says, but his tone is more stiff than cutting. And he doesn't call me "pipsqueak," which I'll take as progress.

The town is a small one, with several shops surrounded by a cluster of a few dozen homes. Nothing about it looks particularly remarkable to me.

Rollick took all the information from our report and mapped it out with whatever details he's gathered from his past investigations. He marked this area of the province as the likely center of the strange activity. There are only a few human settlements within it.

If no one here can give us a hint about where to go next, we've got a lot more combing the wilderness ahead of us.

In the convenience store, Jonah ambles over to the counter and strikes up a conversation with the cashier by asking for directions. As he veers from that subject into a comment about how few other tourists we've run into up here, I scan the shelves for new snacks I might want to try and notice a teenager in a bright, off-the-shoulder sweater and dark jeans. She picks up a magazine and flips through it with a dissatisfied expression.

I stroll over to join her. "Hi! Any good articles in there?"

It seemed like a decent opening, but the girl's eyes dart to me and narrow. She shoves the magazine back into the rack. "I dunno."

Her scowl contradicts the trickle of emotion flowing off her—all fishy insecurity and chalky determination. How can I cater to those feelings?

I motion to her outfit. "I love your shirt! It looks great on you."

To my delight, her posture straightens up, a flash of a smile she tries to suppress crossing her lips. Pride washes away her uncertainties. "Thanks. Your hair is pretty awesome too. Are you just passing through?"

Imagine if she saw it glow.

I nod. "We're stopping to get snacks. It seems like a pretty quiet town. Do you have to worry much about wild animals with so much forest all around?"

Her laugh is a bit scoffing, but it gets me an answer. "*We* don't. They don't bug people usually. But my neighbor stupidly lets her cats go roaming outside. One of them got snapped up by a coyote or something last week."

Or something. She doesn't know for sure what did it.

She turns away from me, disinterested in continuing the conversation. I file away the tidbit of information I got.

I pick out a couple of candy bars, and Jonah rings those up along with some spicy chips Hail grabbed.

As we head across the street, Jonah frowns. "It doesn't sound as if anyone's passed through who's drawn people's attention."

"The shadowkind creatures might have," I say, and tell him about the poor cat.

Hail shrugs. "It *could* have been a coyote. Humans should take better care of the animals they claim they're going to look after."

I taste genuine frustration in his comment. He doesn't like that an innocent animal was killed—the same way it bothered him to kill the shadowkind creatures that attacked us.

I touch his arm. "You're right. They should."

Hail's gaze flicks to me with a flex of his jaw, and then we're walking into the café. He shifts his attention to the patrons sitting at the tables that fill most of the room.

We end up seated between a couple of affable local families. In the space of a quick lunch, we find out that they haven't seen any notable tourists either—but someone else in town had their dog go missing from their yard a few days ago.

"Hopefully it wasn't taken by the same thing that tore up

those wild rabbits in Mr. Johnson's field," one of the kids pipes up before his mother shushes him.

Some creatures have been on the hunt around here lately, more than the town is used to. Jonah and I exchange a knowing glance—for an instant before he jerks his gaze away.

Did he think of some other implications? He doesn't say anything.

We return to the van to find Raze prowling around it and Mirage perched on the roof. The fox shifter leaps down with a flare of at least two tails and an illusionary cheer.

"What did the intrepid explorers discover?" he asks.

Jonah opens the driver's door. "Shadowkind creatures might have been clashing with animals in and around town, but we still don't know where they're coming from. We'd better head to the next town and see if we can find out more."

By the time we reach our second destination, the sun is starting to set.

This settlement looks even smaller than the last one, just a spiral of scattered buildings surrounded by uneven hills with scruffy trees. But a building at the edge of the town has a big parking lot packed with at least twenty cars. Artificial light beams through the hazy windows, and a mix of laughter and music spills out when a new arrival steps inside. The sign says it's the Blueberry Sunshine Restaurant and Bar.

Blueberries and sunshine are both delicious. Seems like a good omen.

Jonah pulls the van into the parking lot. "This looks like the best place to chat up the locals."

He pauses and looks at the rest of us on the benches. Even Mirage has drooped after the long day of travel.

Jonah offers a faint smile. "Do you think you can all behave yourselves long enough to grab dinner and make a little conversation?"

The fox shifter springs up and gives our team leader a jaunty salute. "Eager and ready to follow orders! I'll fox out all their secrets." He manages to grin without revealing the points of his fangs.

Raze's thumb strokes over my wrist, and he pulls his massive form straighter. "I'd like to help."

Hail casts a skeptical glance toward the basilisk shifter. "And to keep an eye on the cream puff."

I feel Raze start to bristle next to me—but he wills down his temper with a huff of an exhalation. "Yes, that too. If *you* can't rile me up, I think I'm safe for now."

The corner of Jonah's mouth kicks higher, but somehow his smile looks more strained. "It's settled. Let's go in."

We tramp into a restaurant big enough to hold everyone from this town twice over—but maybe people come from farms and other places nearby. At least two thirds of the tables are taken, and several figures sit along the varnished wooden bar counter.

The locals must immediately clock us as newcomers. Several heads turn and watch with open curiosity as the hostess seats us.

Jonah purposefully steps around Mirage to take the chair farthest from mine. Does he not want me sitting close?

Our waitress glides over a moment later, as sunshine-y as the restaurant name. "Glad you could make it! Let me go over the specials…"

By the time I've ordered myself a burger and fries, Hail has turned on the charm. Maybe he feels he needs to prove himself after Jonah and I dug up all the info in the last town.

"I hear it can be pretty dangerous living out in the wilds," he drawls, cocking his head. "You must be very brave."

Something about his smooth tone niggles at me, I think because I know he's faking it. But when he aims his cool smile at the waitress, she giggles.

She shakes her head as she jots down Mirage's order of nachos. "Oh, not much happens around here. I like how peaceful it is. Hanging out at the Blueberry Sunshine is usually the most excitement of my week."

Hail slides his graceful fingers over his napkin in a way that's weirdly provocative. "We were hearing about pets going missing and wild bunnies hunted down. I guess the predators know to leave humans alone."

The way he says human has a slightly terse cadence to it, but the waitress doesn't seem to notice. "If people are careful enough, even the animals should be fine. You have to know how to live in harmony with the elements."

Jonah eases into the conversation. "You must hear a lot of stories, working in here—about all sorts of things. We're actually collecting local legends. Ghosts, bigfoot, all that kind of thing. Does Pilverton have any fables like that?"

The waitress taps her pen against her lips. "Hmm. I'll have to think on that. Let me get your order in, and maybe I'll have something for you when I come back with the food."

She walks away emitting nothing but subtle satisfaction, but a smack of avid interest hits me from a different direction, as crisp as the french fries I can't wait to devour.

A middle-aged man is sitting at a table behind us with a couple of other humans around the same age. He's watching us while the other two laugh over some joke.

I aim a bright smile his way. "You look like you might have a story. If you do, we'd love to hear it."

Surprise flickers across his face, and his friends turn toward us too.

One of them elbows him. "What's up, Henry? Got bored of our company?"

"They told Marcy they're collecting strange stories." Henry chuckles and runs his hand over his hair. "I don't really go in for that stuff. I was just thinking they should talk to Ted McGaffery."

The other friend's eyebrows shoot up. "He's just crazy."

Mirage leans toward them with a glint in his eyes. "Crazy stories are good too. What does Ted McGaffery talk about?"

The three men exchange a glance.

Henry shakes his head. "I'm mostly kidding. He's an old-timer, usually keeps to himself on his property out in the middle of nowhere. A regular hermit. But he comes by the bar every now and then. A few days ago, he was waving his hands around with these ridiculous claims."

My own curiosity wriggles up inside me. "What claims?"

Henry pauses. "He said his house got attacked by *monsters*."

29

Hail

No matter how I try to focus on the jangly music, the varied human figures around the restaurant, or the shine of artificial light across the posters on the walls, my gaze keeps sliding back to the short, curvy shadowkind woman in the hooded leather jacket.

It doesn't make sense. If I'm evaluating human-esque visual appeal, there's at least one face in even this small crowd more striking than hers. The hood is covering her vibrant hair. She isn't *doing* anything except perching on a bar stool and gabbing with one of the locals.

But maybe it does make sense. I'm still wrapping my head around the idea that Periwinkle's short but generous hourglass frame held enough power to sear my skin raw in the time it takes to blink.

Watching her beam at her conversational companion, I

can't help thinking that there's a glow to her even when her hair is out of view.

The cream puff has some kind of energy beyond anything I've encountered before, crammed into a deceptively innocuous package. Of course that fact would gnaw at me.

It's not even the only power she possesses. As little as I care about the feelings of the humans we're surrounded by, I'd have to be blind not to notice how the older woman Peri's talking to has lit up after just a couple of minutes of chatter.

Peri pats the woman's hand. "It sounds like you're doing your best. The way you describe them, I can tell how much they matter to you. You shouldn't let anyone tell you not to give it your all."

I have no idea what she's going on about, but clearly her new friend does. The woman smiles even wider. For fuck's sake, are those tears shimmering in her eyes before she blinks them away?

"I'm so glad you stopped here tonight," she says. "Are you sure you have to leave town right away?"

Peri laughs, the sound sweetly apologetic. "We've got some work to take care of. But maybe we'll be able to drop in again on our way home!"

I don't give a shit about the happiness of any of these humans. If they've made themselves miserable, it's their own fault.

So why can't I stop watching Peri work her weird magic? What is this stupid tug inside me as if I'd want to go over and bask in her presence up close?

I yank my attention away and find myself looking at Raze, who's sitting at a table with our fearless leader and a few regular restaurant-goers. His eyes flick toward Peri more often than they're fixed on his supposed companions.

The big lug has gotten somewhere with her. That kiss...

The image pops into my mind with a twinge I don't like at all.

How the fuck would a brute like him know how to handle any woman, let alone one as soft as Peri? Why would she look so pleased about it?

My jaw clenches. No matter what I do, I end up thinking about her.

After all this time forced into her vicinity, she's gotten under my skin.

How many other powers does she have that we don't even know about? Maybe she's some strange variation of succubus?

I want to unwrap her and understand exactly what she is. How she works. What would fascinate her the same way she's hooked my attention.

Maybe if I got as close to her as Raze seems to have, the questions would stop nagging at me. I'd see she's just another being, with the same desires and weaknesses as any other, just different trappings than I'm used to. Then she wouldn't have any hold over me.

The idea steadies my mood. I polish off my chili fries with their kick of spice while only stealing a few more glances toward the cream puff.

Before I decide whether to start implementing my plan right here, Jonah gets up from the table. Peri turns immediately as if attuned to his movements.

She always notices things quickly. I'm going to have to be careful to convey exactly the right attitude.

The sorcerer in our midst waves us toward the door. "We'd better get some rest."

He'd better get some rest, he means. All I have to do is slip into the shadows for a matter of minutes, and any fatigue this human-esque body took on will have melted away.

We all have to maintain our sham of mortality, though.

We head out of the restaurant, Peri and Mirage waving

goodbye to the locals they chatted with. I force a small smile so I can't be accused of sabotaging our mission.

Jonah waits until we're in the van before commenting on everything we've learned. "I think we should head up to that hermit's property first thing in the morning. Find out exactly what monsters he's been seeing."

Peri nods eagerly. "That's our best lead."

As Jonah drives a little farther outside of town so we can settle in for the night without unnerving the locals, she sinks back on the bench as if getting cozy. Raze rests his large hand on her knee with a possessive air that rankles me.

He didn't eat anything at the restaurant, only drank some soda. They don't serve the kind of bloody meals he needs. Which means he'll have to go on a hunt once we've found our spot for the night.

As I expected, the moment our sorcerer pulls off onto an overgrown lane, the carnivore murmurs something to Peri and lunges into the shadows. Mirage bounds after him.

While Jonah gets out his sleeping bag, I aim the warmest smile I can summon at Peri. "We've been stuck in one box or another almost all day. Want to take a walk with me?"

Jonah shoots me a wary glance, but all that matters is the brightening of Peri's face in response. How do her eyes sparkle so vividly?

She springs off the bench to join me. "That sounds great! Thank you for inviting me."

My senses aren't as honed as the basilisk's, but I can pick up traces of our companions' presence well enough to set off in a different direction from both Raze and the ridiculous fox. It's a pleasant enough patch of forest. Pines and birch trees loom tall around us. A light breeze rustles through their leaves.

The terrain is bumpy with protruding granite, but that

only makes it feel wilder. Unhampered by human expectations.

I breathe in the cold night air and let it ripple through my nerves. With the natural world all around me, it's easier to shed my qualms and focus on my goal.

And that's especially important when the cream puff insists on being attuned to my mood.

She aims a softer grin at me, her hood pulled back now so her teal hair tumbles over her shoulders. "You really like being out in nature, don't you? I guess you don't have many chances to enjoy forests back at the school."

I think about the arid desert around the academy, the hot sun baking my skin to the point of pain. "The environment there has some aspects I appreciate… but I am most at home in greener places."

Something about my being resonates with the woods, as if I was made for this setting even though I came into existence on the other side of a shadowy rift.

Peri inhales deeply with a satisfied sound. "It is nice being somewhere so peaceful… I need to be around people some of the time, but all the emotions can get a little overwhelming."

I wouldn't have thought she could appreciate the stillness the way I do. But possibly she's only saying that to cozy up to me the way she seems to with everyone.

That's fine. Right now, I'm aiming to cozy up to her too.

A particularly steep jut of the forest floor gives me the excuse to take Peri's hand and help her up. Once we've clambered onto flatter ground, I keep my fingers wrapped around hers. My thumb traces patterns across the soft skin on the back of her hand.

The rest of her must be even softer.

I need to get on with finding that out so I can set aside this absurd attraction.

Peri provides the perfect opening before I need to. "Thank you for trying to get Gloss to stop bothering me back at the school. I know sometimes I've bothered you too—I never meant to. I hope we can keep getting along better."

I stop and turn toward her, tugging her hand so she faces me at the same time. "I hadn't taken the time to get to know you," I say, picking the words I think will hit the mark best. "There's a lot more to you than I realized. It's hard not to appreciate that once I've noticed."

When I skim my fingers along the arcing line of her jaw, Peri's eyelids dip. A ruddy light wavers through her hair that matches the hunger stirring inside me.

Good. My usual skills work just as well on her as almost every other being.

She's not so special after all.

I lean down and brush my lips against hers.

Peri kisses me back, resting her free hand against my chest as if to steady herself. As her fingers curl into my shirt, the warmth of her touch spreads through my usual chill faster than I anticipated. A pang of need shoots straight to my dick.

She shouldn't have that effect on me. I shouldn't want her this much.

Just get it over with. Prove that she's nothing more than all the other fawning women who've thrown themselves at me. There'll be nothing intriguing about her then.

Deepening the kiss, I nudge her against one of the trees. A quiver runs through Peri's body where we're pressed together.

She eases her head away from mine. Her voice comes out breathless. "Wait. Where do you want to go with this?"

I can show her without any words. I trace her side from the slope of her breast to the curve of her hips, and the gasp that slips out of her has me fully hard in an instant.

That's right. Just like this. It's always so fucking simple.

I dip my head to kiss her neck. Her honey-sweet scent floods my lungs, her skin temptingly tender against my lips. All that power she holds in this marshmallow of a body, and she gives herself over to me so easily.

It's a fluke. The effects she can provoke—all of them—are totally meaningless. Accidental stumbling. She doesn't really see anything.

She doesn't know me. How could a being like her have any idea—

Peri's hand tightens where she's clutching my shirt. All at once, she's pushing me backward, stepping to the side at the same time to put more distance between us.

I blink at her, frustration and unfulfilled desire swelling up inside me in tandem. What the fuck is she doing?

Those gem-like eyes peer into mine. "I can't do this without talking to Raze first. But I don't think it's a good idea anyway. You're not really happy about it."

A jab of irritation hardens my voice. "Of course I'm happy. I wouldn't kiss you if I didn't want to."

Her brow knits as she studies my face. I have the sudden, shameful urge to flee into the shadows so she can't see me at all.

"Maybe," she says, so gently it sets my teeth on edge. "But it's also making you upset. What's the matter? Are you nervous about running into more of those strange shadowkind tomorrow?"

How can she veer off onto that random subject when I was working over her body less than a minute ago?

I step closer. "I wasn't looking to talk."

But when I dip my head and reach for her face to draw her mouth back to mine, she jerks farther away.

A deeper crease forms between Peri's eyebrows.

"Something's wrong. It's okay if you don't want to tell me about it, but I can't ignore it."

A twisted mass of anger and helplessness knots in my chest. "Well, forgive me for wanting to fuck you," I snap, and stride off without looking back.

My heart is thudding too quickly, my limbs still flushed from the feel of her.

Where did I screw up? How could she shrug off what I was offering like it was nothing?

And why do I feel so awful that my caustic last words might have cost me another shot?

30

Periwinkle

I get the feeling we're heading into trouble before Jonah has even parked on the gravel driveway that belongs to Ted McGaffery.

There's nothing I can put my finger on. Across the yard, the two-storey house looms quiet and still. The yellow clapboard siding has transformed into a dingy beige most places, but I can't imagine house painters are in large supply all the way up here. No artificial light glimmers in any of the windows, which isn't surprising when it's late morning.

Not that it's particularly bright out here. The gray clouds smothering the sky only add to the ominous mood. When I step out of the van, a damp breeze licks over my skin.

I pull up my hood both to conceal my hair and to ward off the chill. Why does the wilderness have to be so spooky half of the time?

The house stands in a cleared span of lawn about ten times bigger than the house's foundation. A patchy garden lies to the left of the house, sprawling to a rocky hillside. Tall pines surround us on all other sides like a fence that's sprouted.

A pick-up truck is parked farther down the driveway by a shed not quite large enough to serve as a garage. If Ted is the only person who lives here, that should mean he's home, unless he has more than one car.

Jonah walks tentatively toward the house. "Mr. McGaffery? We've just come up from Pilverton."

His voice rings through the hush of the wilderness. If the house's owner is around, he should have heard our engine several minutes before we reached the house, crawling along that narrow dirt lane.

No one comes to the door or any of the windows. As Hail makes an impatient sound, Jonah strides toward the porch.

He's still a few paces away from the stairs when a stronger gust of wind washes over us—and the front door swings open with a squeal of its hinges.

I'd jump out of my skin if it was looser. Raze springs to my side in an instant. Mirage lets out an uneasy hum.

Jonah has frozen in his tracks. "Mr. McGaffery?" he tries again.

No one appears on the threshold. It looks like the door was unlocked and blown open by the wind.

But if the owner is home, why isn't he answering? If he *isn't* here, then where has he gone?

Jonah walks to the door and leans his head inside. He calls out a few more times to no response before turning back to us.

"He doesn't seem to be home. I don't feel right tramping

in there when we don't know what's going on. We could start by looking around outside, and maybe he'll come back."

"Seek and you shall find!" Mirage declares, and springs off to inspect the shed.

Hail aims a cool glance at me and Raze before heading toward the trees. "I'll see if I notice anything unusual in the woods."

I watch him go, only picking up a trace of indecipherable emotion from him. A wobble runs through my pulse.

The winter fae tried to be sweet with me last night—to get closer with me than I'd ever have thought he'd want to. There was something thrilling about having him let down his guard and reach out to me.

But he *didn't* totally want to. Why would he touch me or kiss me if it unsettled him? Even if he kind of liked it too.

And he got angry when I tried to talk to him about it, which means it's probably bothering him even more than I could tell.

Is this some complicated fae thing I've never learned about?

I shake off those thoughts and nudge Raze. "Let's see what's around back."

Whatever's going on with Hail, he couldn't have made it more obvious that he doesn't want me meddling. If I've learned anything from my time at the academy, it's that trying to soothe emotions people don't even want to admit they're having only pisses them off.

If he ever decides he wants to open up properly, it's not like I'm hard to find.

As we approach the side of the house, my skin starts creeping. Scratch marks mottle the siding, some thin and shallow, others deep gouges.

Apparently some beast decided it needed to claw the house down, and I don't think it was a big bad wolf.

Raze frowns. "It looks like his house did get attacked."

He marches ahead of me and sniffs the area with a flick of his basilisk tongue. The shake of his head reveals his disappointment. "It was too long ago for the scent to linger. At least a few days."

I swallow thickly. "Maybe the creatures didn't come back after he told people in town about it."

But where is Ted McGaffery himself?

I venture into the backyard. A chicken coop stands next to a fenced area where the birds must have been allowed to wander, but there's nothing except scattered feathers on the grass now.

When I get closer, splotches of dark red stand out against the scuffed earth.

I hesitate. "I think whatever came through here, they ate his chickens."

R.I.P., birdies.

Raze comes up beside me with a hint of a snarl. He motions to the patchy lawn next to the chicken coop. "They tore up the yard too."

More clawed spots rake the soil between the patches of grass. I can't restrain a shiver. These creatures had a major beef with the entire property.

Mirage and Jonah come around the other side of the house to join us. I point out the signs we've noticed.

Jonah's eyes darken. "We don't know for sure that shadowkind creatures did that."

Mirage cocks his head. "Are there any mortal creatures that would try to tear down a house?"

Our team leader grimaces. "Not that I can think of."

Hail steps out from between the trees, his gorgeous face unusually grim. "Some of the tree trunks near here have been battered with claws and maybe spikes. It doesn't look natural to me."

Jonah exhales in a rush. "We have to be careful, considering how the creatures came at us the last time we encountered them. Raze, can you make a wider circuit through the woods and see if you pick up any fresh scents? Shout if you get any indication that shadowkind might be nearby. The rest of us will take a look inside the house."

Raze is the only one he trusts to be able to defend himself if there's a sudden attack. I can't argue with Jonah's judgment, even if my heart gives a little squeeze watching the man I've come to adore lope off into the woods alone.

I follow the others into the unlocked house.

We wipe our shoes on the doormat and pad carefully through the rooms. Ted keeps his home tidy—a magazine lies on the living-room coffee table and a mug sits by the kitchen sink, but just about everything is in its place. Upstairs, his bed is made and his clothes hang neatly in the closet.

No monsters rampaged through here. I rub my arms against my rising apprehension. "It doesn't look like there was a struggle."

Hail scowls. "A human wouldn't live out in the wilderness just to spend all his time inside his house. He must go out regularly. Maybe he's taking a hike."

But all kinds of things could happen to a human strolling around in the forest, even if there weren't disturbed shadowkind roving around.

Raze's gruff voice carries through the bedroom window. "Team! I've got something."

He doesn't sound worried, but I hustle out into the yard as quickly as my twinging feet will take me. Another holler brings us tramping through the woods east of the house.

Raze backtracks until he comes into view and waves for us to follow him. "I caught one fresher trail. Something passed by here earlier this morning—another of those strange shadowkind scents." He pauses. "Should we see where the creature went or where it came from?"

"Where it came from," Jonah says immediately. "That's what matters the most. And that's the trail that'll fade sooner."

I smile more to raise everyone's spirits than because I feel particularly upbeat. "That makes sense to me. Let's get this mystery unraveled!"

As we set off through the forest, no one else helps break the silence. Raze sets as swift a pace as Jonah can keep up with on his human legs, and pretty soon I need to slip into the shadows so I can keep up.

Mirage is still bounding through the underbrush in the physical world, but Hail has shifted into his most ephemeral form too. I sense him through the darkness, his presence like a slightly brittle chill.

Despite my earlier resolve not to push the subject, I veer closer to him. There has to be some way to give last night's conversation a better ending.

"I know you might not want to talk to me right now," I say. "But I'm sorry if I upset you last night."

Hail's response travels through the shadows in a mutter. "Don't worry about it."

I don't think he means he's actually fine, but I do have plenty of other things to worry about. Like whether we'll encounter more feral beasts while we wander through the woods. Like what the sorcerer who commanded them is up to now.

"All right. I'm still glad you invited me to walk with you!"

Hail simply snorts.

As we keep pace behind Raze, the sun reaches its peak over the treetops and begins descending to the west. Jonah swipes at the sweat on the back of his neck. I re-materialize to keep him company and dip back into the shadows when my ankles are throbbing.

Finally, the basilisk shifter jerks to a halt. He stares at something farther ahead of us, his stance rigid. "That's… I've never seen one like that before."

I flit forward through the shadows. Before I've quite reached him, a current of energy tremors through my being.

That feels almost like—

I pull myself into physical form and find myself staring at the most formidable rift I've ever encountered.

It's true that I haven't observed a whole lot of the portals that connect the shadow realm with the mortal world. I only returned to my native habitat a few times after I first stumbled into this realm and realized how invigorating human emotions were.

And then, after I got away from my captor… I stuck to just one place, traveling through the same rift to sample the emotions of the local mortals. Practice makes perfect!

Except when it doesn't.

But all of the rifts I've passed through were easy to miss if you weren't specifically looking for one. The hum of shadow energy normally blends into the general thrum of mortal life. There's nothing really to see unless you squint just the right way to make out the blurring of the terrain on the other side.

And they've all been up off the ground, not accessible except through the shadows.

This rift… With just a few more steps, the sense of the world of darkness beyond it jitters right through my skin. The vast, hazy maw stretches up above the treetops—but it also gapes all the way down to the forest floor.

It's several times bigger than any of the rifts I've encountered before. You could toss Ted McGaffery's entire house in there without scraping the edges.

I peer at the forest around us as if the trees might offer

some explanation. My gaze catches on a bit of thread snagged on a twig.

The olive-green color makes my pulse hitch with a flash of memory—the suit jacket my former captor liked to wear, the same color of fabric stretching across his wide shoulders.

I inhale the cool forest air and peer closer. When I consider the details, this thread looks like yarn from a sweater, nothing that would have come from a suit jacket.

I can't keep panicking at scraps that mean nothing.

Jonah is still studying the portal in front of us. He lets out a low whistle. "Now that's a rift. How could the shadowkind community not already know about this one?"

"Maybe it's new?" I suggest, but that idea seems absurd considering how huge it is.

A shudder ripples through Mirage's lean form. His fox ears pop from between the strands of his bright red hair. "It feels too big. Like it's... pushy."

Hail inclines his head in a slight nod, his gaze fixed on the rift. "All the ones I've come across in the past give off a neutral impression. This one makes my hackles go up."

I hug myself. "What do we—"

Before I can finish my question, a shadowy figure tumbles out of the rift. It transforms into a physical body as it hits the ground just in front of the portal: a creature standing a little taller than my waist, with four bowed legs, a squashed face, and scales that lift into jagged tips.

Someone drew the shortest straw.

Raze's nostrils flare. "It smells like the other strange creatures."

As if to confirm his remark, the beast spasms. Its legs shrink while its jaw juts several inches longer. Not an improvement.

Only mild emotions waft off it, like a thin broth.

"It's curious and a little confused, but not hostile," I tell the others.

Hail's stance has gone rigid. "For the moment."

Jonah looks from the creature to the rift. "I think we've discovered where the influx of new, unusual shadowkind are coming from. Now what are we going to do about it?"

31

Jonah

My foster mom leans over the map, her eyebrows drawing together in concentration. "And what exactly was funky about this rift?"

It's strange seeing Sorsha take anything very seriously. The phoenix shifter may be in the running as the most powerful shadowkind in existence—partly because she's an incredibly rare hybrid with strengths from both her human and monstrous sides—but she manages to face everything the world throws at her with a lighthearted attitude.

As a kid, growing up under her watch, her breezy approach gave me an escape from the trauma of having my parents murdered in front of me. Which I guess she understood better than I realized at the time. I later found out that she went through a similar tragedy at around the same age.

As an adult, I appreciate how she mixes humor with

compassion and determination. It often makes difficult situations less intimidating to tackle.

But it also means that when even she turns solemn, I know we're in trouble.

"I couldn't sense it the same way the shadowkind on my team could," I admit, peering at the spot we've marked on the map. "It was definitely closer to the ground than any rift I've encountered before, so I don't know if the sensations I picked up on were because of proximity or something else. But the energy it gave off felt kind of… twitchy, erratic."

"Is that how your shadowkind teammates described it too?"

I nod. "Something like that. Like it was larger, more imposing, and more unsettling than they'd expect. None of them were willing to step through it to see what would happen, even though they've all traveled back and forth between the realms plenty of times before. It unnerved them enough that going inside felt like a significant risk."

Sorsha hums to herself, tucking a stray lock of bright red hair behind her ear. "I've never come across a rift that shadowkind were repelled from. The weird, morphing creatures that've come out of it—do you think the rift changed them into something odd, or does it connect to an odd part of the shadow realm we're unaware of?"

I spread my hands in a gesture of helplessness. "I have no idea. Have you heard of either of those things happening before?"

"No." She sucks her lower lip under her teeth to nibble at it and then flashes a smile at me with her usual lively energy. "But the mysteries of this world are endless. It'll be interesting seeing what comes of this one. At least the worst threat you've had to deal with is some minor sorcerer."

I don't know how "minor" the sorcerer who's controlling some of the strange shadowkind creatures is, but it's true that he hasn't posed much of an obstacle to our investigations so far. We can't be sure whether he intended that one aggressive pack to attack us in particular or just anyone who crossed their path.

He might not even realize that anyone's investigating him.

I rub my jaw. "The creatures are causing problems too. From the reports we've gotten and what we've seen, they don't have the normal shadowkind instinct to be wary of humans. Some of that is due to the sorcerer's influence, but at least one of them wasn't under any sorcery at all and was still frightening people."

Rollick's voice carries through the doorway. "And that's why we need to get a better understanding of this unusual rift."

The demon strides into the small meeting room with an assured air—and Peri hurrying behind him. At the sight of her vibrant hair, my pulse hiccups. I can't help tensing up in an effort to lock my emotions down.

I've been grappling with my attraction to her almost from the start, but it wasn't always this hard. I'm her teacher and the closest thing to an authority figure on our small team —she's a student and dependent on my evaluation. I know pursuing anything more than friendly with her would be one hundred percent wrong.

But when she fell into my arms the other day, when I gazed into her eyes and her bright scent flooded my lungs, all my better intentions flew out the window.

She makes me *feel* brighter, from the inside out. As if a light flicks on inside me when she's around, when she smiles at me, when she makes one of her encouraging remarks.

I don't know how to turn that light off. An increasingly large part of me doesn't *want* to.

I've met a lot of shadowkind over the years, but never a

being like her. Why did it have to be like this, in a position that threatens every shred of my integrity?

Rollick doesn't appear to notice my reaction. He strolls over to the table to join us in studying the map. Sorsha, knowing me much better than he does, raises one eyebrow slightly but doesn't comment.

I avoid looking at Peri, figuring I'm less likely to reveal more if I pretend she's not here.

Sorsha taps the marked spot on the map. "I'd like to take an up-close look at this thing. It'd be good to bring Snap along and see what he can taste with his power. Omen might be willing to take a leap through it and see what's on the other side."

Her four partners—the men who acted as my sort-of dads—stopped by the academy with her today to offer guest talks on their specialty subjects. My spirits lift at the thought of having my makeshift family back together for our next road trip.

Rollick shakes his head. "There'll be time for that later. My little team has been making good progress, but my colleagues aren't prepared to let them rejoin the regular academy program yet. I'd like to give them more opportunity to prove themselves."

He catches my eye. "I have a few instruments I'd like you to bring along on your next venture. The readings they take will help us make a more objective assessment of what exactly is different about this rift."

I lift my chin, ignoring the knot that's formed in my gut. I'm going to be in charge again, wrangling the four very different shadowkind who sometimes seem more interested in harassing each other than finishing our mission.

We have made it through without anyone resorting to murder so far, though. Peri deserves a chance to prove herself even if I'm not sure about the others.

"Of course," I say. "It shouldn't take long now that we know where to go."

"I'll be sending equipment for trapping one of the morphing shadowkind as well, if you have the chance," the demon adds. "But that's a lower priority. I'd also like you to test if you can 'convince' the rift to shrink even a small amount with your sorcery. Its size and power concern me."

That makes two of us. I swallow past the sudden dryness in my throat. "I'll give it my best shot. I've never tried to use sorcery on a rift."

He claps me on the shoulder. "There's a first time for everything. You can have the rest of the day off—no teaching necessary. I'll get the equipment loaded onto the jet for departure tomorrow morning."

Sorsha folds her arms over her chest. "You really believe in throwing people into the deep end, don't you, Rollick?"

He grins at her. "At least I don't have any intention of burning the whole world down. But they won't be without backup. I was hoping you and your associates would show off the speeds that RV of yours is capable of and take me on a trip up the same way, so we'll be nearby if the team needs additional assistance."

Knowing he'll be close eases my nerves and appears to mollify Sorsha too. With a satisfied expression, she swipes her hands together. "There's room in the Everymobile for one more. Or two or three, if *your* associates—"

Rollick cuts her off with a raised hand. "We have other matters keeping us busy, or I'd have been more involved already. I'm hoping this will be a quick trip."

Sorsha laughs as if accepting a challenge. "Omen will make sure of that."

Rollick pats Peri on the shoulder. "You wanted to take another look at the map, so go ahead. Then you should get some rest too, shiny one."

As he ambles out of the room, my gaze follows him. I want to ask what other business has been keeping him and his colleagues busy, but I don't think he'd tell me. The demon likes to keep his cards close to the chest.

Has Quinn had a lapse with her heart condition? Her health has always been shaky.

Sorsha lopes out after Rollick. My skin tingles with the awareness that I'm now alone with Peri.

I step to the side to put more distance between us. "I'll get out of your way. If you notice anything new that you think might be useful, let the rest of us know."

I'm planning on taking a casual stroll out of there, but Peri fixes me with her vivid blue gaze. My legs stall.

She hesitates before speaking. "Did I do something to upset you?"

My stomach drops. I haven't been hiding my internal conflict well enough.

"Not at all," I say as firmly as I can. "You've been great, Peri. I'm not sure we'd have gotten this far without you."

She only looks more puzzled. "Something's been making you uncomfortable around me in the past couple of days. You don't *have* to talk about it, but if there's anything I can do to fix what went wrong, I'd want you to tell me."

I know she would. Fuck, what do I even say?

I grope for an answer. "It isn't your fault. I'm just sorting out some things that are mine to deal with."

She steps closer, making my pulse skip a beat. Then she touches my forearm as if trying to solidify a connection between us. "The one thing I'm good at is helping people sort through their feelings. If you'd ever want a hand with that, I'm right here."

Heat blooms through my arm. I ease back as gently as I can so I'm out of reach. "Thank you for the offer. This is the kind of thing I should work out on my own."

Peri is watching me even more intently now. She takes another step toward me with an experimental air.

The wall stops me from retreating any farther. She lifts her hand to trace her fingers along my jaw, and a zing of desire shoots to my groin.

I'm about to yank myself away even knowing it'll confuse her more when she pulls back instead. Her eyes widen.

Her voice comes out even softer. "Why does it bother you that you like being close to me? I wouldn't *expect* anything from you or—"

Shit. The cat's out of the bag now.

I interrupt before she can spiral into anxiety. "Like I said, it isn't your fault, Peri. It's just not… appropriate, when I'm your teacher and evaluating your performance on the mission. We can't control our feelings, but we control how we act on them. And I can't act on those feelings at all."

I'm afraid she might not understand the subtleties of those dynamics, but a ruddy orange sheen ripples over her hair as a blush crosses her cheeks. "Oh. Oh, I didn't even think about— I wasn't trying to be pushy."

"I know." I manage a small smile that's genuine enough. "It's all right. I'm just being careful to make sure *I* don't do anything that wouldn't be fair. You don't have to worry about me. I'll leave you to the map."

I duck out of the room without looking back, hoping my explanation will satisfy her… and regretting how much I've inadvertently revealed.

32

Periwinkle

"Peri!" Fen catches me in the dorm common room while everyone's heading out for breakfast. My friend exudes happiness like a shower of gumdrops.

I have to grin back at her. "Did you get good news?"

"Not exactly. Last night, I met a new being who just arrived at the academy. She's a selkie, so she knows all about watery powers. And she's really nice. She gave me some tips on keeping mine held in. I think it might be enough for me to finally get the hang of it! You'll like her too. She's in one of the other dorms, but we can sit with her in the cafeteria."

I keep smiling through Fen's deluge of excitement, but my stomach tightens. She made a new friend twelve hours ago, and they might already have solved her biggest problem?

She's never been this overjoyed any time we've spent together.

Why should she have been? I gave her company and encouragement, but it isn't as if I ever really *helped* her, is it?

I brightened her day a little, stopped her from feeling lonely, but my presence hasn't had any more impact than one of those flickering glows that passes over my hair and disappears.

"That's great!" I tell Fen, and I mean it. If she can stop herself from accidentally conjuring water in awkward situations, the other students won't have any reason to make fun of her. She won't be at risk of exposing her powers to humans.

She'll be able to move through the levels at the school, visit the voluntary student building, make lots more friends…

She's been nothing but kind to me since I arrived here. Of course she deserves to find her footing and her place in the world.

It isn't her fault that alongside my happiness for her, I'm deflating like an undercooked souffle.

Fen rubs her hands together eagerly. "She used to live in the sea. I've never been to one of those. Have you seen an ocean before?"

I have vague memories of a big expanse of water almost the same color as my hair, from long before I knew about sorcerers and cages. "I think so. One of the first times I came to the mortal realm."

In my distraction, I bump against one of our fellow students in the hall. Or maybe she bumps into me, but because it's Vim, our classmate who's always posturing like a pro wrestler, she looks peeved anyway.

She rolls her eyes at me and grimaces. "Can't even walk straight, and you think you have so much amazing advice for the rest of us."

As Vim strides off, Fen knocks her elbow playfully

against mine. "She just wishes she had as good a friend as you. How soon do you have to leave again? Brine is starting at level two, but she might be in one of our classes this afternoon anyway."

Her compliment combined with the reminder of her much better friend twist up my gut into a heavy if petty lump. I suddenly can't imagine forcing any food down my throat.

The words tumble out before I have a chance to think better of them. "Actually, I can't even come to breakfast. We're supposed to leave early this morning—I need to finish preparing."

Fen frowns, but my excuse only dampens her joy a little. "That's too bad. Well, you can meet Brine the next time you're back. How much longer do you think Rollick is going to keep you on this special assignment before he decides you're safe to go back to regular classes?"

"I don't know. Hopefully we'll be done soon." Although what Rollick is going to decide based on how much—or little—I've contributed, I have no idea.

Does being the team cheerleader count for something?

I grab her hand in a quick squeeze. "We'll be able to hang out again soon. I'm glad you'll have Brine to keep you company while I'm gone."

Part of controlling my powers is knowing when to back away from a situation that's stirring up unruly emotions, right?

I tell myself that, but parting ways with Fen at a split in the hall still feels like running off with my tail between my legs.

How can I be a good friend if I'm getting upset the second she makes a new one?

I don't actually have any final preparations to make. I

wander aimlessly until I spot one of the sliding glass doors that leads to the building's inner courtyard.

Most of the reform students are at breakfast. There are only a couple of beings lounging together on one of the benches, and a few others sitting cross-legged on the patio stones playing a game with shiny tokens.

I veer away from them toward the garden area at the other end of the courtyard. Amid the flowering bushes, I sink down on the firmly packed dirt and lean against the slim trunk of a small tree.

I draw my legs up to rest my chin on my knees. An ache I don't totally understand spreads through my chest.

A burn of tears that makes even less sense forms behind my eyes. What's wrong with this human-like body?

I squeeze my eyelids shut as if I can push the moisture back that way.

Everything is fine. We've made progress with our mission. My best friend is closer to moving up in the levels. I'm keeping my emotions in check right now, not letting them overwhelm me or burst out.

But I can't stop myself from seeing Vim's mocking sneer. Jonah's uncomfortable expression yesterday when he explained that the way I make him feel is in violation of his job. The anger flashing in Hail's eyes before he stormed off the other night, because I wouldn't ignore the uneasiness I could tell *he* was feeling.

I open my eyes again, trying to dismiss those memories, and the bushes in front of me rustle. A furry red face pokes between the leaves with ears perked.

The fox cocks his head at the sight of me and then leaps through the gap between the plants. He rolls onto his back with a whirl of his five tails like he's a helicopter about to take off. With another flip, he flings himself right up into the air, seeming to actually hover for a few seconds.

Then he whips his body around so that he lands cushioned on those same tails with an immensely pleased expression.

A giggle breaks through the ache that's gripping me. The animal offers a very foxy smile and ripples into Mirage's human-like form, other than the furred ears above his human ones that he doesn't bother to retract.

He tips his head to the side much like he did as a fox and speaks in a mischievous hush. "What are you doing hiding away in here, Rainbow? Some new sneaky mission?"

Another laugh bubbles up, but my tumultuous emotions stew around it.

I rub my face. "I needed a little time alone."

Mirage's smile vanishes. He moves to retreat. "I won't bother—"

"No." I catch his sleeve before he can pull out of reach. "I'm glad you found me. Watching you play cheered me up."

The fox shifter smiles again, but in a more subdued way than before. His ears flick away within his ruddy locks.

He lifts his hand to trail his fingers over my hair. "Why are you blue, Rainbow?"

My lips twitch with a hint of amusement at his phrasing, even though the question is serious. "No good reason. I guess I'm trying to figure that out. It feels like… like I know what I want to be doing in the world, but I have no idea how to do it. Nothing I try works."

Mirage hums. He sits down by my side, facing me, and keeps twisting a strand of my hair into a corkscrew curl. "What do you want to be doing?"

"Making people feel good," I say automatically. "Happy, safe, excited, proud… All those things."

"And what makes you think that you're not?"

An awkward flush creeps up my neck. "Other than my outbursts where I literally hurt people? I don't see it happening very much, and I do see people getting annoyed or upset with me."

Mirage lets out a soft huff. "You don't annoy me."

I look over at him, meeting his bright brown eyes. "I did sometimes. You seemed irritated the first time I talked to you."

The fox shifter opens his mouth and closes it again. He droops his gaze with an abashed expression. "It wasn't really you bothering me. You were being kind. I... It's scary feeling that someone is safe to be around, because if they're safe then there are other things I might want to talk about, but I don't even want to think about them, and—"

He cuts himself off, his eyebrows rising as if he's surprised himself.

With a rough laugh, he nuzzles my cheek in a way that sets off giddy quivers over my skin. "Like that. But now that I've been around you more, I think maybe... it will feel good to talk when I let myself. Better than running away. You let me see that."

A lump fills my throat. I don't know everything that's haunting this charmingly erratic man, but there's no mistaking the gratitude in his voice.

Is it possible I've helped Fen in ways I haven't seen too?

I touch the side of his face, running my thumb over his smooth brown skin, the arch of his high cheekbone. "Mirage—"

Before I can go on, a larger form pushes through the bushes. "Peri, are you all right? I—"

The second he sees us, Raze freezes. His lips pull back with a low growl, his eyes narrowing at Mirage. "What are you doing here?"

I hold up my hand to bring his attention back to me, but the fox shifter has already jerked away. He hunches his shoulders in a submissive posture. "Not getting in your way or making a play. Only trying to cheer her up. She seemed to need it."

I suck in a breath to add my confirmation, but Raze's posture relaxes. He crouches down amid the shrubs, considering Mirage and then me with a twist of his mouth. "I saw you didn't come to breakfast. Something's wrong. Who upset you?"

I manage a wry smile. "Mostly just myself. I feel better now."

"Because of him." Raze studies Mirage a little longer. "You noticed. It mattered to you enough that you looked after her."

The fox shifter dips his head in a nod. His eyes gleam when he glances at me. "She's got a whole rainbow in her. A being that special needs to be taken care of right."

His words and his gaze send a flutter through my chest. I don't know if Raze can tell or if he's simply going by Mirage's reaction, but he hesitates and then says, "You care about her a lot. You like her… in a lot of different ways."

Mirage's voice turns tender. "She *is* very special. And it's very enjoyable to show her that. However I can. As long as it's welcome."

A heated energy tingles through the air. Raze meets my eyes again, careful and maybe a bit curious. "You enjoy being around him too."

I reach out to stroke my lover's jaw. "I do. But it has nothing to do with enjoying *you*, which you know I do, very much. He really was just cheering me up. If anything else would make you upset—"

Raze inhales sharply, cutting me off. "I think… I think it shouldn't. Mirage wouldn't hurt you."

He pauses again as if grappling with something inside himself. A glimmer lights in his eyes that isn't so different from the fox shifter's usual sly glint.

Raze lifts his chin toward Mirage. "She could feel even better. I want to see how she'd look if you kiss her."

Mirage blinks at him. For a second, I think he's offended by the domineering request. My pulse skitters.

Then the fox shifter turns the full force of his grin on me. "Would that make you even happier, Rainbow?"

My heart thuds faster, but nothing about the rhythm is fearful now. When I peek at Raze, he's watching avidly.

I wet my lips. "Yes. I think it would."

Mirage scoots toward me and teases his fingers into my hair. Anticipation shivers through me.

He tips forward and catches my mouth with his.

The gentle press of Mirage's lips summons a whole swell of giddiness that wraps around my heart. As I kiss him back, Raze takes a rough breath with a trace of a groan.

The basilisk shifter edges closer and rests his hand on my back with a bloom of warmth.

Then the PA system crackles to life with Shanty's voice. "The students scheduled for this morning's trip north should report to the admin room now."

33

Periwinkle

Jonah looks at the trees around us and back at his phone. "It should be *right* here."

Mirage tips his head to one side and then the other before spinning around with a brief swoosh of a couple of fox tails. "If there's no rift, there's no work to do!"

Raze adjusts the bag of equipment slung over his bulky shoulder and frowns. "It can't have disappeared, can it? Do rifts move?"

"They aren't supposed to." Jonah's forehead furrows. "But this wasn't like any other rift we know of, right?"

A wobble travels through my veins. "And the creatures coming out of it change like no other shadowkind do. Maybe it's all part of the same energy—always morphing."

Hail folds his arms over his chest. He offers a typically blasé tone. "If Rollick's been getting reports of the strange activity up here for months, then the rift mustn't move very far. Let's get on with finding the stupid thing."

Jonah motions to the rest of us. "We should spread out. Pay attention to the atmosphere—if you sense anything like the vibe the rift gave off, shout for the rest of us."

As we fan out from the spot where the weird rift stood before, my skin creeps. I stay where I can still see Raze's huge, sinewy form between the trees.

We haven't come across any sign of more strange beings so far on this trek, but that doesn't mean we won't. And I'm not all that confident in my ability to protect myself.

I extend my awareness as far as I can, but I'm built for picking up on emotions, not bizarro shadow-realm energy. I haven't noticed anything at all when the fox shifter lets out a bark.

"What is it?" I ask, hustling over to him.

By the time I reach him, Mirage's emotions have calmed. He points to a crumpled mass of shiny paper on the ground. "No rifts, no worries. I stepped on that, and it startled me. It's not part of the forest."

I bend down. The paper is shiny because it's coated with aluminum foil, the surface flecked with dirt... as well as dried smears of a dark red substance.

My pulse hiccups. I pick the paper up and give it a sniff.

The spicy tang of tandoori fills my nose. I drop the wrapper as if it burned me.

Jonah and Raze lope over from opposite directions. Raze takes one look at my face and bares his teeth. "What's the matter?"

I shake my head quickly. "It's nothing. Just some garbage. Another random coincidence."

Lots of people eat tandoori. We had it at the academy just days ago. There's no more reason to think this piece of trash is connected to my former captor than our cafeteria meal was.

Other than the fact that we know there's a sorcerer with questionable intentions operating nearby.

As I rub my arms to will down the goosebumps, Jonah picks up the crumpled wrapper. "We need all the evidence we can get."

Mirage sniffs the breeze. "The air is a little... wobbly this way."

I step forward, ignoring the twinge that's creeping up my ankles. "Maybe that's where the rift wandered off to. We can find it!"

Raze has only taken a few more steps before his tongue flicks over his lips. "I can smell one of those unusual creatures. Not too fresh. The trail's at least a few hours old."

Jonah perks up. "Follow the trail back to where it came from."

We tramp on through the woods, all together now. After a couple of minutes, a tingle of energy passes through my essence.

My head jerks up. "I think I can feel it."

Hail nods, his pale face more intent than usual. "We're close."

We pick up our pace, twigs crackling under our feet. The energy reverberates more thickly through the air, and my nerves start jittering again.

We reach a small glade with a ridge of rock at one side. The rift looms right in front of the low cliff, blurring the vegetation I can see through it.

Jonah taps the new coordinates into his phone. "It moved half a mile in a couple of days. I wonder how often it drifts around?"

Hail grimaces. "Hopefully we'll be done with this mission before we have to find out."

"Well, let's get started…"

Our leader takes another step toward the rift—and a small, blue-and-gray form careens out of the nearby trees with a piercing shriek.

The creature is only a little bigger than a blue jay, with moth-like wings rather than feathered and at least ten slim pointed legs. But it dive-bombs Jonah's face with those needly legs extended and its wings battering the air.

What kind of demented butterfly is this?

Jonah grunts and smacks the thing to the side. Its legs draw scarlet scratches across his knuckles. A few sharp sorcerous syllables burst from his lips.

As the wacko butterfly whirls back toward Jonah, Mirage leaps in. He springs up to bonk the creature with one hand like he'd spike a volleyball.

Apparently the insane insect isn't interested in playing ball. It whips away from him and shoots off between the trees.

The five of us stare after it. Would laughing or screaming be more appropriate?

"That was… interesting," Hail says, sounding equally bemused.

Jonah wavers on his feet and then grabs the first aid kit from his pack. "If it's gone, it can't bother us. No way to track it when it's flying anyway. What's most important is getting a read on this rift."

But where was that creature going in such a hurry? Jonah's sorcery didn't stop it from wanting to attack. Did it really get so scared of Mirage?

I didn't pick up any emotions from it at all, now that I think about it.

Uneasiness crawls down my spine, but I can't say what exactly I'm nervous about.

Jonah wraps a length of gauze around his scratched

knuckles and gestures to Raze, who hefts the bag off his shoulder and unzips it. They pull the metal boxes with their knobs and buttons out of their padded containers, as well as a couple of folded cages that we could open up if a less-flighty creature comes through the rift. Hail moves closer to watch.

I don't understand how the devices Rollick sent with us are supposed to operate, but there's something reassuring about the pings and ticks as Jonah holds the first one up to the rift. As if he's bringing this strange phenomenon back into the realm of things that can be explained and catalogued. It won't remain an unsettling mystery for long.

Since I have no experience with technology, there isn't much for me to do. I wander through the woods near the rift, testing whether I can catch hints of emotion from the forest's inhabitants. Are more odd shadowkind lurking close enough for me to sense their presence?

I taste Jonah's satisfaction at fulfilling Rollick's request and Raze's at helping with the job. Mirage exudes delight while chasing sunbeams that dart with the swaying overhead leaves. Hail has his feelings tightly under wraps as usual.

A little fear reaches me from a few forest animals who don't know what to make of our presence, but I don't taste anything that matches the shifting emotions the strange shadowkind give off.

After a while, Jonah switches from one device to another. "Once we've gotten all the readings, I'll see if I can affect the rift with my sorcery. Maybe you should give yours a try too, Raze—see if basilisk poison will shrink it. If you're all right with making the attempt."

Raze dips his head and murmurs an answer I don't hear, because at the same moment a different sort of energy zings right through my skull.

My heart lurches.

The energy crackles around in my head. Like when Jonah gives us his sorcerous commands, the words jabbing into my will like tiny fish hooks… except this zing has a darker, sharper flavor to it.

Every inch of my skin chills as if it's been coated with ice.

I know this feeling. Like tarnished medals behind glass. Like tandoori chicken wrapped in aluminium foil in a dim basement room.

As my pulse pounds frantically, I throw my awareness in the direction the energy came from with all my concentration. A few whiffs of emotion—mortal, human— reach me.

Frustration like meat charred to black.

Anger like bursting peppercorns.

Greed like vanilla mousse that's spoiled.

I know those feelings too. I've tasted those exact flavors.

All from the same source.

My throat constricts so fast I lose my breath.

All those little bits and pieces I've stumbled on—they weren't just coincidences. The sorcerer messing with this rift *is* the man I knew, the same one who flung his shimmering net over me, shut me away in a cage, and dug his blades into my body to make me his anguished tool.

He's here. He found these strange shadowkind and decided to turn them into his new slaves.

Any second now he's going to realize that his attempt at latching on to my mind didn't catch hold, that it bounced off the brief instruction Jonah gave me earlier. Then he'll hit me even harder.

I don't know for sure that my former captor has stronger magic than Jonah's—but he is a lot older. He's had much more practice. He commanded an army of shadowkind creatures a couple dozen strong.

If he captures me again—if he traps my teammates in his power—

Horror sears through my veins alongside the blare of panic.

A shudder wracks my body, and my vision hazes. The dark emotions roiling beneath my skin heave to the surface.

The command Jonah gave me to control my power has faded since yesterday's iteration.

Oh, no. I'm going to hurt them again. All of them, and every animal nearby, and—

There's one specific being I *do* want to hurt.

The idea hits me just as the agony blasts from my body. Darkness surges in every direction.

No!

I grope for a shred of control, picturing the man's stocky body and pock-marked face, focusing on the place where I sensed those noxious emotions.

With a grunt that bursts from my throat, I heave all the fear and misery gushing out of me toward only him.

The wave roars around me, warbling through the trees. Somewhere farther off, it smacks into a form with a flare of acid-sour pain that echoes back into me.

Good. If there's anyone in this world who doesn't deserve happiness, it's him.

More darkness careens through the woods. I have to stop him. I have to—

Jonah's voice pierces my head in a shout of sorcerous syllables.

The power rushing out of me contracts in a jolt so abrupt I stumble forward and fall to my knees. The distant pain flickers and dwindles—I think the man who meant to capture us is running away.

I sent him fleeing before he could dig his awful sorcery into any of us. A grin crosses my lips.

Footsteps thud toward me.

"What was that?" Disappointment rings through Jonah's voice and wafts off his presence. "Peri, you seemed fine. If you were getting worked up, you were supposed to warn us."

Mirage shuffles over, rubbing a wound on his arm that's dribbling smoky essence.

As I look at him, guilt clamps around my gut. "I'm sorry. I didn't mean to hurt you. There was—I had to—"

"You *had* to screw up the whole mission yet again," Hail interrupts in a caustic tone. He holds up one of Rollick's devices. "All of the tech we brought is going haywire thanks to you, pipsqueak."

What? I scramble to my feet, my pulse racing. "I tried to direct it away from you, away from the rift, as quickly as I could. I was throwing it over there—I mustn't have been fast enough."

Raze's forehead furrows. "You let out that blast of darkness on purpose?"

Jonah's mouth twists, and Mirage winces.

They don't understand. If my former captor tried to aim his sorcery at my companions too, they didn't recognize the effect.

Of course they didn't. I'm the only one who knows this sorcerer. I've been recognizing him all along and not wanting to believe it.

I don't even know for sure that he's gone.

"We have to be careful!" I blurt out. "He was close—I could feel it. If he tries again—"

Hail sneers. "You lost your head in more silly paranoia and exploded your crazy energy all over. Now we've got to go back and get new equipment to start the whole job over again. What do you figure Rollick is going to say when he finds out how everything got broken?"

A clammier chill sweeps through me. I've caused another

incident, and this one was so much more destructive than the one before.

Destruction we can't gloss over.

Before I can say anything, Jonah rakes his hand through his hair. "We have to give Rollick the whole story. I don't know, Peri. I've tried—but maybe you need something more to get you stabilized than any of us can offer."

"No!" Another tremor shakes my body. "Please. I was only trying to help. The sorcerer was trying to catch us like he always does—"

Raze holds out his hands, a flicker of worry crossing his face and wavering through the air between us. "Just calm down, Peri. We'll figure it out."

They think I'm freaking out over nothing again. They're *afraid* that I might lose control.

What can I say that'll convince them?

Is there anything I could say that'll matter?

I finally got some handle on my powers and pointed them toward the right target… but I still ruined everything we were working on.

And when Rollick finds out, even he's going to want to banish me.

A sob breaks from my throat. I can't protect anyone. I only make things worse.

Blinking away tears, I hurl myself into the shadows and dash away as fast as I can go.

34

Mirage

Her name breaks from my throat automatically. "Peri!"

Our rainbow-vivid companion has already rippled away through the shadows. I move to leap after her, but Hail stops me with a burst of frost that melds my feet to the ground.

"Don't you go running off too," he snaps. "We don't even know how else she might lash out."

Jonah has taken a step in the same direction, but he halts with a firming of his jaw. "If she needs some space, we should probably give it to her."

Does *he* think she'd explode at us again?

A memory wavers up: her plaintive voice carrying through the night when I left her behind in the forest several nights ago. "She might get lost—not be able to find her way back."

Our sorcerer aims a firm glance at me. "I'd imagine Peri can look after herself."

I think I hear a thread of uncertainty in his voice. But it also occurs to me that he might believe it's better if she can't return.

Coming back means facing the judgment of the school administration. Maybe being banished.

Does Peri deserve that?

If she runs away, she might be able to stay free here in the mortal world, feeding on the emotions she needs.

I rub the wound on my arm that's already sealing, just a thin wisp of essence still drifting up. It only hurt for a moment—she'd already yanked her brutal energy away from me before Jonah intervened.

She really did get control over it.

I scowl at Hail. "She wasn't trying to break anything."

"But she did, didn't she?" He turns toward Jonah. "You should have told the administration the whole story in the first place. Let them decide how significant a threat she is instead of letting her cutesy exterior distract you. Now we've got a huge mess and nothing to do but go back empty-handed—and *we're* the ones who'll pay, not you, oh great sorcerer."

Jonah winces. "I'll make sure they know none of you did anything wrong. She wasn't even interacting with us when it happened."

Raze starts to pace. Uneasiness wafts off his hulking body, potent enough that I can feel it without any special emotion-sensing awareness. "She said she was *trying* to send out her power. Why would she do that? She hates it."

Hail scoffs. "She got caught up in her delusions about

this sorcerer she tangled with before. We never should have brought a wimp like her along in the first place."

All five of my tails swish out of me with a furious swipe through the air. "She isn't weak. Anyone would be bothered by getting captured and mistreated."

I should know.

Hail aims his glower at me. "What does it matter if she's too unstable to hold herself together?"

Jonah drags in a breath. "We don't know if that's the case. If she's getting better at deciding when and where she lets out her destructive impulses, that's a good sign."

Hail shakes his head. "Only if we can trust her to point them in a reasonable direction."

My gaze falls on the broken equipment, the data on their displays fragmented into distorted light. The first wave of searing darkness washed over them and me and our other teammates—behind Peri.

She didn't mean to do that part. After the power had already burst out, she pushed it somewhere else.

"What if the sorcerer *was* here?" I ask abruptly. "The one she knew before or whichever one's messed with the shadowkind up here? You're just assuming she's delusional."

The fae man grimaces. "Because she's been set off by ridiculous things every time before."

"But before, after her outburst, she knew she'd just gotten scared. This time she was still worried about us." The image of her standing before us, pale and trembling, flits through my mind. "She looked in the same direction where she sent most of her power, like she was worried about what's over there."

I don't wait to see if the others will agree. I just wiggle my feet free from the melting frost and lope between the trees.

The bark on some of the trunks looks as if it's been

scraped like my arm was. Some of the leaves scattering the ground have shriveled and grayed.

My skin creeps, but I hurry onward, lifting my nose to make use of my fox senses.

Raze hustles over beside me, his muscles flexing through his brawny body. "We need to know what provoked her that badly."

Somewhere behind us, Hail grumbles words I can't make out. The crunch of footsteps through the brush tells me both he and Jonah are following us.

All at once, Raze stiffens. He pushes forward twice as fast as before, his tongue forking into its lizard shape as it flicks over his lips.

He comes to a stop at a small clear spot between the trees and throws out his arms to block me. "Wait!"

As Hail and Jonah catch up with us, the basilisk shifter tastes the air again and again. His hands ball at his sides.

"Someone *was* here. It's the same human smell I picked up near the cabin the other day."

My pulse skips a beat. I duck closer to the ground to peer at it. "I see the impression of shoes. The dirt looks stirred up, like he was having trouble on his feet."

Jonah inhales sharply. "If Peri's energy hit him hard, it would have injured him at least a little."

When I glance at Hail, his pale face has gone completely taut. I draw myself up to my full height, nearly meeting his eyes on the same level. "She *did* notice someone dangerous in the woods. She wasn't messing things up—she was protecting us."

The winter fae opens his mouth and closes it again. His shoulders start to slump. "How were we supposed to know after everything before?"

Raze growls. "Because she's *always* trying to help us, every way she can. You kept insulting her before she had a chance to totally explain."

Jonah is still staring at the churned up earth. "We need to know where the sorcerer went. She wasn't sure he'd left. If he's still lurking around…"

His gaze darts across the nearby trees and then back to us. "I should give you a stronger command of my own to bolster your defenses, in case he tries to impose control on you."

For once, Hail doesn't argue. He lifts his chin. "Fine. If I'm going to listen to any sorcerer, better it's you than some creep."

Jonah's mouth twists, but he speaks his weird sorcerous language to all of us. I shiver at the command poking into my skull.

But there are worse ways of controlling someone. I know that too.

I spin around. "We need to find Peri. *She* doesn't have extra protection. The sorcerer might go after her for revenge."

Raze's head jerks after me. His voice bellows through the trees. "Peri!"

Jonah touches his arm. "We'll get Peri back, but someone needs to follow the sorcerer's trail while it's fresh. And probably not alone, in case he causes more trouble than we expect."

To my surprise, Hail wipes his hands together and speaks in a more forceful tone than usual. "I played the biggest part in running the cream puff off. I owe her the biggest apology. Come on, fox. Let's track her down and let the sorcerer and the basilisk hunt the villain."

He wouldn't be my first choice of company, but my preferences feel a lot less important than making sure Peri's okay.

We head back toward the rift. The pushy atmosphere it gives off weighs on me even from many bounds away.

"Peri!" I call, as loud as my voice will carry. "Please come back!"

Hail adds his voice to mine, sounding a little hesitant. "Periwinkle! We know you were right!"

He makes a face at those words. As we stride around the jutting rock face behind the rift and venture into the shadows Peri fled through, I peer over at him. "Why are you so mean to her all the time? Why are you mean to any of us?"

Hail's stance tenses. "Why should I be 'nice'? What have you done for me?"

"You don't think it'd make the mission easier for everyone —including you—if we're getting along?"

"I didn't ask to be here," Hail mutters.

I click my tongue. "But you are and I am and she is. The job is what it is. And whatever you think about the rest of us, *she's* been nice to *you*."

I've seen it with my own eyes. He can't deny that Peri extended her generous gentleness to him just as much as the rest of us.

Hail doesn't try. He's silent for a few rasping footsteps.

Then he sighs. "I don't see why. It doesn't make sense. Nothing about her makes sense."

I have to laugh. "I think she's the *only* being I've ever met who makes sense. The problem is that the rest of us try to make everything so complicated."

Even me, for all I try to simplify my life to jokes and games. Maybe *because* I do that.

A pensive expression comes over the winter fae's face, but I like it better than the sneering one he often puts on.

"Peri!" he hollers again.

I pitch my voice even louder. "Come talk to us, Rainbow!"

Hail cuts his gaze toward me. "Rainbow?"

His tone is puzzled but not disdainful. I let myself grin at him. "It's more accurate than 'cream puff.'"

But none of that matters when Peri still hasn't returned.

I pause, listening hard, but I can't hear her curvy body rustling the underbrush, can't smell her sunny-sweet scent or feel the impression of her presence within the shadows.

If she kept running after she left, she could be beyond hearing us already. I don't know how we'll ever find her.

"Rainbow," Hail murmurs to himself with a slight roll of his eyes, and an idea lights in my head.

I clap my hands. "Yes! We need a rainbow to call back our Rainbow."

My powers tingle through my body. I form the picture I want to create in my head and will the image out into the world.

Cascading colors streak across the sky. Their mottled light radiates between the trees to cast their sheen down to the forest floor.

The illusion I've conjured, a massive splash of rainbow, stretches above us as far as I can propel it toward the hidden horizon.

Hail stops, his jaw going slack. "You… Mortals will see it too."

I can't break concentration to answer him. Already, the effort of extending my magic so far is turning the pleasant tingle of power into a sharper prickle. Soon the strain will be jabbing at me like little knives.

I don't care. I push the illusion farther, drenching every inch of forest I can with the multi-colored light.

Peri needs to see it, needs to know I'm reaching out to her.

Here comes the jabbing. I tune out the pain as well as I

can, though my fingers twitch. The longer I can maintain this image, the more likely she'll—

"Mirage?"

The tentative voice breaks my focus. The rainbow shudders away, and I find myself panting, standing amid the trees with not just Hail but Jonah and Raze by my side.

How long was I lost in my conjuring?

Long enough that a pale face framed by teal hair is peeking over the top of a bush at me, still a few paces distant, as if she's waiting to see whether she'll need to race off again.

A smile springs to my lips. "Rainbow! You saw me calling."

Peri shifts her weight from one foot to the other, her gaze sliding from me to our companions. She tugs her leather jacket closer around her chest.

Hail jumps in before anyone else can. "I'm sorry. I was a jerk to you. We saw that the sorcerer really was there by the rift."

His apology is brusque, but I'm not sure I've ever heard him apologize before at all. Peri blinks at him.

Jonah picks up the thread in his calmer voice. "We're all sorry we didn't hear you out the first time. Why did you go straight to attacking him? I'm assuming you had a good reason."

Peri's voice comes out quiet but steady. "He tried to latch on to me with his sorcery. Your command stopped him, but I knew he'd try again, stronger. And I recognized the flavor of his magic. It *is* the man who trapped me before."

Her head droops. "I felt so horrible, knowing he was that close—I couldn't keep the awfulness in. But I could throw it at him so it didn't hurt anyone who didn't deserve it." She hesitates, with an apologetic glance at me. "Not too much."

Jonah pulls his posture straighter. "We have a lot to talk

about, then. If you're willing to give us another chance to listen, that is."

Peri looks at him for a long moment, a pale blue glimmer passing over her hair. Her jaw firms. "Yes. I think I'd better tell you everything."

35

Periwinkle

Even after I've made the declaration that I'll spill every detail, my insides stay as tangled as a heap of spaghetti. With each breath, my lungs contract.

Raze moves first, scooping me off the ground into his muscular arms. As he tucks me close to his broad chest, he turns toward the others. "She's been through a lot today. And we don't know how thoroughly the sorcerer is monitoring the forest. Shouldn't we wait until we're back at the van before we talk about anything important?"

Is he offering to carry me there? He trusts himself enough not to hurt me all that way?

The thought lights a warm glow inside me. I *am* tired—from grappling with the power that surged out of me, from my headlong hurtle through the woods, from the hike that brought us to the rift in the first place. My feet are aching with little jabs racing up my calves.

In Raze's embrace, the tension melts enough that I can nestle my head beneath his chin. His hold tightens just a little, as if to reassure me that he's got me.

At the edge of my vision, I see Jonah nod. "We're going to have to make the trek back anyway. Peri can take the time to rest and decide the best way to tell her story."

A rough laugh hitches out of Mirage. "Story time. Gather 'round."

He comes up next to me and brushes gentle fingers over my shoulder. "You don't owe us anything, Rainbow."

The nickname reminds me of the brilliantly colored illusion that flooded the sky just minutes ago. The beautiful image he created to call me back.

Simply because he wanted me here, safe and sound.

I half expect Hail to grumble a protest despite his initial apology. Instead, the winter fae shrugs. "We'd better get walking, then. The longer that degenerate sorcerer has to plot his next moves, the harder he'll be to tackle."

He hefts the bag of damaged equipment without complaint.

We set off between the trees toward the distant spot where we had to leave the van. For the first few minutes, I'm lulled by the heat of Raze's body and the rhythm of his steps. His scent, tart but musky, wraps around me.

I can't completely forget the conversation we're going to need to have soon, though. The commitment I made to revealing all the awful things I've been a part of.

This might be the last cuddle I get.

A lump rises in my throat, but a more urgent concern dislodges it. "You found evidence that the sorcerer was nearby. Did you figure out where he went after I blasted him?"

"It seems clear he was injured," Jonah says evenly. "But not so much that he couldn't run off—by whatever means.

He might have had shadowkind under his control close by to help him."

That remark sets an idea pinging through my brain. "That butterfly-bird that attacked you—do you think it was one of his?"

A moment of unsettled silence follows my question. Jonah's tone turns grimmer. "It could have been. Like a sentry. It only attacked me, and when Mirage got close, it flew off. He might have ordered it to divert any humans who came close to the rift and alert him to new shadowkind in the area."

I frown. "A crazy butterfly alarm system."

Unfortunately, a very effective one.

Raze's rumble of a voice reverberates from his chest into my body. "I followed the man's trail to a dirt road a few miles from the rift, one that wasn't on any maps so we didn't know we could use it. There were fresh tire marks. He must have driven away—as soon as the road connected to a paved one, I couldn't tell where he went from there."

"Then we still have no idea where he is or where he'll turn up next."

To my surprise, it's Hail who speaks the next words of encouragement. "Maybe your story will help us with that, Cream Puff."

He says his silly nickname with a lilt that sounds more amused than disdainful. Like he thinks I might actually be delectable.

His new friendliness sends a pang of guilt through my gut.

Would we have ended up in this much trouble if I'd spilled the beans from the start? Or at least back when we found the cabin and I had my first outburst?

I was so afraid of what they'd think of me, of revealing the villainous things I've done, that I might have laid out a red carpet for the real villain to hurt us. If they'd had the full picture from the start, we might have put the pieces together as a team.

They might have been holding me up like they are now, so I wouldn't have exploded with anguish yet again.

Imagining telling them everything makes my stomach churn, but I know that I have to. After all the mistakes they've given me a pass on, I have a very large bill to pay.

It's a good thing talking is my best currency anyway.

By the time we reach the van, the sunlight is starting to dwindle. Only a faint twinge shoots through my ankles when Raze sets me down.

As we sit on the benches inside the vehicle, tension coils around my insides again. But the only emotions I pick up from the men around me are tangy curiosity and concern as comforting as fresh-baked bread.

This *is* my team. We're more than just fellow students— and bonus teacher—now. We might have argued and clashed with each other, but we've accomplished a lot too.

All the same, I find I can't look anywhere except at my hands, clasped tightly in front of me. "I told you the sorcerer captured me and kept me caged for a little while. It was actually… a pretty long time. I think. It was hard to tell how many days and weeks passed, but it was definitely years altogether."

Raze lets out a fierce growl. "He's going to pay for that."

I can't appreciate his protectiveness when he doesn't know the full situation yet. "He didn't just keep me caged. The mementos he kept—the people he wanted to hurt—he figured out my power, how I could do so much damage if I got upset… He made clothes that protected him from the worst of the effect. He'd bring me to places where he wanted to sabotage people, and then he'd hurt me—say horrible things and stab my feet until all the awfulness burst out of me…"

Jonah's voice stays even but quiet. "That isn't your fault, Peri. He was using you."

"But I still *did* it." Tears well in my eyes. I swipe at them, swallowing hard. "I hurt so many humans. Lots of them were people he didn't even care about, they just happened to be nearby. Hundreds and hundreds… Because I couldn't stop myself. I couldn't control my powers. Just like I can't now."

Mirage makes a dismissive sound. "Extreme circumstances mean extreme impact."

Hail's tone is drier but almost soft. "If someone smashes a nest, you don't blame the twigs for spilling the eggs."

"Still…" I inhale shakily. "I hated him, and I didn't want to do it, but some part of me was made to lash out. I don't know why. I want so much to make up for it now that I can —to bring more joy than I ever caused pain—but I don't know if that's even possible."

Raze slips his arm around me and strokes his hand up and down my arm. "It will be."

Mirage cocks his head. When I let myself glance at the fox shifter, something in his expression sends a wobble through my pulse. He doesn't normally look so serious.

"How did you get away from him?" he asks.

I cringe away from that memory too. Why does every good thing come with a dollop of bad?

But they need to know everything.

"The sorcerer had a daughter. Gracie. That's how I know a bunch of time passed—she was just a kid when he first brought me to his house, and by the time I left, she was a teenager. He didn't tell her much, but she knew about the beings he kept in the basement. She'd come down when he was out and talk to us, bring us bits of food… One day she managed to break the power source that kept the blazing lights on us all the time, so we could run off through the shadows."

Jonah smiles. "That was very brave of her, going against her father."

I duck my head. "I know. I heard him yelling at her while I was dashing away, and I wanted to help her, but it bothered me so much—I was afraid I'd end up hurting *her* too. So I just kept running. I have no idea what happened, if she's okay. She used to talk about going to college in this one city. I want to look for her, when I'm sure I'm safe."

A shiver runs through my body. "If he's gathering shadowkind up here now… When he was keeping me, he lived where it was a lot hotter, more like around the academy but rainier too. He's come a long way. We don't know if he dragged her with him."

Our sorcerer's voice stays soothing. "You don't know how long it's been. She might have grown up and gotten away from him too."

Yes. If she was strong enough to stand up to him for us, she must have been able to stand up for herself, right?

Pretty, pretty please with sugar on top.

Hail turns to look at Jonah, unexpectedly deferring to the other man's authority. "We need to track this prick down, don't we? We can't do much about the rift if he's going to keep meddling—if there's a chance he'll break any protection you give us and capture us."

"He's definitely the biggest threat in this situation." Jonah's dark gaze fixes on me. "Peri, I know you don't like thinking about that time, but we need to know everything you can remember about who this man was, how he behaved —anything that might help us find and stop him."

I square my shoulders. Of course. This is why I spoke up to begin with.

"I think I know his name. Sometimes he'd answer his

phone when he was in the basement with us, and if he was close enough I could make out the voice on the other end. Someone called him 'David' and a couple of other people called him 'Mr. Blaver.'"

Mirage perks up. "David Blaver. We find out what he's up to, and then we smack him down!"

One corner of Jonah's mouth quirks upward. "There might be more than one. David's a pretty common first name. What else can you tell us about him, Peri?"

I think back to all those days I spent in the sorcerer's basement. "He collected those trophies and medals. He liked to eat tandoori chicken. Like I said before, he was on the shorter side and kind of wide—he had light brown hair, but it might be going gray now. Dark brown eyes. Oh! I think he went to college at a place called Stanford. He ranted a lot about how stupid other humans are, and sometimes he'd mention things that happened when he was 'at' Stanford."

Jonah taps notes into his phone. He aims a wider smile at me. "That's really helpful for narrowing things down. Keep going."

I open my mouth and then close it again, my gaze lingering on the device in his hands. "After… after we talk about all this, are we going to meet up with Rollick and Sorsha and the others to tell them what happened?"

Jonah hesitates.

Raze's hand goes still against my arm. "It wasn't Peri's fault that the equipment got damaged. She *saved* us."

"I know." Our sorcerer rubs his hand over his face. Then he looks around at us. "Are all of you ready to be a real team? To go all in on working together, no sniping or second-guessing? Do you think you can trust the rest of us that much?"

A glimmer of hope lights in my heart, bright as sunshine.

"Yes," I say without needing to think about it.

It's Raze's turn to hesitate, but only for a moment. "I trust that everyone here wants to crush that sorcerer more than anything else."

Mirage grins. "I'll give it my all with all of you."

We shift our attention to Hail.

The winter fae grimaces, but I can only taste discomfort from him, not anger.

"I know I've been the least interested in buddying up to anyone," he says, "but you have done some useful things." He catches Jonah's gaze with an arch of an eyebrow. "Even you, sorcerer boy. I'd rather take on this asshole with the bunch of you than with anyone else."

A quiver of anxiety flits out of Jonah, but he sets his jaw defiantly. "Then I say we handle this problem ourselves and prove how solid a team we can be. That's what Rollick sent us out here to do."

36

Periwinkle

I know it's only been half an hour since I last asked. I know Jonah will tell us as soon as he hears anything. But after he finishes his dinner of canned stew, I can't help asking again, "Any news from your friend who knows how to dig up info?"

Jonah lets out a soft laugh. "Not yet, Peri. It could take a while yet. We didn't have that many details, and this sorcerer is probably covering his tracks. Ruse doesn't know how to search the online records himself—he's just very good at persuading other people with the skills we need."

I pace on the other side of the campfire, unable to contain my restlessness. Now that I've spilled my guts, there isn't really anything for me to do. I have no idea how much use I'll be in the coming confrontation—whether I can help tackle David Blaver, my former captor, without hurting my teammates and innocent bystanders in the process.

Whether my searing blasts are a gift or a liability comes down to my brand-new and incredibly shaky ability to aim them. Would it have been so hard for the shadow realm to bring me into being with an instruction manual in hand?

Hail went off into the woods as evening fell, saying he thought the mortal creatures of the forest might be able to convey something useful to him. As a fae, apparently he's attuned to the natural world in ways he's barely mentioned before.

Raze has been prowling beyond our campsite, keeping watch for sorcerer-controlled creatures. And Mirage…

The fox shifter walks over with his usual jaunty stride and catches my arm, his grasp gentle. "Why don't we go for a walk, Rainbow? You're having trouble staying still, and I've always got extra energy to burn."

I hesitate, not wanting to be out of range if news does come, but Jonah waves us off. "Even if we get word back soon, it'll take a bunch more planning before we can leave. Just don't go too far."

"We won't wander right off the edge of the earth," Mirage assures him cheerfully.

I let the fox shifter guide me toward the trees that surround this overgrown lookout spot. There isn't much of a view in any direction now. The forested hills around us cast deeper shadows through the deepening night.

We've only walked for a few minutes when Mirage pauses, his head jerking toward me. His fox ears flick out and swivel back on his head. "Your feet—you said the sorcerer who tortured you would cut them—sometimes you've said they're bothering you. Do they still hurt when you walk on them?"

His concern sends a tingle of warmth through my chest even though I don't like acknowledging the weakness. "Only if I'm walking a lot, or moving around very quickly or in awkward ways. Most of the time it's fine or so mild I can easily ignore it."

The fox shifter hums with a hint of a growl. "I don't want you to be hurt at all."

I shrug. "It's just… the way I am now. Everyone ends up picking up scars, right? I'd rather tune out a little pain and enjoy the world in all its wonders than stick to the shadows where the old injuries won't ever bother me."

"I guess that makes sense. But if it means they'll hurt less, you can put a little weight on me."

He eases closer so our shoulders nearly brush and tucks my hand around his elbow. The tingle of warmth turns into a waft of heat.

We walk on, taking a winding route between the trees. An owl hoots somewhere in the distance.

Mirage speaks up again, this time without stopping or looking at me. "When I was captured, it was different than for you. The people holding me wanted to poke and pry at me, taking 'samples' and testing my reactions. Scientists."

I shudder, my grip on his arm tightening. "That's horrible. Why would they do that?"

"I don't know. They wanted to understand shadowkind nature better, but not for good reasons. So they could get rid of us, I think."

"I hope someone got rid of them instead."

Mirage gives a faint chuckle. "Someone must have. One night the building collapsed and the cells they were keeping us in burst open so we could break free. I've never heard of them again. The Company of Light, they called themselves."

My forehead furrows. "I've never heard of them either. So maybe they are gone now."

"I just…" Mirage's voice wavers. He ducks his head. "I don't like to talk about it. I try to run in the opposite direction. But what you said about how the sorcerer used you

—it happened to me too. They'd mess with my mind to get me to conjure illusions that would help them lure other shadowkind in."

I stop and turn to face him. "That's awful—of them, not you. You'd never have wanted to do it."

Mirage leans forward and nuzzles my temple. "Not any more than you would have. But that doesn't make the regrets go away, does it? I wanted you to know… in case maybe it's easier to forgive yourself if you see how easily you can forgive me."

"There isn't anything *to* forgive you for," I start indignantly before his point hits me over the head. "Oh."

Mirage chuckles again, more relaxed this time, and dips his head lower so his lips brush my cheek. "You shouldn't feel bad about *anything*. Out of all the beings I've ever met, mortal and shadowkind, there's no one else who shines with goodness like you do."

A blush flares across my face. "I try. So many times it doesn't work out. How can I feel good about having my powers if I can't use them without causing all kinds of problems?"

Even picking up on emotions has bothered the beings I wanted to help at least as often as it's encouraged or comforted them.

Mirage teases his fingers over my hair. "You're getting better at controlling them. You only gave me a little scrape this afternoon, but you sent that stinking sorcerer running. I bet he's afraid of you now instead of the other way around."

My throat tightens. "Maybe. Sometimes I still feel like I really am just a pipsqueak."

As Mirage makes a scoffing sound, another voice rumbles out of the darkness. "You're much more than that, Glowbug. No one will dare call you a pipsqueak when you finish learning how to wield your power."

Raze emerges from the shadows—he must have crossed paths with us on his patrol.

His words send a pang through my heart. "I don't want to scare anyone."

He shakes his head fondly. "Of course you don't. That's how I know you'll keep improving your control."

Mirage tips his head to nip the shell of my ear. The spark of pleasure propels a gasp from my lips.

The fox shifter grins at me and then Raze. "Maybe she needs a reminder of *all* the power she can wield. I know she's got me under her spell. We were very rudely interrupted this morning…"

A thrum emanates from Raze's brawny chest. He steps closer to sling his arm around my waist. "You're right. She deserves a reward after all of today's stresses."

He presses a kiss of his own to the crook of my jaw. "There aren't many beings who can overcome a basilisk, you know."

The stroke of Mirage's hand across my hip and the slide of Raze's mouth leave me breathless, but I can't restrain a protest. "I haven't really *overcome* you—"

"Of course you have," Raze says. "My heart beats faster whenever I look at you. My whole body heats up when you're near. There's nothing I want to do more than talk with you, protect you, pleasure you…"

My heart is just about jumping out from my rib cage at his words. I set my hand against his chest, soaking in the sensation of his muscles flexing beneath his shirt. "As long as you know that you have the same effect on me. I'm never afraid of you. I like knowing how powerful *you* are."

Raze exhales roughly, and then he's tugging me around to claim my mouth. His fierce kiss sets off a rush of desire that condenses between my legs, as fiery as Mirage's hair.

Before I can fret that the fox shifter might feel left out,

Mirage's hands settle on my waist. As Raze kisses me again, Mirage strokes his fingers up and down my sides and then around to cup my breasts.

I whimper into Raze's mouth. Mirage pinches my nipples as if in reward, sparking twin pulses of pleasure.

He presses a little closer and nibbles his way along the back of my neck. "Mmm. You could melt me into a puddle of jelly with just that brilliant smile."

I quiver against Raze, feeling pretty jelly-like myself, and the basilisk shifter grips my hips. In one smooth motion, he shows off the strength I praised earlier by hefting me up against him.

For a fleeting moment, our mouths meld even closer together as my pelvis locks against his. The ridge of his erection rubs against my core to draw another, needier whimper from my throat.

Then Raze spins me around in front of him, so deftly he might as well be an acrobat. Even though I'm hardly slim, he handles me as if I'm light as meringue.

With my back flush against Raze's chest, he slides his hands beneath my thighs to support them. Spreading my legs, he releases a scorching breath across my jaw. His tongue teases my skin with its basilisk fork.

"Why don't you take off those tough girl clothes so Mirage can worship your light every bit as much as you deserve?"

Another giddy shiver passes through me, but my nerves jump at the brazenness of his request.

When I look at Mirage, my uncertainties evaporate. The fox shifter kneels before me, his eyes gleaming so eagerly they might as well be flames too.

With a nudge of my essence, I blink into the shadows and back to Raze's arms, returning utterly naked.

"Such a beautiful Rainbow," Mirage says slyly, and buries his face between my legs.

A gasp escapes me at the first swipe of his tongue. He delves deeper, his fangs skating over my sensitive flesh, his lips working over my clit.

A flood of bliss sweeps through my body until I have to grasp his hair to stop myself from spiraling completely away. My own hair casts a ruddy pink haze into the night.

My hips rock toward Mirage's mouth of their own accord. His approving chuckle reverberates through my core with a pulse of pleasure that has me moaning.

Raze groans and massages my thighs. His mouth brands the side of my neck and all across my bare shoulder. "Keep bringing out that gorgeous glow. I love seeing how good we're making you feel. Show off your power. Tell him exactly what you need, Glowbug."

A shaky breath escapes me. Mirage laps across my opening and sucks hard on my clit, and I shudder in Raze's embrace. The ecstatic sensations are flooding me so swiftly I feel like I'll break right apart, but in the most delightful possible way.

I want even more. And Mirage will offer it if I ask, won't he?

I tug on his hair. "I want you inside me. I want you coming with me."

The fox shifter makes a sound that's half groan, half growl and surges up to meet me. His clothes waver away with the same trick I used. He catches my mouth and presses into me where I'm braced against Raze, sliding the head of his hard cock over my folds.

"Right here, Rainbow?"

I can only manage an inarticulate noise of approval, but I must get my meaning across. With a ragged sigh, he plunges into me.

It isn't the same immense fullness I experienced with Raze, but Mirage's thrust brings just as much heady pleasure. I sway to meet him, urging him on.

With every buck of his hips, Mirage pushes deeper. Soon he's stroking right against the special spot within that seems to be the source of my body's capacity for bliss. Every time he hits it, I careen farther into a giddy delirium.

But I'm not so far gone I forget about my other lover: the stalwart, statuesque being who's supporting me.

My mouth collides with Mirage's in a wild kiss, and then I tip my head against Raze's shoulder, groping behind me at the same time. "Want… you… too."

The basilisk shifter grunts and adjusts his hips to help me find his rigid shaft. Sometime during our interlude, he shed his clothes without my even noticing.

I wrap my fingers around his hardness and pump him up and down. At his ragged breath, I increase my grip and my speed.

We crash together, a storm of desire and pleasure. I know nothing beyond the press of the bodies on either side of me and the bliss they're conjuring in my own.

I shatter apart first, the wave of my climax whiting out my vision. At my cry, Raze jerks against me. Moments after his release splashes over my wrist, Mirage bows his head and surges into me a final few times.

For several moments, we stand there locked together, breathing hard. Then Mirage lifts his head to place one more lingering kiss on my lips.

"There's no one mightier than you. Every evil sorcerer in this world had better watch out."

37

Periwinkle

We're still in the same old camper van, but it's never felt as stealthy as it does this morning. I peek through the window at the motel on the other side of the narrow highway, my heart thumping fast.

There's nothing really to be worried about. Mirage is using his talent to create illusions that haze the windows so no one can see me anyway.

But we got word hours ago that a computer expert connected my former captor to an alias he appears to have been using for the last several months—and that alias has been staying at this motel regularly. Raze slunk through the shadows to confirm that the scent he picked up near the rift is wafting fresh from room 107.

The man who controlled me and tormented me is on the other side of that door. At any second, he could emerge.

With a fierce rumble, Raze adjusts his weight impatiently. "The second we see him, I should tear him to shreds."

Jonah shoots the basilisk shifter a chiding look. "You know we can't do that. We need to find out if he has anything to do with the state of that rift. We're not going to figure out anything if he's dead."

"And we need to free any shadowkind he's got trapped now," I remind Raze with a reassuring caress of his arm. "The influence of his sorcery might disappear when he's dead, but if he has them caged with lights and metals—it could be years before they'd be able to get free."

He lets out a huff. "Right. We follow him to his evil lair, see what he's doing, and *then* tear him to shreds."

My stomach clenches at the thought of that kind of violence, but I can't say the villain we're surveiling doesn't deserve it. "That's a much better order of things."

At the other side of the van, Hail lets out a dry chuckle. "When even the cream puff wants you dead, you know you really screwed up."

I glance over my shoulder at him. "I don't really want *anyone* dead. I just… don't see a better solution."

As soon as my former captor realizes we're around, he'll try to force his sorcery on us. Jonah gave us more potent commands to shield us from other influence, but even he admitted that his talent probably isn't as strong as the older man's.

Our opponent is too dangerous for us to try to imprison and interrogate him. I don't want to watch any of my companions fall under his sway or Jonah be torn up by his captured shadowkind.

Hail offers me a crooked smile that feels surprisingly

genuine. "Of course you don't. And it's a good thing we've got you around to tame the beast, hmm?" Before Raze can do more than start to growl at the implied insult, the winter fae adds, "I consider myself lucky that you still think I'm salvageable."

I blink at him, startled by the self-deprecation that sounds awfully genuine too. I knew Hail felt bad that he dismissed my efforts to protect them, but I had no idea he saw it as that huge an offense.

"Everyone makes mistakes," I tell him. "What this man's doing is deliberate awfulness, over and over again. I've never seen anything good in him."

Hail's chuckle expands into a brief laugh. "If you see goodness in me, I suppose I'm doing all right then."

Mirage has kept quiet as he concentrates on his illusion, but he reaches across the bench and gives a strand of my hair a playful tug. "Our Rainbow doesn't realize that she makes all of us better."

None of the men around me argue. A faint sheen hazes the windowpane with the pinkish glow of my hair, matching the affection that's lit in my chest.

Then the door to room 107 swings open, and the man I never wanted to set eyes on again steps out into the dreary morning.

As David Blaver glances up at the overcast sky, my heart stutters and squeezes tight.

It can't have been that long since I fled his cage—years but not decades. His brown hair is grayer now, and he's grown a short moustache and beard that cover the pudginess around his jaw, but I still recognize him in an instant. He walks over to his truck with that slightly bow-legged gait that used to carry him around his basement workroom.

He's wearing an olive-green sweater—like the bit of yarn I noticed snagged in the woods.

All our gazes track him as he slides into the driver's seat.

The moment the truck has headed north along the highway, Jonah starts the van's engine.

"On these quiet roads, we should be able to stay a good distance back and still see where he goes. We don't want him suspecting that he's being followed."

Mirage sinks down on the bench with a soft sigh, releasing the illusion that's no longer necessary. "I can hide the whole van in a pinch!"

Jonah shoots him a tight but grateful smile. "I know you can, but I think we should all preserve our strength for the end of this journey, wherever it leads us."

I scoot forward on the bench so I can watch through the windshield. Without comment, Raze scoops me up and offers his lap so I have a better view. The steadiness of his body helps settle my spirits, so I ignore the indignity of needing a living booster seat.

The man we're trailing is never going to hurt me again. We're going to make sure of it.

We follow David Blaver into the nearest town, where he parks on the main street and goes into a café. For a tense hour, we wait for him to finish his meal and eat. When he returns, he drives for another half an hour before turning off at a parking lot for a local beach. He takes a folded chair and a bag with a rolled towel out of his trunk.

The five of us peer at him. I can't help breaking the silence. "He's going to spend the day sunbathing?"

Jonah swipes his hand across his mouth. "Maybe he likes to relax for a little while before getting on with his business?"

"Or maybe he's decided not to *do* any business for a few days after he tangled with Peri yesterday," Hail says. "If he recognized her powers, he might have been just as surprised as she was to run into her… It could have made him think he should lie low."

Raze inhales roughly. "He doesn't look all that scared—

he's not moving like prey. I don't think he cares all that much, even if he's pretending to be normal just in case."

It's true. Having shut his trunk, the sorcerer is strolling through the parking lot as casual as can be.

He slows briefly near one of the other cars. After a quick glance around, he eases closer, glances through the back window, and then heads down to the lake.

My stomach flip-flops. "I think he's scoping out a new target. Someone he's going to send his brainwashed shadowkind after when he thinks he can get away with it."

Hail frowns, his pale face turning abruptly pensive. "Maybe we should—"

The peal of Jonah's phone cuts him off. Our sorcerer grabs the device. "It's Rollick."

My body tenses up. Even the gentle tightening of Raze's arm around me can't stop my nerves from dancing a jitterbug as Jonah answers the call.

We were supposed to meet with the demon today to report on what we found out at the rift—which isn't anything all that useful right now. Is Jonah going to decide there's no point in continuing the investigation on our own?

Will Rollick let me stick with the mission once he finds out that my powers exploded all over again?

Jonah's voice stays even. "Yes. It didn't go exactly as planned. We're following up on another lead. We've found the sorcerer who's been messing with the warped creatures. I didn't want to reach out until we see where that takes us."

He pauses, and his jaw works. "Yes, you're right. It could be we'll want some backup. You can track the van, can't you? And we'll call you if we need you here faster."

After he ends the call, he slumps in his seat. "Rollick wants to monitor the situation directly. He's going to give us a couple more hours, and if we're still uncertain of what to do by then, he, Sorsha, and her shadowkind partners are going to come join us."

One of Mirage's tails twitches into view for a second. "And take over."

"Something like that."

Hail grimaces. "They're all shadowkind, even Rollick. What can they do against a sorcerer that we can't?"

"I don't think Sorsha will be affected—benefit of being hybrid," Jonah says. "But it's true, even Rollick avoids tangling with hostile sorcerers. They might go straight to the tearing apart option."

My heart sinks. In a couple of hours, David Blaver might still be lounging in the sun, scheming against his neighbors and giving us no help solving this problem.

All Rollick will see from our efforts is a bunch of burnt out equipment, not proof our team can shine.

Unless we get on with the shining…

I turn to Hail. "You were going to suggest something before."

He stares at me as if surprised that I remember—or that I'd want to know what it was. Then he sits a little straighter.

"If the problem is that this prick doesn't feel like prey—doesn't think he has anything to worry about—maybe we should *give* him something to worry about. If we make him nervous, he'll check on whatever's most important to him or go wherever he feels safest, right? Which is probably wherever he's got his enslaved shadowkind and the rest of his sorcerer things."

Mirage perks up. "I can conjure something to terrify him."

Jonah holds up his hand to stop them. "That's a reasonable idea—but we'd have to be subtle about it. If you throw any illusion that's too intense at him, he'll realize it's supernatural influence. Especially if it's a generically scary thing. If we knew what he'd personally find most frightening…"

As he trails off, his gaze slides to me. My heart skips a beat in understanding.

I tasted my former captor's emotions while he kept me caged. I have insight not just into his external life but everything that was going on inside him.

My skin crawls at the idea of dredging up those darker emotions, but it's better than sitting here like lumps.

"Let me think," I say quietly, and close my eyes to concentrate.

When did the sorcerer feel scared? What would make him anxious about protecting whatever awfulness he's created in his new life?

I riffle through the scraps of my experiences in his cage. There's so much I ignored or tried to tune out to keep my sanity.

A fragment comes to me, vivid enough that the sour-metallic flavor of the fear passes over my tongue in an echo. "There was something… One time his daughter let someone into the house when he was down in the basement and not expecting it. I think he was terrified they'd find out what he was up to. He yelled at her a lot. He'd always get uneasy even if he was talking on the phone and the other person suggested they'd come by."

Jonah hums to himself. "He was afraid of being discovered."

"Maybe if he thinks he's in danger of being discovered now, he'll want to make sure everything is still hidden."

"Yes." Our sorcerer grins at me and then at Mirage. "Do you think that's enough material to work with?"

The fox shifter's eyes gleam. "I'll sneak and creep through the shadows to spy. Make him imagine the other people are looking at him suspiciously, whispering about him, plotting plans and planning plots."

"Not too overboard," Jonah reminds him.

Mirage nods eagerly and leaps away.

There's nothing for the rest of us to do but continue waiting. I lean against Raze. He strokes his hand up and down my arm, but my pulse keeps thumping away.

Did I pick the right fear? Will it be enough?

Jonah sucks in a breath. "He's coming back to his truck."

I jerk upright in time to see my former captor hustling over to his vehicle with his beach gear wobbling in his arms. He shoves it into the trunk and practically dives behind the wheel.

A giggle bubbles up my throat. "It worked!"

As the truck peels out of the parking lot, Mirage materializes next to me with a cheeky grin. "He didn't like the stares or the suspicious airs. Let's see where he goes!"

Jonah is already taking our van out of park. We rumble down the road on our target's tail.

David Blaver takes a winding route onto increasingly narrow and rundown roads. We stay far behind, but when we see him turn onto a dirt track amid thickening forest up ahead, Jonah motions to Mirage. "We do need the whole van hidden now— there's no way he won't be suspicious if we follow him in there."

The fox shifter crosses his legs on the floor of the van, an expression of total concentration gripping his handsome face. Magic tingles over my skin as his illusion surrounds the vehicle.

We have to slow down on the bumpy track. Jonah closes the distance between the van and the truck, but we still almost miss it when the other sorcerer pulls off onto an even smaller laneway several miles later.

We follow him for another mile down that overgrown

lane, the leaves of overhanging trees warbling across our windows, before the truck parks… at the edge of what looks like an empty clearing.

Please don't tell me he's figured out the secret of invisibility.

My former captor gets out and hurries across the clearing. As I crane my neck to watch, he bends over and appears to yank up a chunk of the grass.

Ah ha! There's a trap door in the ground.

David Blaver clambers into the hole he's opened up, shuts the grass-covered door over him, and it's as if he was never there.

The five of us exchange a glance.

"We can either wait here for backup, or risk going down there and taking a look ourselves," Jonah says. "Well, *you* can take a look—there's no way for me to get into that bunker without him seeing me."

The men all turn to me. Raze nuzzles the side of my head. "The three of us could go. You shouldn't have to face that brute again."

But I'm the only one who knows this sorcerer and how he works. They might need me.

I'm the only one in danger of getting banished if we sit around waiting for Rollick to handle the problem for us.

I take a deep breath. My emotions are roiling around, but I don't feel out of control.

I know who we're going up against. I know I didn't deserve what he did to me.

He won't ruin any more of my life.

"No," I say. "I'm coming. Let's find out all the vile secrets he's been hiding."

38

Periwinkle

We slip into the shadows before we enter the clearing. A tang of anxiety follows me from where we've left Jonah braced in the van.

Raze, Mirage, Hail, and I slink through the patches of darkness amid the grass and weeds. The trap door may be shut, but that doesn't pose any problem to us. A thin shadow seeps between the door's edge and the frame that holds it.

Raze's voice sounds slightly muffled in our current state, but I can still make out a hint of a growl. "I'm going in first. If we need to take him down, I should be ready."

A quiver of fear passes through me, but I don't argue. It's not as if I'd be much help if it comes to a fight.

Mirage's buoyant presence sidles closer to me. "Are you all right, Rainbow? Not too many blasty feelings welling up?"

Despite the fact that I'm about to come as close to my former captor as I have since I fled his basement, I feel strangely calm. Maybe because this time I'm prepared. I'm making the choice to approach him rather than being taken by surprise.

The new Periwinkle, girlboss version.

"I think I'll be okay," I say. "But if I start feeling overwhelmed, I'll get away from all of you before I have an outburst."

Hail lets out a cool chuckle. "Or you could point it all at the asshole. He'd deserve it."

I guess he would. Still, the thought of purposefully battering my old captor with the full force of my powers when he's technically minding his own business makes me queasy.

Before, I did it because I had to aim all that energy somewhere. I had to protect my friends. But I've hurt so many people in the past because of this man.

I want to be something different than the weapon he turned me into.

I helped get us to his secret lair. That means I contributed to the mission without needing to cause anyone pain, doesn't it?

Raze darts into the tiny gap. The rest of us follow side by side.

We emerge into a garishly lit room that has me cringing in the sliver of darkness along the trap door. The artificial illumination blazes from the walls on one side of the space, where searing lamps are pointed at dozens of barred cages. The metal structures emit even more light from their floors and ceilings.

Within all that glare, knots of filmy darkness wriggle: shadowkind who've been captured and restrained, kept far from any shadows they might leap into if the sorcerer's control fades.

My entire being winces. I jerk my attention away from that area to take in the rest of the room.

The other end appears to be David Blaver's main workspace. Three corkboards hang on the walls, one pinned with photographs and newspaper clippings, another with sketches and handwritten notes, and the third with a large map. On the floor between them stands a desk. A storage cabinet and a table holding a camp stove are set up in the middle, a folding cot propped nearby.

The sorcerer himself is nowhere to be seen.

In the corner of the room near the desk, there's another trap door, larger than the one we came through. It's open, showing mostly darkness below.

"The basement has a basement," Mirage says in a singsong tone.

A rustling sound emerges from it, suggesting the sorcerer went down there. The only human-like thing in view is a headless, armless sewing dummy poised next to one of the corkboards for some purpose I can't guess.

"What's he got stuck all over the walls?" Raze mutters.

I can't make out the details from here, but shadows dapple the wall behind the ladder below our perch and the floor beneath the furnishings on the side away from the cages. I nudge my companions. "Let's go down and take a closer look."

I flit through the narrow bands of darkness and into the larger splotches offered by the table and desk. Tucking myself in a shadow next to a pencil holder, I study the corkboards up close.

The photographs and articles seem to be clustered into groups, each around a specific person. Some have jagged words scrawled on them in marker, like *BRAINWASHING MENACE* and *RIGHTS GOUGER*, whatever that's supposed to mean.

I sense my companions' presences gathering around me in the shadows. "Those must be the people he's targeting," I say. "He's fixating on a whole crowd. There'd always be people he decided were making his life difficult on purpose, that he wanted the beings he was controlling to get rid of. He didn't use to say—or write—stuff like that, though."

Hail's tone is disdainful. "It looks like conspiracy theory craziness. Humans make up all kinds of insanity even though they can't handle the actual strangeness in the world."

My former captor was a little unhinged to begin with. Has he spiraled even farther into vengeful delusion?

Please let Gracie have gotten away from him all right.

I shift my attention to the next board. The drawings tacked to it remind me of some of the warped creatures we've stumbled on—mismatched features, arrows that maybe show them shifting from one awkward form to another. The erratic notes are difficult to read even from here, but the bits I can decipher record the writer's observations of the creatures' characteristics and behavior. It looks like he was trying to figure them out too.

So he could make better use of them rather than so he could protect people from them, of course.

Some of them are dated. Raze grunts. "He's been keeping track of them for almost a year now."

"And keeping track of the rift too, I think," Mirage pipes up, adjusting his position to peer toward the map.

As I study it alongside him, I decide he's right. The map looks a lot like the image I've seen on Jonah's phone when he stops to navigate, showing the area we've been driving around in. It's marked with at least fifteen red push-pins—different locations the rift has galivanted to, maybe?

I frown. "I don't see any pattern. Maybe Rollick would be able to find one."

Hail's presence twitches. "If we can get it to him."

He's barely finished speaking when the stout, pasty man climbs out of the lower cellar into the room.

Even though I knew my former captor was down here, my essence clenches up at the sight of him so nearby. Closer up, it's clear his skin has gone blotchy, his graying hair patchy, as if he isn't eating all that well.

He's obviously not preparing haute cuisine in this remote place. Is he even getting enough sunlight? I think he might be wilting like a plucked flower.

Possibly his mind as much as his body, because as he walks over to the corkboards with a stiff gait, he starts muttering. "It all stinks, Sam. Every one of them. We have to pelt them all with justice."

It's only when he pats the sewing dummy on its armless shoulder that I realize who he's talking to. Or rather, what.

How does he think it's listening to him when it doesn't even have a head to put ears on?

There's unhinged and then there's whatever this is. All hinges have departed the area.

The sorcerer stares at the pictures I assume are his current targets, tapping his lips. Disgust and anger roll off him in a noxiously bitter sludge I can't in good conscience call soup.

"What do you think, Sam?" he asks the dummy. "Stomp on him first? Or her, who's always flinging her eyes around?"

Who's doing what now?

I can't help stating the obvious—at a murmur, as if there's any chance of the sorcerer overhearing me. "He definitely doesn't like those people."

Hail snorts, similarly subdued. "No fucking kidding. Somehow I don't think they'd like him either."

While David Blaver glowers at his photographs and

carries on his one-sided debate with the fabric torso who's apparently his only friend, I slink away to the opening to the deeper cellar. At a peek into the dim space below, a flinch ripples through my essence. "Oh, no."

The men shoot over to join me. Mirage's voice roughens. "That's not fair play."

A vaguely human figure slumps against the wall beyond the opening. Vaguely because there's little left but bones stuck with shreds of fabric and scraps of flesh. Intestines loop around the knobby spine in a gruesome belt.

A patch of face remains—a tuft of short white hair, an eyeless socket, a jutting nose. Enough for me to guess the victim was male.

Next to me, Raze's presence shudders. "I think we found Ted McGaffery."

He might be right. Did the sorcerer decide Ted was talking about his "monsters" too much and toss him down there as punishment? Was it a sick experiment to see what those monsters would do when egged on?

On second thought, I'll skip the answers, thank you.

In the upper room, David Blaver is shuffling toward the side with the cages. I slip back beneath the table to watch.

He picks up a thin metal rod and slides it back and forth across his palm as he paces in front of the cages. After a few rounds, he stops by one. He says something in the sorcerous language and turns down a control on that cage to dim its lights.

A beast like a reptilian raccoon materializes from its cringing mass of shadow. It stares through the bars at its captor, jagged scales lifting and ruffling across its back.

The sorcerer thrusts the rod into the cage. With a flare of sparks, the creature jerks and spasms as if it's being electrocuted. A thin shriek pierces the air.

A jolt of horror zaps through me in turn. Raze lets out a

snarl, his presence twisting. Hail gives a hiss of revulsion, and Mirage simply whimpers.

I don't know which of our reactions my former captor picks up on. Maybe it's all of us at once. My only warning is a spurt of startled panic before he whirls around, already shouting out sorcerous orders.

This time, he doesn't take any chances being tentative. This time, he hurls his magic at us with a punch of force that shakes the hold of Jonah's command in my head.

I hurl myself away, as if I can flee his compulsion just by moving. My mind wobbles, grappling with the instruction to show myself. The sorcerous demand clashes with Jonah's insistence that I refuse all other orders, but the hold of that earlier command is crumbling.

Mirage and Hail waver into physical form, their faces taut with anguish. Panic flashes across the sorcerer's face as he shouts more commands at them.

One of his yells must hit Raze too, because the basilisk shifter jerks into the physical world with a rasp of breath. Every muscle in his sinewy body strains against his skin as if he's fighting to escape his very body.

The sorcerer's commands must be stopping him—stopping all of them—from using their powers. But whether because I've fought against his magic before or because my presence was the smallest and least noticeable of the bunch, I'm still holding on to some small shred of control, hidden in the dark.

That control is slipping through my grasp. Even if my former captor doesn't hurl any more sorcery at me, in a matter of seconds I'll be popping into view too.

Frustration and terror blare through my mind. The caustic flavor of those emotions surges into a rising wave.

No. This isn't how I wanted this to go.

What if my power isn't even enough? What if he catches deeper hold of me too quickly?

I just want everyone to be *happy*.

But even as that thought passes through my head, a more potent realization hits me, all the way down to the center of whatever soul I have.

I can't always make everyone happy. Sometimes I can't make anyone happy at all, and that's just the way it is, because there's already too much awfulness being spread around.

So maybe the best I can do in those moments is to stop the villain who's stealing everyone else's joy. Bring back the possibility of happiness, whatever it takes.

I can do that. I can shatter the crimes this awful man is committing and give all his captured creatures the chance they deserve.

With a swell of conviction, I propel the churning energy inside me toward the other side of the room as hard as I can.

The dark wave roars over my companions and my former captor, but that's not where I was aiming the main force of the impact. The fiercest currents smack into all those burning lights inside and around the cages.

In an instant, every bit of illumination except the single lamp poised over the corkboards blinks out.

The imprisoned creatures spring through the bars in a whirl of energy. The sorcerer was already stumbling, skin scalded by my sudden flare. The onslaught of shadowkind hurtles into him, knocking him right off his feet.

Scrambling up, he teeters left and right. His hands catch hold of the bottom rungs of the ladder. He starts to haul himself upright—outside, to escape.

No. No. *No.* I'm not going to let this man deal out even more pain.

Another spurt of caustic energy flares in my chest, and I throw it at his hands.

His fingers spasm apart, and the flood of shadowkind flings him onward. With flashes of fangs and glints of spikes and spines, the deluge of hissing, screeching beasts in their muddle of ephemeral and physical form pummels him across the room.

"Sam!" he hollers, groping toward the dummy, apparently forgetting that his friend doesn't have arms any more than it does ears.

The deluge of shadowy creatures heaves him again, and he topples right over the edge of the cellar door.

David Blaver tumbles through the opening headfirst. A crack reverberates from the concrete floor below, vivid enough to send an image of a skull cracked open like an eggshell flashing through my mind.

As the jumbled creatures whirl on around the room as if unsure of where to go next, I pull myself out of the shadows at the edge of the trap door. Peering down, I make out my former captor's crumpled body.

His neck is twisted at an unnatural angle. A puddle of blood expands beneath his head like crimson yolk.

A breath rushes out of me, with a flutter of sickly relief I won't feel guilty about.

Three figures draw up around me. Raze sets his hand on my back.

"He's gone," the basilisk shifter says gruffly.

The sorcerer's commands died with him.

I grasp Raze's arm and tuck myself into the embrace he offers.

Mirage spins around in a giddy circle. "And now everything he's found is ours! We'll make much better use of it. Thanks to our Periwinkle."

The fox shifter beams at me and dips his head to give me a quick peck.

When Mirage pulls away, Hail is watching the three of us with a bemused expression.

"Thank you, Cream Puff," he says in a mild voice that makes the phrase sound more like a fond nickname than an insult. "Come on. Let's tell *our* sorcerer how you saved the day."

39

Sorsha sets the last block of iron beneath the rift and steps back with her hands on her hips. "That should be enough to keep any creatures from coming through. I guess we'll have to wait and see whether the metals lock the rift in place or if we need to scatter the protections around more widely."

She turns toward us with a swish of her flame-red hair and an easygoing grin. One of the benefits of the phoenix shifter's hybrid nature—born to a human father and a shadowkind mother—is that she isn't bothered by iron and silver the way pure shadowkind are.

The men who came with her in her strange, huge vehicle can't say the same. They're full shadowkind, as unnerved by the protections as the rest of us, so they've been prowling through the forest for any sign of additional trouble while she's worked here.

Rollick nods approvingly where he's standing with me and my team several paces back from the rift's current position. Here, the aura of the metal blocks stacked around the base of the portal and the thick chains hanging from the trees on either side only nip at our skin rather than searing it.

The demon was able to arrange for some human associates to drive a truck of supplies nearby and carry them most of the way over, but he didn't want them getting too close to the rift itself. Sorsha had to take on the bulk of the final work.

"And I have a lot of reading to do," he says. "Sorting through all the notes this addled sorcerer made and separating madness from fact. I'd thank him for leaving a few of his captives weak enough for me to catch them for further study and potential rehabilitation, but I don't think he deserves even a fragment of good will."

I can't hold back a shudder. "No, he doesn't."

Raze's growl echoes my reaction.

Rollick turns to look at the five of us, his cool gaze assessing.

"You've done an impressive job working in collaboration, even with unfortunate circumstances stirring up personal trauma." The dip of his head acknowledges my private struggle. "I'm pleased with all of you, but I'd like to hear from your own mouths whether you think you and your teammates can safely return to your regular studies at the academy—and how you've addressed the problems that you'd have been banished for."

My heart skips a beat. He's going to trust our judgment about each other? What will the men I've worked with say about me?

The demon motions toward Raze first. "You were ignoring the rules about maintaining physical form and avoiding interacting with the other students rather than trying to integrate. Can the academy's staff expect to see that change?"

Raze squares his shoulders. "Yes. I… I've realized that I don't need to be as afraid of my powers as I have been. That's the main reason I was keeping to myself—for everyone else's safety. And feeling less unsettled in general will make it easier for me to avoid losing my temper."

Rollick glances around at our group. "Will the rest of you support his assessment?"

I jump in immediately. "Definitely. Raze has gotten a lot more comfortable around… all of us, since I first met him."

Especially me, but I don't think Rollick needs *all* the delicious details.

"He has," Jonah agrees. "And I've seen fewer kneejerk responses from him, even when he's provoked." He arches an eyebrow at Hail.

The winter fae shrugs. "I'll admit that I've given him a hard time, and he hasn't unleashed any evil eye or venom at me."

Rollick moves to Mirage. "What about our fox shifter of the many tails, which he finds so difficult to keep hidden, along with his ears and other features? Have you managed to moderate your pranks so you're only provoking laughs and not injuries?"

Mirage swipes a hand through his ruddy hair, where no ears except his human-like ones show. "I'm not perfect at tucking away my foxy bits yet, but I didn't show them at all when we were talking to humans for our mission. And I didn't confuse anyone except when it helped the team."

Jonah nods. "That's all true."

Raze forms a warm rumbling sound. "Mirage has been very considerate of the rest of us."

In various meanings of "considerate," at least one of which might set my hair glowing pink again.

"And he makes us laugh, which is a good thing too," I put in.

Rollick fixes his gaze on Hail. "Have you been preventing your cool attitude from afflicting the humans *you've* had to talk to?"

Hail's normally nonchalant gaze drops. "I've seen reasons to be annoyed with them, but I haven't tripped anyone up. I knew our mission was more important than my frustration."

To my surprise, Raze speaks in agreement first. "Hail did hassle me to begin with, but he's also defended us every time he needed to. And he's become less harsh the more we got to know each other."

Mirage hums. "Fewer insults, more in-jokes!"

As Hail rolls his eyes good-naturedly at the fox shifter's remark, I find Rollick's attention has shifted to me. I resist the urge to hug myself protectively.

"And you, our glowing mystery," he says. "You felt very guilty about how you've hurt those around you in the past. Can you say for sure that your powers won't explode all over the school again?"

The certainty that came over me in the sorcerer's lair gathers inside me again. I'm alive and free, and my former captor is scrambled eggs in a dingy basement.

I knew how to do what was right, even using my wrongness.

I take a deep breath. "I feel like I can avoid hurting anyone. Now that I've faced the man who scared me the most, nothing that happens at the school seems all that bad. And I've found ways of aiming the outbursts when they come on, even if I can't completely stop them. If I have to, I can direct the energy somewhere harmless."

"Peri's come a long way," Jonah says quietly. "I don't believe she'd say she's ready unless she's sure of it."

Raze grasps my shoulder with a gentle squeeze. "She

protected all of us from the sorcerer who was capturing those shadowkind—he'd already worked his magic on us. If she hadn't reacted so quickly and so well, we'd be under his control."

Hail looks at me with an upward quirk of his lips. "She's still a cream puff, but definitely not a pipsqueak."

"She's a rainbow," Mirage insists. "And her glow makes it easier for us to see everything we need to."

Their words spark a different sort of light inside me, tingling around my heart. I find myself grinning back at all four of them. "Thank you."

Sorsha nudges Rollick. "That sounds pretty definitive to me."

The demon chuckles. "I'm suitably convinced that you'll all contribute to the school in a positive way from here on. Thank you for uncovering and dealing with even more problems than I'd considered might exist."

Sorsha pumps a fist in the air and swivels toward the spot where we left our vehicles. "That means it's time to celebrate! You'll all eat human food, right? We brought a picnic."

As we march back between the trees, the full relief of the moment washes over me. It's a four-course banquet with bread and butter on the side, savory and spicy and sweet, the most satisfying meal I've ever enjoyed.

We defeated a sorcerer who's hurt so many beings, human and shadowkind alike. We did it *together*, standing shoulder to shoulder as a real team, accepting and respecting what we all can offer.

We understand each other now. Who knows what else we might accomplish?

The only thing I'm sure of through the giddy thump of my pulse is that I want to do so much more side by side with these four men.

The joy of that knowledge swells inside me—and surges straight out of my skin.

I stop with a gasp, caught up in the rush of happiness and harmony. The sunny light streaming out of me isn't the blinding blaze that's burst out before, but four concentrated beams that streak through the air from my torso straight toward the men on my team.

The glow hits their chests, lighting up their clothes and skin with a flare of warmth I feel echoing back into me.

Jonah stumbles, shock flashing across his face. Raze whirls toward me with a bewildered expression. Mirage simply laughs, but his good humor falters when he paws at the beam penetrating his side. Hail freezes up, staring down at himself stiffly.

And all at once I feel not just my own heart pounding, but four other heartbeats thumping along in tandem. My chest constricts around them.

What in the realms have I done?

About the Author

Eva Chase lives in Canada with her family. She loves stories both swoony and supernatural, and strong women and the men who appreciate them.

Along with the Pack of Outcasts trilogy, she is the author of the Royal Spares series, the Rites of Possession series, the Shadowblood Souls series, the Heart of a Monster series, the Gang of Ghouls series, the Bound to the Fae series, the Flirting with Monsters series, the Cursed Studies trilogy, the Royals of Villain Academy series, the Moriarty's Men series, the Looking Glass Curse trilogy, the Their Dark Valkyrie series, the Witch's Consorts series, the Dragon Shifter's Mates series, the Demons of Fame series, and the Legends Reborn trilogy.

Connect with Eva online:
www.evachase.com
eva@evachase.com